before
you die

Samantha Hayes grew up in the West Midlands, left school at sixteen, avoided university and took jobs ranging from private detective to barmaid to fruit picker and factory worker. She lived on a kibbutz, and spent time in Australia and the USA, before finally becoming a crime writer.

Her writing career began when she won a short story competition in 2003. Her novels are family-based psychological thrillers, with the emphasis being on 'real-life fiction'. She focuses on current issues, and when she writes, she sets out to make her reader ask, 'What if this happened to me or my family?'

With three children of her own, Samantha is well versed to talk about how the aftershocks of crime impact upon families and communities.

To find out more, visit her website:
www.samanthahayes.co.uk

Samantha Hayes
before you die

arrow books

Published by Arrow Books 2015

2 4 6 8 10 9 7 5 3

First published in Great Britain in 2014 by Century

Arrow Books
Random House, 20 Vauxhall Bridge Road,
London SW1V 2SA

A Penguin Random House Company

Penguin
Random House
UK

www.randomhouse.co.uk

Addresses for companies within The Random House Group Limited
can be found at: www.randomhouse.co.uk/offices

The Random House Group Limited Reg. No. 954009

A CIP catalogue record for this book is available from the British Library

ISBN 9780099584834

Typeset in Sabon LT Std 12pt by
Palimpsest Book Production Ltd, Falkirk, Stirlingshire

Printed and bound by CPI Group (UK) Ltd, Croydon, CR0 4YY

MIX
Paper from
responsible sources
FSC
www.fsc.org   FSC® C018179

Penguin Random House is committed to a sustainable
future for our business, our readers and our planet.
This book is made from Forest Stewardship Council®
certified paper.

For my dear parents, Avril and Graham.
With all my love.

ACKNOWLEDGEMENTS

As ever, I am indebted to the wonderful people I work with. I couldn't possibly do it without you, so huge thanks and love to everyone involved – Selina Walker, my editor, for brilliant advice and friendship, as well as Georgina Hawtrey-Woore, Philippa Cotton, Jen Doyle, Sarah Page, Andrew Sauerwine, Vincent Kelleher, Richard Ogle, Dan Somerfield, Dan Balado and everyone else at Cornerstone involved with my books. Big love and thanks to Oli Munson, my agent and champion, and also to Jennifer Custer and Hélène Ferey for taking me around the world, and thanks too to all the wonderful staff at A M Heath. Gratitude and thanks to all my foreign publishers, and very special thanks indeed to Alexis Washam and her team in New York for making me feel so welcome. I am indebted to Smeg and Berry for their remarkable tales, inside knowledge, help and advice – all so invaluable as I was writing this book. (I take full responsibility for any mistakes!)

Finally, as always, my love to Terry, Ben, Polly and Lucy.

ONE MONTH EARLIER

I cling to him as the wind blasts over my body, cutting through my mind, sweeping clean my thoughts. The trees and hedges are dark flashes of danger streaking past in a midnight blur. As his right hand twists the throttle, I grip his waist and press my face against his T-shirt. His back feels warm and his muscles are tense through the fabric.

'You OK?' he yells, half turning his head.

'This is am-*azing*!' I call back, but I don't think he hears me from behind my visor. There was only one helmet dangling from the handlebars when we nicked the bike. He insisted I wear it.

'Want to go faster?'

My heart kicks out a frightened yet exhilarated beat. I glance over his shoulder at the speedometer. Fifty-six miles per hour yet it feels like twice that.

'Yes!' I scream out, nodding my helmet-head to make sure he knows I'm up for it.

We round the corner and I see the road pulling

out long and straight ahead of us. They call it Devil's Mile.

I give him a squeeze beneath his ribs, so he knows I want to go all the way, that I'm up for it. He opens up the throttle with his right hand. The bike strains, the engine noise increases, and I slide back in the seat as he releases the clutch. I hold on to him tighter and grip the bike with my legs. The road whips past us in a tarry, moonlit ribbon.

He notches up the accelerator, pushing the bike to its limits. The engine screams its power, carrying us through the desolate night-time landscape, sucking out everything that's been blowing up my head from the inside out. It's the release I need.

The end of the straight section of road approaches faster than my thoughts. I feel my fingers digging into his ribs as I wonder when he's going to brake. If we take the corner at this speed, we'll end up in the ditch.

'Slow down!' I yell.

Immediately the engine noise decreases and I lurch forward, my hips pressing against his, my body feeling like a great weight against him. He's laughing; half turns to let me know it. His white teeth flash sheer fun. As we slow down, my hands take hold of the curved metal bar behind me and I tip back my head.

'That was fucking amazing!' I say.

We bring the bike to a stop and it purrs throatily beneath us. His feet go down on the muddy verge to steady it. He's only wearing flip-flops.

'You're not exactly dressed for the occasion,' I say, swinging my leg over the back of the bike. 'Nice machine, though.'

I sound as if I know about such things, but the reality is that I've never really been into motorbikes. Now, after just one ride, I feel addicted to the thrill of speed and the temporary amnesia it brings. The engine makes a grumbling sound as I unstrap my helmet, pulling it off over my ears. My hair crackles with static and sticks up.

'I knew you'd like it,' he says, kicking down the stand and pressing up against me.

A white van comes slowly round the corner, the man inside texting or doing something with his mobile phone. I can see the glow reflected on his face. He doesn't pay us any attention.

'We haven't got long,' he continues. 'Someone's going to miss this beauty pretty soon.' He strokes the bike's seat with one hand, my backside with the other.

My stomach lurches and twists from what we've done, and my head spins from the alcohol and whatever it was I smoked.

People like me don't do things like this.

'Perhaps we should stop now,' I say. 'You know, just dump it and get out of here.' I'm suddenly terrified of getting caught – police cars, blue flashing lights, officers, cuffed hands, spending the night in a cell . . . *prison.*

'What? You don't want to take her for a spin?' He sounds disappointed. 'After all the trouble I went to?'

I stare at the motorbike and feel the rev of my heart again. The bike's sleek lines, shimmering paintwork, chunky silver exhaust – the sheer thrill of its hidden power – win me over. 'You think I can do it?'

His mouth swipes over mine. I've never felt like this before.

'Of course. Get on the front.'

He shifts aside, steadying the rumbling bike as I climb on. I pull my helmet back on, visor lifted up. The handlebars seem too far away and I have to stretch to reach them. Even just ticking over, the engine vibrates a thrill up my legs, my spine, and into my fuzzed-up brain.

'You know how to drive, right? Well, it's not so different.'

His breath smells of beer mashed up with vodka. I wonder if mine is the same; if we'll be locked up together for ever.

I move in to kiss him – *what am I doing?* – but the opening in the helmet is too small and I end up bumping him on the forehead. We burst out laughing in uncontrollable fits of loose-limbed hysteria, which nearly causes us to drop the bike between us.

'You'd better show me how it all works before I lose it completely,' I say. Then I reach and grab hold of his wrists in a surge of horror as another moment of clarity strikes me in the face. 'We've stolen a fucking motorbike! We're going to get into a crazy load of trouble for this.'

My hands and arms and shoulders are shaking and even holding on to him doesn't ease the trembling. I start to get off. This is so very wrong.

'Chill out,' he says with a cocksure laugh. 'Now, do you want to have some fun or not?'

Then his hands are on the side of the helmet, gently easing it up off my head again. His mouth is pressing down on mine, searching out the fear, kissing it all away. Making everything better.

I nod. 'Yes,' I say, loving him all the more, never wanting him to stop.

He shows me how to pull in the clutch, when to accelerate, where the gear and brake levers are and, finally, how to slow this great beast of a bike with my right hand and foot. I run through it virtually, pretending to work the controls.

'I'll be sitting right behind you and we'll just go slowly. I'll tell you exactly what to do. Now, put this back on.'

He gives me one last kiss, deeper and more tender than ever before, then slips the helmet back over my head, snaps down the visor, and climbs on.

I feel a brief pang of guilt that he should be wearing one too.

With his feet fixed on the ground, he helps me turn the motorbike around. Once again we are faced with the long stretch of road ahead of us. Its slick surface glows in the moonlight, shiny from the recent rain. All I can think of are his hands wrapped tightly over mine on the handlebar controls. He tweaks the right one back and the engine immediately responds.

'Ready?' he shouts above the noise.

I nod, and allow my hands to follow his prompts. As he releases the clutch, we slowly creep forward.

I glance at the display. Thirteen miles per hour, but it feels faster sitting at the front. He's still balancing us with his toes tapping on the ground each side. After only a couple more bursts on the accelerator, he picks up his feet and rests them on the posts.

'Keep the revs up,' he shouts. 'You don't want her to stall.'

He still has control, even though I am the one in contact with the bike. We slip seamlessly through the gears, as he kicks down on the lever.

'This is fantastic!' I cry out, but I don't think he hears.

I glance at the speedometer. I want to go faster, push it a bit before we hit the end of the straight, so I twist my right hand backwards and feel the machine respond. As the engine begins to strain, he changes up another gear and it feels as if we must be doing a hundred.

Everything is flowing out of me as we rush to the corner. I am being cleansed, filtered by sheer madness.

'I'm doing it by myself!' I call out.

I twist my right hand towards me and the thrill in my heart kicks up with the engine. I know he will be feeling the same. A few flicks of my eyes to the display:

fifty-five, and then we're creeping up through the sixties. There's room to push it more, a chance to show what I'm made of.

'You're a natural!' he yells from behind.

Without another thought I turn the accelerator towards me as far as it'll go.

There's no time to think. No time to take action. Fear and inexperience and stupidity blanket any chance of rationality in less than a second. The bike screams forward, smacking my head back against his face. I cling on, not knowing what to do, realising immediately it's too late.

The tree is a silhouette against the inky night sky. We are heading right at it, doing seventy, maybe eighty.

He's shouting. I feel his feet searching, kicking against mine. His hands don't reach the handlebars in time. His feet never make it to the controls.

We must be doing nearly a hundred when I feel a sharp shove in my ribs, hurling me sideways.

I'm flying. The ground is above me, below me, battering my back, my legs, my head, earth forced between my fingers, and smashed into my face. The bike is gone, stripped away.

Then the loud bang, the crashing thud of my skull inside the helmet as it comes to rest. A sharp pain grabs the length of my back. My left leg is twisted behind me. I can taste blood.

✳

When I open my eyes, a tree is seared on to my mind, the negative of an image I'll never forget.

My fingers claw at the cool, wet verge, reaching, searching for something, anything. I can feel the night air blowing on my face – does that mean I'm alive? I want to scream but can't.

'Where are you?' It's just a whisper.

I listen for a reply but hear nothing – nothing except . . . I take off my broken helmet, try to move, but everything hurts. The night is silent around us now with just the sound of the breeze rustling through the hedge above me. I am in the ditch.

'Hello?'

My hands come up to my head, but not without pain. I am shaking uncontrollably as the tears pour down my face. I'm not sure if it's from pain or fear or the urgent need for help. What have I done?

Please God, let him be OK. Let him be OK.

Then I spot him. A twisted creature curled and crumpled at the base of the tree. My first thought is that it's someone else, that it can't be him, that it's the chewed-up carcass of a wild animal. But as I slowly drag myself to my feet and hobble towards the tree, I recognise the green shorts and stripy T-shirt. The flip-flops are nowhere to be seen. The motorbike lies a few feet from him, bent into a barely recognisable chunk of red and orange metal.

I drop to my knees. He isn't moving.

'Wake up. Talk to me!'

My hand goes out to his shoulder. He is still warm. He is covered in blood. One side of his head is gone.

I shake him, letting out a noise that doesn't sound like me.

There is a purplish bone pushing through the skin of his right forearm and his neck is snapped too far back. His skull is open and fresh, the contents scenting the night air. I can't make myself think of the word *dead*, even though it's pushing up my throat like a hand emerging from a grave.

Stay sane, I think. Keep calm. Take his pulse. Check his breathing. Call for an ambulance . . . phone the police . . . flag down a car . . .

I stand up, fighting the pain that grips me, trying to make the darkened landscape around me stop spinning. Everything seems bigger, scarier, twisted and evil, as if the trees are gathering and marching towards me and the hedgerows are curling around to grab me.

Evil, evil person the countryside is whispering.

I have no idea what to do.

I could call an ambulance or the police, but they'll arrest me, throw me in a cell for the rest of my life. It's what I deserve.

I was driving. I was drinking. We stole a bike. Now the man I love is dead.

Then something clicks inside me. It's as if he's telling me what to do.

I go back to the ditch and retrieve the buckled helmet I was wearing, tucking it under my arm. And then I limp away. I don't look back. I don't want the memories that will haunt me, torment me in my dreams, soak my bed with night sweats. As far as I'm concerned, I was never a part of this.

I stop again – my feet unable to move for a second. There's a car approaching. Panicking, I see a gate leading into a field and scramble over it, chucking the helmet ahead of me. Headlights arc above me just as I drop down behind the hedge, illuminating everything dark in my mind. I hear the engine slow, imagine the driver's horror when he sees the scene.

Making sure I stay close to the hedge, crouching, hobbling, escaping, I disappear into the night. What will happen to me now, I have no idea.

1

Detective Inspector Lorraine Fisher slowed as she pulled off the main road. The journey from Birmingham was less than an hour but still long enough for her to make it only two or three times a year.

There was no space in her life for regrets and should-haves, therefore time spent with her younger sister in the country was usually limited to Christmas, birthdays, or the routine summer holiday visit as she was doing now. An entire week away from work suddenly seemed like an awfully long time. Or was it that an entire week in her sister's company was daunting?

She loved Jo, had always protected her, watched out for her, picked her up and dusted her off, but there was usually a price. Lorraine wondered what it would be this time.

She glanced down at her daughter's lap. 'Don't you feel sick?' Stella had been staring at her phone for the last forty-five minutes, texting, tapping messages into Facebook, playing games.

Lorraine had been hoping to catch up with her, find out about her end-of-term test results, see how she was getting on with her Geography project, but instead she'd ended up filling the rumbling void of the M40 with a programme on Radio 4, which was now coming to an end. Stella had not been pleased by the early start, and had had to be cajoled into the car, still in her pyjama bottoms and an old sweatshirt, with the promise of hastily made bacon sandwiches and crisps for breakfast.

'Dad would have a fit if he could see this lot,' Stella giggled as they'd wrapped the food in foil and dropped various other junk into a carrier bag.

'Then we won't tell him, will we?' Lorraine said, feeling slightly smug.

'Dad can force Grace to eat his organic yoghurt and bucketloads of berries later,' Stella said, also enjoying the subterfuge.

Lorraine had said goodbye to her older daughter the night before, knowing she wouldn't be up before they left. Grace was meeting a friend later and they were off to an athletics camp. She'd been looking forward to it for ages.

Their week together would be, Jo had said on the phone a few days ago, just like old times. Lorraine hadn't said anything, but that's exactly what worried her. 'Old times' implied Jo getting herself into an emotional pickle, making ludicrous decisions and bad choices – and, as ever, Lorraine bailing her out.

She'd always called her a restless soul. Jo, it seemed, was never satisfied with what she had.

'Why do you have to drive so bumpy?' Stella asked.

Lorraine rolled her eyes and smiled. 'It's not my driving, it's these country lanes. We're not in the city now you know. If you look up from that phone you'd see . . . cows or something.'

She flicked her hand towards the windscreen. Endless fields dotted with dark green wooded areas, ripening crops scattered across the undulating earth, and the meandering lane tacked on to the farmland spanned the breadth of their view. Everything was vibrant and lush, as if it had been coloured in from an entirely different palette to that of their built-up neighbour-hood in Moseley.

If she was honest, Lorraine envied her sister still living in the country. It was where they'd both grown up. Moving to Birmingham at the age of eighteen had been an escape for her at the time – twenty-five years ago now – and she admitted the city was in her blood, part of her life, a place she couldn't imagine not being in.

But these Warwickshire villages, especially her child-hood home of Radcote, would never leave her heart. The mellow ginger stone of the local buildings, the low brows of thatched cottages, the cow parsley verges, the tiny post office with its musty wooden floor and big jars of penny sweets on crooked shelves, the land-mark churches with their towers and spires marking the route on endless summer bike rides – it was all tattooed on her heart.

As the road narrowed and curved, bending between farms and livestock, crops and Dutch barns with stacks of hay, Lorraine wound down the window and breathed in deeply, tasting the air. It was sweet and slightly cloying. Just how she remembered it. Already she felt the feeling of coming home seeping into her skin.

She smiled. This week was going to be just what she needed. A damned good rest.

She indicated right and turned down an even narrower lane. The hedges pulled in close, cloaking their passage with varying shades of green, as well as brighter patches of white or yellow flowers. Every so often they passed a gateway with a crusted muddy entrance where tractors had been coming and going.

'What happens if another car comes?' Stella asked, dropping her phone into her bag. Her arms were folded across her stomach as if she might be sick at any moment.

'One of us has to back up to a passing point,' Lorraine stated.

'But what if no one will?'

'Then I guess we sit there all day,' Lorraine replied, quite used to her daughter's endless questions. Occasionally her wayward line of thought would contain a shred of what seemed like brilliance or unusual insight, which prevented Lorraine from silencing her when other mothers might have grown impatient. As far as she was concerned, Stella could babble on. It was white noise that she enjoyed, a welcome contrast to her job. 'But people are generally friendly in the countryside.'

'What if they have a gun?'

'Well, you're in trouble then,' she said, speeding up again as the lane straightened into a more driveable stretch. 'Know what they call this road?' Lorraine asked, pointing ahead. It used to scare her as a kid, give her a creepy yet slightly irresistible feeling. She'd always pedalled that bit harder when cycling along it to the next village to visit a friend.

'A road?'

'Devil's Mile,' Lorraine said, with a slight growl to her voice. Before Stella had a chance to ask, she added, 'I have no idea why.'

'Probably because the Devil lives here or something,' Stella said matter-of-factly. She was obviously feeling less nauseous all of a sudden as the phone came out of her bag again in response to the bleep of an incoming text. 'It would liven this place up a bit if he did. It looks dead boring.'

'There's another straight road not far from here called the Fosse Way,' Lorraine continued.

She'd been going to explain about the Roman road's route but slowed at the sight of a dozen or so wilted bunches of flowers laid at the base of a tree to their left. There were a couple of notes and cards pinned to the trunk, drooping and soggy from all the recent rain. Lorraine hated seeing these temporary shrines to lost loved ones. Usually these cases were tragic accidents rather than anything sinister, but occasionally she'd have to deal with the clean-up, the painful aftermath of assessing what had happened when Traffic, the first officers on the scene, called her in. She'd worked a number of times with the Serious Collision Investigation Unit when initial findings weren't entirely clear-cut and a more disturbing outcome was suspected.

She glanced in the rear-view mirror at the faded floral tribute as they passed and wondered if it was anyone local.

'Very sad,' she said.

'What is?'

'Those flowers. Someone must have died in an accident.'

Lorraine flicked the indicator again and turned down the final lane that would take them to Radcote.

'Maybe the Devil killed someone,' Stella said, pulling open another bag of crisps and stuffing a handful into her mouth.

*

'I can't believe you didn't bloody tell me,' Lorraine said, easing out of the sisterly embrace. 'It's pretty up there as family crises go.'

They'd barely got out of the car before Jo had

emerged from the front door, picking her way across the gravel with bare feet, cotton skirt swishing at her ankles. She was at her sister's side, unperturbed by Stella's indifference to their arrival, and had simply stated, calm as anything, 'Malc's buggered off.'

'When?' Lorraine beeped the car locked, thrust a bag at Stella to carry, and walked across the drive with Jo.

'Two months ago.'

'Two months? And it didn't occur to you to pick up the phone and tell me?'

'I didn't want to worry you. You're always so busy.'

Lorraine felt a surge of familiar guilt. Her work spilled into family time, into *everything*. It was the way it was, always had been. Yet Jo was making it sound as though the break-up was somehow her fault.

'And I knew you were visiting soon anyway, so thought I'd tell you in person,' she added.

They went inside the hallway of Glebe House. The cool, slightly musty air immediately transported Lorraine back to her childhood. The smell of the place never changed. She wouldn't have been in the least surprised if her mother had come through from the kitchen to greet her, wiping flour-covered hands on a faded floral apron, her hair twisted behind her head in a tight grey knot, a handmade skirt over the dark tights she always wore, winter or summer.

Lorraine shook the memory of her mother from her head. This was Jo's house now, and she was glad.

She gazed around and gave a little shiver, realising she'd left her cardigan in the car. It was cooler inside. The thick-walled house remained a constant temperature all year round. Only once all three fires had been blazing for at least half a day during the winter months did the pervading chill lift, allowing them to stretch out of all but the essential layers of clothing.

'Oh, come here,' Jo said as they dumped the bags on the uneven flagstones.

It was then that they hugged properly. Lorraine felt her sister's slightly leaner body pressed against hers, felt her ribs and slim waist beneath the cotton of her white blouse. She suddenly felt ashamed of the two rounds of bacon sandwiches and crisps she'd consumed on the journey. But Jo's bucolic lifestyle was more conducive to keeping healthy than her own frantic, grab-any-food-going, busy-working-mum routine as a detective inspector.

'Are you OK for money?' It had to be asked. Jo hadn't had a paying job in years.

They were in the kitchen now. Nothing much had changed in here since her last visit either. In fact, you wouldn't even know that Malc had left, Lorraine thought, noticing a pair of man's sunglasses on the dresser and a tweed cap hooked over the peg beside the back door.

She'd never thought of Malc as a cap man. He worked in the City, commuting some days, but more often than not he'd be holed up in his Docklands studio flat, returning to Radcote at weekends.

Lorraine would never have guessed he'd give up the country life so easily. But if she was honest, she thought Jo looked better for being single. Her skin seemed healthier and brighter, and her eyes had a mischievous sparkle to them.

'Malc's being generous. Giving me what I need.'

Stella dragged a wooden chair from under the table, making a terrible noise on the quarry tiles. She slumped down, earphone wires winding out from within the unbrushed tangle of her hair. She rested her head on the table and made an overstated yawn.

'Oh, poor little Stell,' Jo said. 'Didn't you get all your beauty sleep last night?' She rubbed her back playfully. She had always doted on her nieces.

Stella made a grumbling sound from within the nest of her arms.

'You can do me a favour if you like and wake Freddie up. He's still in bed. A couple of bombs and an earthquake should do the trick.'

Another indignant moan and squirm from Stella made Jo stop teasing.

'Shall I make some tea?'

Lorraine nodded, trying not to show her irritation with her sister's news. Whatever she felt about Malcolm and the way he'd so speedily stepped into Jo's life eight years ago (although that was almost certainly down to Jo's impulsiveness at work) and now his sudden retreat, he was the man her sister had chosen to marry, the man who had adopted her son, the man who'd looked after her and supported her financially. And knowing Jo as she did, that was no mean feat.

But she still thought he was a complete shit for deserting his wife.

No doubt, she thought as the kettle boiled, he'd found something younger, something less tarnished by the nagging drudgery of running a large house and bringing up a teenage boy mostly alone while he was living it up in London.

They sat outside in the mid-morning sun, the tray set down on the white-painted iron table that she remembered her father sanding and lacquering every couple of years. It was clear to Lorraine that Jo had kept up their mother's high standards around the place since she'd moved in five years ago. It looked as if she'd worked her fingers to the bone weeding and maintaining the acre of garden. It was immaculate, and the crammed-in shrubs and herbaceous plants were in full bloom. The thick scent of the overhead jasmine winding around the pergola and the nearby thicket of roses made Lorraine feel almost dizzy. She marvelled at the patchwork of coloured borders that she knew had taken years to mature.

It was nothing like her modest, sun-deprived suburban patch that only ever got used a few times in the summer when they threw a last-minute barbecue for friends or work colleagues, or when she ducked outside for a sneaky cigarette, usually at the end of a long day during an investigation that didn't allow for any kind of routine. She hadn't done a scrap of gardening this year, and Adam had only cut the grass a handful of times.

'You're going to tell me it was an affair, aren't you,' she probed, but with a casual inflection so it didn't sound as if she had an issue with the word. Jo wouldn't respond to an inquisition.

She thought she noticed a small nod.

'You know, if dog-ends grew into flowers, mine would look way better than this,' Lorraine said with a laugh, sweeping her hand out in front of her.

'Yes,' Jo said with a curt nod. 'And I mean about the affair, not the dog-ends.'

'I'm sorry to hear that, Jo. I hope you kicked him out in a good and proper village-rousing, suit-slashing display of emasculation, rather than allowing him to slink off with his tail between his legs when no one was looking.'

Jo fished the teabag out of Lorraine's mug, added milk and stirred in some sugar. 'He left quietly of his own free will.'

'I bet he bloody did.'

'Lorraine . . .' Jo sighed. 'It's me having the affair, not him.' She slid the mug towards her sister.

Lorraine took a breath. 'I see,' she said, picking up her tea.

The first thing she thought about was the house. It had belonged to their parents. It was their family home – Freddie's inheritance now. When their father had died ten years ago, their mother, June, had continued to live there for several years. But the place was no good without him, she'd said. *Too big, too empty, too heartbreaking* . . .

Too much to cope with, Lorraine suspected but never said.

And then, one day, her mother had packed up a few essentials and, without telling anyone, moved into her caravan on the north Cornish coast. It was a month before they knew where she'd gone. She'd since re-located to a more substantial park home, and had never set foot inside Glebe House again. No one really understood why. It was just the way she was.

In the meantime, she had made arrangements for the property to be signed over entirely to her youngest daughter, as if she was already dead and buried. Lorraine's theory was that she wanted to leave a family feud in her wake that she could actually witness and enjoy. She gave nothing to Lorraine.

Lorraine had barely finished reeling from the unfairness of this transaction when, without prompting, Jo did the right thing and bought out her stunned sister's imaginary share – or rather, Malc bought it out soon after he'd married Jo.

'She'll have to try harder than that, sis,' Jo had said once the paperwork was finalised.

Lorraine was grateful. There had been no family feud for her mother to enjoy. But the gesture had made her feel indebted to Jo – something she continued to feel uncomfortable about, and even, if she was honest, a bit resentful of.

'Tell me he wasn't . . . you know, hurting you or anything,' Lorraine said now, taking a sip of tea.

There was silence, interrupted only by the buzzing of insects driven wild by the garden scents. Lorraine had brought this up a couple of Christmases ago, after noticing a pale green bruise around Jo's upper arm, but had been told in no uncertain terms to let it drop, that she'd bashed herself while hauling the tree inside.

'I just met someone else,' she finally responded. 'We clicked. Malc's job was taking him away all the time. We weren't really getting on.' She batted a wasp away with her hand, flinching when it returned.

'You were lonely, then?'

'No, I wasn't lonely.' Jo seemed certain about that.

'Then what?'

'I can't honestly say,' she replied.

Lorraine wasn't sure if it was more a case of *won't* say or that she simply didn't know. Or, she wondered, was it another of Jo's manically bad decisions that she would live to regret?

Either way, the moment of finding out had passed because Freddie emerged from the kitchen door, stumbling out on to the terrace wearing pyjama bottoms and a tatty blue dressing gown. His feet were bare and huge, Lorraine noted, thinking back to the last time she'd seen him – far too long ago, considering they only lived an hour or so from each other. Every time she saw Jo and Freddie she made a mental promise that she'd come up more often, every month or every couple of months at the very least. But promises soon fell by the wayside when work took over.

'Freddie, my God, you've grown another six feet!' Lorraine stood up. She opened her arms wide, trying to ignore the pained expression that spread across her nephew's face.

Freddie absorbed the hug as best he could. Lorraine was grateful for that. She released his limp body and held him at arm's length. She thought he looked a little pale, washed-out, and he smelled of sleep.

'You look well,' she said tentatively, with a forced grin and a wink at Jo. 'What's your mum been feeding you?'

Freddie laughed pleasantly, humouring his aunt. He'd always been a good-mannered boy, brought up properly by his mum and stepdad. By *Jo*, Lorraine thought to herself, not wanting to give Malc too much credit. She hoped by the end of the week's stay she would know more about what had gone wrong, but for now she wasn't entirely prepared to give him the benefit of the doubt. There must be a good reason for Jo to have acted this way, she told herself.

'You look well too, Aunty Lorraine,' he said, pulling the dressing gown tightly around his chest. He folded his arms, wrapping himself up as if it was winter rather than the twenty or so degrees it must already be.

'What's the plan before we go to the theatre this afternoon, then?' Jo said to her son in an expectant way.

Lorraine knew that tone of voice well, having used it on her girls many times. It contained the vague hope that the morning might consist of something other than lounging around watching TV, and military manoeuvres on the fridge every half hour.

Freddie shrugged. His hand paddled through his hair, as if sweeping away the idea that he might be required to do something useful. 'Dunno. Not sure I'm coming. I haven't woken up yet.' He shifted from one foot to the other and his eyes narrowed to slits in the sunlight. He was clearly wishing that he hadn't come outside.

'Did you say hello to Stella?' Jo asked him.

At the mention of his young cousin, Freddie allowed a slight grin. 'Yeah, but she's asleep at the kitchen table. Sensible girl.' That endearing laugh again, followed by another ruffle of his unruly blond hair. There was nothing short back and sides about it.

'Why don't you take her up to the Manor?'

Lorraine immediately noticed the change in her sister's voice. It was lighter, expectant.

'What for?' Freddie said.

Jo hesitated. 'You know,' she said, looking across the garden, shielding her eyes with her hand. 'Take

Stella to see the horses or something. Maybe you'll bump into Lana. It's such a nice morning. There's no point spending it indoors.'

Freddie made a noise – a cross between a laugh and a snort. He stared at the ground and shook his head a couple of times. 'Yeah, OK, I'll take Stella out. But you wake her up.' He turned and disappeared through the French doors into the darkness of the kitchen.

Once he was out of earshot, Jo frowned. 'How do you think he seemed?' she asked.

'Tall,' Lorraine replied flippantly. 'Why?'

Jo wrapped her fingers around her mug. She brought it to her mouth and took a long sip, taking a moment to gaze around the garden again. Lorraine could see she wasn't admiring the flowers, rather trying to figure out how to say what was on her mind.

'I've been worried about him, that's all.'

'How come?'

'He's just not been himself recently. He's quiet, sullen, rude even. Some days he doesn't even get out of bed. And he's stopped seeing his mates.'

'Sounds like a normal eighteen-year-old. Girl troubles, perhaps?'

'I wish,' Jo said. 'That would mean he'd actually made an effort, bothered to go out, meet friends, socialise, be normal. He's just spent all his time in his room on his computer the last few months.'

'Probably just a phase.' Lorraine looked at her sister, admired her deep blue eyes and glossy blonde hair, and sighed. 'But maybe he's taken your separation harder than you thought. He is really close to Malc.'

Jo shifted uncomfortably. 'I wondered about that too, but he was like it before Malc left.' She rubbed her eyes, and when she looked at Lorraine again, there was real fear in her face. 'I often hear him crying,' she said. 'Up in his room. Not just normal crying, but a deep, soul-ripping, aching crying.' There was a pause. 'It scares me.' She paused again. 'You know, after everything, I couldn't bear it if anything happened to him.'

2

Freddie lugged Stella's bag upstairs, and left her to change. When she came down to the kitchen ten minutes later dressed in shorts and a T-shirt, he tossed a can of Coke at her, thinking how grown-up she looked. He watched as she held back her blonde curls and drank.

'Are you sure you want to go out?' he asked. He wasn't keen on taking her to the Manor. He had other things to do. He sighed and glanced at his watch. He had that stupid theatre trip to worm out of, too.

'What else is there to do around here?' she asked, shrugging.

'Nothing,' he replied, picking up an apple from the fruit bowl. He gave it to Stella when he saw the look on her face and took another for himself. 'Come on then. Let's get this over with.'

They left the house and headed off down the lane, Freddie with one hand thrust deep into his jeans pocket, striding off at speed. He heard Stella's smaller footsteps struggling to keep up with him.

'I'm sorry you have to do this,' she called out.

He felt a pang of guilt. He didn't want to be mean to her. She had no idea about all the crap on his mind.

'You don't have to look after me,' Stella continued. 'You can just leave me over there and I'll sit in the bus stop for a bit if you like. Our mums won't know.'

Freddie stopped and turned. He stared down at her through the frizzy tendrils of his unkempt fringe, watching as she fiddled with the cluster of bracelets on her wrist. He couldn't prevent a half-hearted smile from forming. She was far from grown-up, he decided, and hoped she stayed that way. He'd hate to think of her dealing with problems like his.

'Don't be daft,' he said in the kindest voice he could manage. 'I needed to get out of the house.' He watched her for a moment before striding off again. 'Come on, I'll take you to see the horses. All girls like horses, don't they?'

'Not really,' Stella muttered, running to keep up.

The entrance to the Manor was well hidden off the lane leading out of the village. It was opposite the church, tucked between two oak trees, and was heralded by a rather crooked and rotten five-bar gate rather than anything grand like the house's name suggested. The drive was a couple of hundred metres long and ended with a shabby little building made of pale red brick and a slate roof. Ivy was knitted into the mortar.

'It's not very big,' Stella commented as they approached. 'And it's grotty.'

Freddie laughed. 'That's not the Manor, that's just the old tack room. The stables are behind it and the main house is beyond that. It's huge.'

'So no one lives in there then?' Stella said.

She walked up to the building and tried to peer in through the ground-floor window, but there were waist-high nettles growing in a skirt around the base, preventing her from getting close. She stood on tiptoe, moving her head from side to side, trying to get a better view through the dirty cobwebbed glass.

'Is it haunted?' she asked.

The look in her eyes made Freddie wish he was her age all over again.

He drew up beside her, putting on a scary voice. 'They say someone who escaped from a mental hospital lives in there, that he's a mad murderer.'

'*Really?*' Stella's breath snagged in her throat.

Freddie didn't get a chance to reply as a figure suddenly appeared from round the side of the ivy-clad building. He tensed but then relaxed when he saw who it was.

'Hi,' she said cheerily.

Seeing her, he felt a temporary wave of lightness. He'd hoped she'd be here. There were things they needed to discuss. He forced himself to speak, to stop staring at her, wondering what life would be like without all the shit going on.

'Hi, Lana,' he replied.

Stella was suddenly beside him, clearly intrigued by the older girl. He put a hand on one of her shoulders. 'This is my cousin, Stella,' he said, pushing his other hand into his pocket when his phone vibrated, feeling the familiar wave of nausea.

'Hello, cousin Stella,' Lana said. 'I'm Lana, Freddie's . . . friend.'

Freddie's heart clenched. Had she been going to say *girl*friend? They weren't a couple, not really, not yet.

'Nice to meet you.' Stella offered her hand politely.

Freddie couldn't help the grin of affection towards his little cousin. However indomitable and sometimes unapproachable his Aunty Lorraine had seemed over the years, she'd brought her daughters up right. He wondered if his mum sometimes got it wrong, that Lorraine wasn't the powerhouse, the workaholic, the never-at-home mother she thought her to be. Surely Stella wouldn't be so nice if that was true? He was still a bit wary of his aunt though – she was a police detective, after all.

'How long are you staying in Radcote for?' Lana asked. She pulled out a packet of mints from her shorts pocket and offered them to Stella.

'A week,' Stella said, prising a sweet from the tube.

'Do you like horses?' Lana said, slipping her arm through the crook of Stella's.

'*Love* them,' Stella replied.

They walked off together, leaving Freddie standing

alone. He sighed. There was no way they'd be able to talk now.

Stella glanced over her shoulder, beckoning Freddie on with her eyes.

They reached the paddock fence, and Freddie leant on the wooden crossbar of the gate. He stared out across the Manor's acreage. The level field was dotted with five or six horses and ponies, most with heads bowed, munching the lush grass. Stella squinted at them, her hand shielding her eyes from the bright sun. Two of the horses looked up and began slowly to plod over to where they were standing.

Freddie closed his eyes and finally dared to take his phone from his pocket. The messages were always similar. He wasn't sure how much more of them he could take.

Beside him, Stella was looking at the Manor looming behind them in a great shadow of red brick, twirling tall chimneys and gingery stone windows. He knew it was very different to her house in Birmingham. Lana lived a privileged life.

Freddie watched, pensively, as the bigger of the two horses – brown and white, with a stubbly beard and massive feet – approached, and Stella nervously stuck out her hand.

'It smells,' she said, wrinkling her nose.

A cluster of flies had followed the horse across the field, forcing the creature to swish its tail every few seconds and shake its head in annoyance. Stella suddenly retracted her outstretched fingers when it wrinkled its lips and threw back its head. It let out a fearsome noise.

'Oh, Bruce,' Lana said, laughing. 'Stop being a grump.'

She removed the mints from her pocket again and levered several of them into her palm, which she held out flat for the horse to take. They were gone in a second. The horse head-butted the fence and scraped at the bare earth with his hoof.

While they were both preoccupied, Freddie took a deep breath and read the message, feeling sick. Would it ever stop?

'Are you OK, Freddie?' he vaguely heard Stella asking.

He was aware of the flush on his cheeks, the tremor in his hands as he put his phone away. 'Yeah, yeah, I'm fine,' he managed, catching sight of someone approaching.

A couple of crows clapped out of a nearby tree.

Stella and Lana turned.

'Hello, Gil,' Lana said affectionately in the same voice she'd used to speak to the horse. 'How are you today?'

There was no reply.

Freddie noticed how Stella stepped back, pressing against the gate. Gil had come right up close, but it was as if he hadn't even seen them. He approached the fence, squeezing between Lana and Stella, where both horses were idly scratching the wood with their foreheads. He stared across the field.

'He doesn't always want to talk,' Lana explained to Stella. 'Do you, Gil?'

Stella nodded nervously. Freddie wanted to tell her it was OK, Gil was harmless, but the text had knocked the air from his lungs.

Die, you useless fuck. Go kill yourself.

'But when he does . . .' Lana trailed off with a giggle. 'He's hard to stop.'

'Who are you?' Gil suddenly asked, staring at Stella. He sounded like a kid reading out loud to a teacher, even though he was an adult.

Stella recoiled visibly and looked at Freddie.

'She's Freddie's cousin, Gil,' Lana said, stepping in.

'Will you be my friend?' he asked Stella, shifting from one foot to the other. 'Good,' he continued, even though Stella hadn't replied. He stared down at the ground. 'You're my friend now and I am glad to have you as a friend because I don't have very many.'

'Do you want to feed Bruce?' Lana asked him, going over to where the grass grew long just outside the reach of the horses' mouths. She picked some, wincing as she bent down, and gave a handful to Gil.

'Shall we go now?' Freddie heard Stella ask. But he was looking at his phone again, wondering whether to reply, see if he could make them back off.

Gil fed the horse, then suddenly spun round and hurled himself at Stella. His arms went round her body, knocking her off balance and pushing her against the gate. Her eyes grew huge and she opened her mouth to scream.

Freddie dropped his phone and was immediately between them, fighting Gil off Stella, getting him in an armlock.

'I'm OK,' Stella said weakly, attempting a laugh. She was hugging herself.

Freddie saw the tears gathering in her eyes.

'Let him go, Freddie.' Lana prised Freddie's arms off Gil. 'He didn't mean to scare her. He just gets over-enthusiastic sometimes.'

Gil was clapping clumsily and nodding, unashamed by what he'd just done. He pulled at Bruce's mane. 'They say I'm bad but I'm not,' he said.

The horses kicked up their heels and galloped off across the field in a chain reaction of bucks and side-swipes. Gil turned and lumbered off down the path.

Freddie picked up his phone and put an arm around Stella. 'You sure you're OK?' he asked.

She nodded, sniffing back the tears.

Freddie ruffled her hair, fighting back his own tears, although for different reasons. 'He could be the one, you know,' he whispered, in a spooky-film voice, forcing himself to be brighter for Stella's sake. 'The evil murderer who lives in the old tack room.'

'He's not evil, you idiot,' Lana said immediately, but her words were obliterated by a sudden shriek from across the garden.

They all turned. Gil was crouching, spit frothing at the corners of his mouth. The muscles in his forearms stood out as if his limbs were attached to his shoulders by thick cords.

'I'm not a murderer!' he shouted. 'I didn't do it!'

Lana ran over to him.

Stella clung on to Freddie, shaking.

'He was my friend but now he is dead. Don't blame me! Don't blame me!'

'No one's blaming you for anything, Gil,' Lana said kindly. 'Let's get you inside.'

She led him off towards the house, looking back at Freddie briefly, allowing him to see the worry written all over her face.

Freddie didn't know if he should go after her and help her or stay with Stella. In the end, he remained frozen, watching until they'd disappeared from sight, feeling even more useless than he already was.

3

Lorraine gave a little smile when she heard Stella's gasp of delight. Her daughter had been looking forward to the play all week.

'Is that the place?' she asked as they viewed the wide red-brick building with its glass-topped tower sitting squarely beside the river. 'Shakespeare's theatre?'

Stella had stopped in her tracks as they'd rounded the corner from Sheep Street. They'd just finished lunch in a quaint bistro housed in a beamy black-and-white-fronted Tudor building with a wonky roof and cobbled courtyard at the rear. It had prompted her to pour out everything she knew about the 1500s. She'd not visited Stratford-upon-Avon for a few years and, now that she was older and had studied the period at school, she was devouring the quirky old buildings that seeped history.

'It's not Shakespeare's theatre as such,' Jo replied, 'but it's home to the Royal Shakespeare Company.' She wrapped her arm around her niece's shoulders. 'It opened in the nineteen thirties.'

Stella nodded and spouted off another stream of facts about Elizabethan times and the Globe Theatre in London, tumbling over her words until Jo had to stop her. 'Come on or we'll be late,' she said, laughing, leading Stella across the road.

Lorraine was pleased to see her daughter a bit more cheerful now. When Freddie had brought her back from the Manor earlier she'd seemed upset about something. Tearful, even. She hadn't wanted to talk about it or say why, and Freddie hadn't provided answers when asked. He'd just sloped off up to his room, saying he wouldn't be coming to see the play. Jo had looked crestfallen.

The Royal Shakespeare Company theatre dominated Waterside, appearing almost factory-like and urban since its refurbishment. The glass and brick was a fitting contrast, Lorraine thought as they climbed the steps, to the historic performances it housed. She loved seeing Stella so inspired and made a promise to book tickets more often.

'It's going to be great,' Lorraine whispered once they were seated. 'But you'll have to concentrate.' She flipped through the programme. 'It's not always easy to follow.'

'I'll try,' Stella replied.

Lorraine felt a pang of satisfaction. She doubted that Grace would have shown much interest in seeing *A Midsummer Night's Dream*, let alone sit still inside for several hours when the weather was so nice. Grace would be having a much better time at her athletics camp.

Moments later, the lights dimmed and three actors appeared on stage, their voices loud and commanding. Other characters entered across bridge-like walkways either side of them, making Stella spin round in wonder, taking it all in. It was instantly magical; they felt as if they were part of the story in the intimate, tiered theatre. Stella's fingers crept on to Lorraine's lap, clasping her hands. She looked across and winked at her daughter. It was a perfect way to spend an afternoon.

✳

'Mum?' Stella said when the play was over and they were outside. The sun flashed from behind huge white clouds that were reflected in the surface of the River Avon flowing slowly through the town. Brightly coloured narrow boats were moored against the bank, several of them queuing to enter the lock. It was a colourful spectacle. 'Was what happened to Pyramus and Thisbe in the play the same as what happened to that boy in Aunty Jo's village?'

Stella stopped and turned round. The expanse of lawn ahead, cut up with neat block-paved pathways, was crammed with tourists crowding round a street performer. Lorraine noticed the look of wonder on her daughter's face as she spotted the juggler's fiery batons flying into the air. But then she looked back up at her mother and Lorraine recognised the telltale furrows of worry and inquisitiveness on her daughter's brow. She put her arm round her slender shoulders and drew her close.

'What boy, love?'

'I know the story of Pyramus and Thisbe is a play within a play. But when Pyramus kills himself, thinking that a lion killed his girlfriend, and then she kills herself because she is so unhappy, is that like when suicide becomes contagious? Like what happened to that boy in Radcote? Will I catch it?' Stella tugged the strap of Lorraine's shoulder bag. 'Mum?'

Lorraine wanted to take a moment to think about this, to formulate a suitable reply. She didn't know what to say.

'Anyway, I need the loo,' Stella said when Lorraine remained silent. 'I'll meet you over there in ten minutes.' She gestured towards a bench and walked briskly back towards the theatre, leaving Lorraine grateful for the reprieve.

She waited for Jo, who was watching the juggler, to catch up. They walked on slowly together and sat down on the bench. The surrounding lawns were neatly mown and the sun was warm on their backs. A band of midges hovered in the late-afternoon heat. It was a typical summer's afternoon, perfect for a day of not thinking about work.

'Stella just asked something a bit odd,' Lorraine

said, squinting at the waterfront, watching the tourists as they ambled alongside the river. She heard all kinds of accents, but mainly American and Japanese. She smiled to herself as a large coach party swapped cameras to get an assortment of shots.

'What's she got on her mind now?' Jo said, smiling.

'It was a bit grim, actually. She was asking about suicide.' Lorraine paused. 'And she mentioned Radcote.'

Jo sighed. 'Welcome home.' The irony was palpable. 'People haven't forgotten yet.'

'But that was eighteen months ago, wasn't it?'

The sudden cluster of teenage suicides had shocked the local community to the core. What had begun as a tragic, isolated death when a seventeen-year-old girl hanged herself in her bedroom quickly turned into front-page news when five more teenagers took their own lives in and around Radcote within the space of two weeks. Boys and girls alike; there was no sense to the terrible loss of life.

'It still seems like yesterday,' Jo said. 'And do you want to know something?'

Lorraine nodded reluctantly.

'Sonia and Tony Hawkeswell, the couple who own the Manor in Radcote, their son Simon was one of the dead. He was second last.'

Lorraine felt a chill sweep up her legs. 'Oh my God, that's awful.' Goosebumps puckered the skin on her arms. 'I'm really sorry to hear that. Did he hang himself too?'

The expression on Jo's face reminded Lorraine that talking about death so frankly was second nature to her, but not necessarily so for everyone.

Jo shook her head. 'Yes. It was terrible. He left a note.'

Lorraine spotted Stella coming out of the theatre and raised a hand as her daughter peered around looking for them. They stood up and began a slow walk towards the water.

'Sadly, clusters like these do happen,' Lorraine told her sister as Stella approached. 'We have to learn from them, to prevent future incidents.' She was, of course, talking as a detective, but her words still rang true.

Jo nodded. 'It just seemed as if everyone local knew one of the dead, or if not, then a relative or friend who was suffering because of it. No one was immune.'

'Immune. Interesting choice of word. Stella mentioned about suicide being contagious just now.'

'It *was* like a disease,' Jo said. 'It *did* seem contagious. Everyone worried for their kids. Freddie was sixteen at the time and I fretted myself sick about him. To be honest, the worry has never gone. You don't forget something like that.'

'Hi, Stell. All OK?' Lorraine said, stepping away from Jo.

Stella hugged her mother round the waist and briefly rested her head on her shoulder. 'Yes. So now you can answer my question. Is it possible to catch suicide?'

They'd reached the water's edge before Lorraine

answered. First they'd bought some ice creams at Jo's suggestion, and spoken about the possibility of a rowing boat ride and what they would pick up from the supermarket for supper on the way home. None of this was enough to dissuade Stella from pressing on as they stood licking their vanilla cones.

'The short and easy answer, my love, is no, you can't catch suicide,' Lorraine said, taking her daughter's hand. 'It's not a disease in the contagious sense, although depression needs treating by a doctor.'

'I'm not a kid, Mum. I know something bad happened near Aunty Jo's house a few weeks back. A boy drove a motorbike into a tree on purpose. Freddie told me. He said it will probably spread like a disease all over again, that everyone's talking on Facebook about it.' Stella licked the edge of her ice cream as part of it slid down the cone and on to her fingers.

'Well, Freddie's being silly,' said Jo. 'You know how horrid big cousins can be.' She rummaged in her bag and handed Stella some tissues.

'Freddie's not horrid,' Stella said, wiping her mouth. 'But that nasty man was. He cried and wailed and said he wasn't a murderer.'

'What nasty man?' Jo said. She licked her ice cream. 'What are you on about, Stell?'

'Freddie says he's called Gil, and he lives in a little house up at the Manor. Me and Freddie . . . Freddie and I . . . we were on a walk and we met Lana and then Gil came and fed the horses and then he grabbed me and when he walked off he got all mad and strange and then that's when he mentioned the man who died, and that he was his friend.'

'Someone grabbed you?' Lorraine looked Stella in the eye. 'Why didn't you tell me before?'

Stella let out a mini-sigh. 'I'm fine. But, Mum, *listen*. Freddie said that the disease had come back. A boy killed himself a few weeks ago and mark his words, more kids would die. I don't want to catch it. I want to go home.'

Lorraine hugged her. 'Sweetheart, when people take their own lives, it's very sad and a terrible waste, but it is *not* a disease that you can catch. Nothing bad is going to happen to you so I don't want to hear any more talk about suicide or having to go home. Now, are you sure you're OK?' She tipped Stella's face up towards hers, and Stella nodded. 'In that case, we're going to have a lovely week with Aunty Jo. What could be better?'

'Going on a rowing boat?' Stella said, crunching down on the side of her cone.

❈

Later, Jo handed Lorraine a glass of wine. They were at home, sitting either side of the kitchen table, each of them incredulous at how the weather had suddenly changed. Lorraine peered out of the French doors that led on to the terrace where they'd been sitting in the sun that morning. Drizzle wiggled down the glass, making the garden scene appear more autumnal than the end of July. Even the light was fading early, a swoop of thick clouds having cast a purple-grey shroud over the landscape.

On the journey home from Stratford, Stella had blurted out that it was an omen, that the rain coming so suddenly meant something sinister was going to happen. 'You wait,' she'd said in a demonic voice.

Lorraine had reassured her, but had made a mental note to discuss it with Adam on the phone later. They needed to be more vigilant about keeping work discussions, however masked in code they thought they were, out of family time. Not that there had been much of that recently. Their professional lives were often entwined – Adam was also a detective inspector with the West Midlands Police – though their caseloads had diverged over the last couple of months. Lorraine was actually grateful for this, given what had happened last time they'd worked as a team. Adam had been the Senior Investigating Officer and Lorraine didn't mind, but occasionally she'd have liked to be considered before him. Together they had over forty years' worth of experience so when it was called upon it usually meant a major investigation was underway – murder, more often than not.

'Freddie's just a big kid when he hangs out with Stella,' Lorraine said with a smile, sipping her wine. She could hear the movie Stella had put on in the other room. *Finding Nemo* was one of her favourites from years ago. 'He adores her.'

'I'm afraid he's not watching it any more,' Jo replied. 'He lasted all of two minutes. He'll be up in his room now on his computer. He can't go more than an hour without it.'

Lorraine understood. Stella loved nothing more than a session chatting with her mates online. Grace, on the other hand, preferred her life to take place in the real world. If she wasn't allowed to be the centre of attention with her group of friends, or to play for her sports teams, or to go to lots of parties, she thought she would literally waste away.

'You sound annoyed about that,' Lorraine said.

Jo drained her glass of wine. 'He just seems so . . .' She hesitated. 'Look, this isn't easy to say. It's awful, in fact, but . . .' She looked towards the door. There was no one there. 'I think Freddie has been cutting himself.' She drew a line across her forearm with her index finger. 'He just seems so lonely and aloof all the time. That's why I encouraged him to go and see the horses with Stella earlier. I wanted him to bump into Lana, actually. He seems to really like her.'

'Wait a minute, back up there. *Cutting* himself? Freddie? Jesus Christ.' Lorraine took a deep breath. She couldn't imagine how she'd feel if she thought either of her daughters was doing that.

'There was a razor blade in his room. I discovered

it when I was changing his sheets. I found blood on one of his school shirts, too.' Jo drank more wine. 'I thought I saw some faint scabs on his arm but he wouldn't show me. He got embarrassed and wore long sleeves for ages. That was a couple of months ago now. I don't think he's done it since and I haven't noticed scars, thank God.'

Lorraine was shaking her head. 'Jo, you should have called me. This is shocking. Has he spoken to anyone about it? Been to see his GP? It's not something that should be ignored.'

Jo closed her eyes. 'I'm so scared for him, Lorraine. I think he might be seriously depressed.' She paused. 'It's just that no one dares breathe a word around here about this sort of thing, not after what happened a few weeks ago. It was bad enough eighteen months ago. Even the newspapers were reluctant to report it in case it started something off again. Admitting that my own son could need help – it's really scary.'

Lorraine reached out and put her hand on Jo's. 'Look, it was probably just a horrible accident rather than suicide. As for Freddie, he's a different matter entirely. He's your son, and he's been through a lot recently with you and Malc. Sadly, kids hurting themselves isn't that uncommon. He needs to see someone, Jo. A doctor. And soon.'

Jo's sigh was a slow river of exasperation. It followed her as she stood up, went to the fridge and pulled out the half-full bottle of wine, and trailed her back to the table where she topped up their glasses. It only stopped flowing when she sat down.

Lorraine stared at the bottle as she set it between them. Within seconds it was coated in a layer of condensation. Beads of water dotted the cold glass.

'The lad who killed himself recently was called Dean Watts,' Jo said slowly. 'He was only nineteen years old. He stole a motorbike and drove it headlong into a tree. The police said there were no tyre marks on the road to indicate he braked. The stories going round afterwards were awful. The only good thing is that it was instant.'

Lorraine allowed herself a small nod, a slow arc of understanding. She'd seen hundreds of deaths over the years and couldn't possibly count them all, let alone recall details of every investigation. While she wouldn't say that she was hardened to it exactly, hearing about an anonymous person losing their life – through their own will or accident or even murder – didn't have the same impact on her as it did on someone like her sister.

She recalled the first time she saw a dead body as a probationer. It was a sight she'd never forget. But the feelings of sickness, revulsion and horror that had reared up inside her had certainly been diluted by twenty years in the force. It had been a road traffic accident, and the pale corpse of the young woman driving, her face still perfectly made-up after an evening on the town, had reminded her so much of her little sister Jo. The only noticeable damage on the girl was a thin red line across her neck where it had snapped. She remembered, too, how while sipping on sweet tea back at the nick later she'd vowed she'd give it all up, hand in her notice the next morning, say she wasn't cut out for the job. Somehow, she'd never got round to it.

'It is really tragic,' Lorraine said, knowing how strong the community was in Radcote. 'But if you saw the figures nationwide, you'd realise it's not unusual.' She sipped on her wine before continuing. 'About five, maybe six thousand people a year kill themselves in the UK, Jo. Having a suicide in your neighbourhood is shocking, but on its own, as an isolated case, it doesn't resonate with what happened eighteen months ago. This area isn't immune to regular statistics just because it had more than its fair share a year and a half ago.'

Lorraine had been going to add that it was just plain crazy, unbelievable, unprecedented that six kids from the locality had killed themselves within two weeks. It was the kind of thing that happened in hopeless and depressed areas of the country, not in an affluent, well-to-do pocket of rural Warwickshire where clay pigeon shooting and Boden were the norm. But she decided against it.

Instead, she put her hand back on her sister's, noticing the lines of worry on her face. 'But none of that means Freddie's going to kill himself, OK?'

4

'I'm going to Wellesbury this morning, would you like to come?' Jo asked.

Lorraine was sitting at the kitchen table, drinking coffee. Freddie hadn't emerged from his bedroom yet, and Stella was lazing in the garden with her book. The day was a pleasant one, but the pattern for the last week or so had been rainy, sometimes thundery, afternoons.

'I'd love to,' she replied, sipping her drink. Jo always made it strong. 'Errands to run?'

'Kind of,' Jo said. 'I promised Sonia Hawkeswell I'd pick up some leaflets from the homeless shelter in town. I said I'd hand them out.'

Lorraine nodded slowly. She didn't recall such a place, but she hadn't been there in a while. As a young kid, Wellesbury was always an exciting source of sweets and toys for her and Jo, as well as trips to the market or the library with their mother. When she was a teenager, she saw it for what it was – a rather boring

Midlands town with nowhere cool to hang out. But on the few occasions she'd visited as an adult she had found it charming, with its stone shop fronts, interesting boutiques and cobbled pedestrian areas.

'Sonia volunteers at the shelter,' Jo continued. 'Actually, she virtually lives there. She works really hard. They're having a fundraising event so I said I'd help promote it.'

'That's very commendable,' Lorraine said. 'Of course I'll come.' She was keen to meet Sonia Hawkeswell, to see if she could find out a bit more about the man who'd upset Stella yesterday.

✳

New Hope Homeless Shelter was housed in an old church hall on the south side of town, only a short drive from Radcote. Lorraine stared up at it as they got out of the car, squinting at the austere building as it sparked a memory. They'd parked opposite, outside a fish and chip shop, which was just opening up; on the other side of the road was a dog-grooming business. The rest of the properties were small terraced houses.

'God, I remember this place,' she said with a grin, eyeing the new sign above the door. 'We did Girl Guides here for a while, didn't we?'

She linked her arm through her sister's, giving her a squeeze.

'We did indeed,' Jo said. 'Until they kicked us out.'

'That was your fault,' Lorraine said with a laugh.

'It was not!' Jo said indignantly, but then fell quiet as they approached the steps of the church hall. She drew to a halt. 'Look, before we go in, you should know something.'

'Oh?'

Lorraine put up her hand to shield her eyes from the sun. Jo appeared serious all of a sudden.

'Sonia has devoted her life to this place since . . . well, since she lost Simon. It's not only her time she gives, but money too. And by that, I don't just mean all the fundraising work she does. She's donated a load of personal cash recently.'

'That's very kind of her,' Lorraine responded, wondering how anyone could possibly cope after losing a child in the way she had.

'But it's way more than a financial investment,' Jo continued, her voice low. She glanced at the door. 'Sonia's suffered no end, and she's become very emotionally attached to all the lads who stay here. She told me once she sees a bit of Simon in each and every one of them. It's really sad, like she's trying to bring him back.' Jo paused, looking uncomfortable. 'By working here, it's as if she wants to . . . to make it up to him somehow. As if she blames herself. She can't seem to let go.'

Lorraine nodded her understanding. 'Grief affects everyone differently.'

They went inside the small entrance porch. Empty

wooden crates were stacked neatly to one side as if they'd recently held bulk amounts of food – potatoes, bags of carrots, loaves of bread – and were waiting to be collected. The black and white chequerboard floor looked as if it had been recently mopped, and a lavender scent hung in the air. There was a noticeboard attached to the wall with a colourful handmade banner saying 'Welcome to New Hope'.

'This won't take long,' Jo said as they went in. 'Sonia puts me to shame with all her voluntary work. It's the least I can do.' She clutched at her cotton skirt, bringing the hem up to reveal her tanned knees in a way that reminded Lorraine of her as a little girl. For a second, her eyes sparkled.

They went into the main room of the building, which was nothing like how Lorraine remembered it from their Girl Guide days. Gone was the dusty wooden floor for a start. Stripped and polished boards now gave a light and airy feel to the place, especially with the sun streaming in through the tall arched windows, and all the walls were freshly painted in white. It was the complete opposite to the inner-city equivalent Lorraine had occasionally visited in Birmingham. Somehow they exuded a kind of fake hope rather than the real thing, as in this place.

They walked between several rows of beds, each one made up with a plump pillow and clean sleeping bag. A small table between each bed separated the bunks and Lorraine noticed that there were little vases of flowers or china ornaments on some. She raised her eyebrows, impressed with the attention to detail.

'It's nice,' she whispered to Jo as they headed to the rear of the hall.

Jo answered with an I-told-you-so look.

There was a smaller area at the back reserved for a couple of settees and a television. A low table with books and magazines sat on top of a rug that looked as if it had come from an antique shop.

'Hello, Sonia, it's me,' Jo called out towards another room beyond. Her voice echoed around them, getting lost in the vaulted ceiling.

The place seemed deserted, even though the front door had been unlocked. For a moment Lorraine wondered if all the homeless people of Wellesbury and the surrounding area had been miraculously re-homed. The reality was, as she later learnt, they got sent out for the day and weren't allowed back in until six p.m.

Jo's voice rang out again amid the avenues of sunlight that sloped through the Methodist chapel's tall windows.

'Odd. She said she'd be here.'

Then they heard a noise coming from the other room, and soon after that a figure emerged through the doorway. 'Sorry, sorry,' the woman said in a flustered voice. 'I was lost in what I was doing.' She offered a small smile.

'Sonia, this is Lorraine, my sister,' Jo said, and Lorraine was struck by the note of pride in her voice.

Lorraine approached the woman and shook hands. She was extremely thin, her skin tinged grey and almost see-through, as if she'd not eaten in months. The pale blue jeans she was wearing would have once fitted snugly, likewise the white T-shirt that hung loosely from her slight frame. The jade-green silk scarf looped around her neck lent a small splash of colour to an otherwise washed-out appearance. Lorraine could tell she'd once been a beauty, perhaps not so long ago, but that recently taking care of herself had not been a priority. There was a tangible air of sadness about her, an aura of grief that was gradually consuming her.

'You've done a great job with this place,' Lorraine commented, and noticed the way Sonia's eyes dipped briefly to the floor. Her hair was thin, once-blonde, but now the grey was pushing through at the roots, suggesting she'd not been to a salon in a while.

'I try my best,' she said coyly. 'I don't know what they'd do otherwise.'

There was a slight pause.

'She means her boys,' Jo said fondly. 'The homeless lads. And there are a few girls, too.'

'They must be very grateful to you,' Lorraine said.

Sonia picked at her nails nervously. Lorraine noticed several were broken.

'You have no idea how excited Jo has been about you coming to stay,' she said. 'She's been telling me about your visit for ages.'

'She might not be saying that by the end of the week,' Lorraine responded with a laugh.

'Freddie took his younger cousin up to your place to see the horses yesterday,' Jo said.

'Yes, Lana told me she'd bumped into them.' At the mention of her daughter, Sonia smiled and her shoulders dropped an inch.

'Stella's no rider, that's for sure, but she enjoyed seeing them. She told me she thought your home was beautiful.' Lorraine wanted to mention Stella's 'nasty man' incident, but wasn't sure it was appropriate to bring it up without asking Jo first.

'They're welcome any time,' Sonia said. 'Lana would be happy to see them.' It seemed as if she'd been going to say more, but she didn't.

'Well, we won't keep you any longer,' Jo said, breaking a slightly awkward silence. 'I'm sure you're busy.' She cleared her throat. 'I just came to pick up the leaflets.'

'It's nice to have a break, actually.' Sonia walked over to a shelving rack next to the television and took down a stack of flyers. 'I was going over the shelter's accounts. Here.' She handed the pile over. 'It would be fantastic if you could spread them about. The event's not until the end of August.'

'Of course,' Jo said, quickly scanning one. She nodded her approval, then slipped a hand on to Lorraine's shoulder. 'Right, let's make a move.'

Lorraine nodded and opened her mouth to say goodbye but was interrupted by a deafening crash. It came from the kitchen. Sonia screamed and Jo jumped while Lorraine, immediately switching into work mode, dashed past them both to see what had happened. It sounded like breaking glass – a window perhaps? Might it be an intruder?

'Wait there,' she called back to them, slamming the door open as far as it would go with a swipe of her arm and scanning the room.

The kitchen work counter and floor were showered with shards and chunks of sparkling broken glass, and a still plugged-in power cable was trailing out of the smashed window. She peered out through the hole but all she saw was a small courtyard housing a couple of dustbins. The wooden gate was flapping open. Even after only a few seconds an intruder could be gone. Nevertheless, Lorraine ran towards the back-door exit of the kitchen, cursing her sandals which were no good for fast movement.

The door was locked. No chance now.

Sonia was crunching her way through the glass. 'They've taken all the chicken we were going to give them for dinner!'

'Please, stay back,' Lorraine said, not meaning to sound rude. It was a natural instinct to keep a crime scene as clean as possible. 'Are you sure it's just the chicken?'

'What do you mean?'

'Was there a laptop in here?' Lorraine pointed at the cable and watched Sonia's expression change.

'Oh *shit*,' she said. It sounded wrong coming from

her. 'It was Tony's computer, not mine. This can't be happening. What am I going to do?' Looking white and even more shaken, she advanced towards the window.

Lorraine raised her arm and asked her again to keep out of the mess. Local uniform would want a look.

Jo was hovering in the doorway. 'Why was Tony's computer here?' she asked quietly.

'I borrowed it for the morning because mine's being mended. I couldn't find him to ask his permission before I left.' Sonia looked imploringly at Jo, then covered her face with her hands. 'He's going to be so angry.'

Jo stepped away, turned, then walked back again, as if she didn't quite know what to do.

'I should call the . . . the police,' Sonia said, and then looked at Lorraine. Jo must have mentioned her job.

'I won't be helping with this one, I'm afraid,' Lorraine said. 'It's not my patch. But I'll make the call if you like.'

*

Fifteen minutes later, two uniformed officers from Warwickshire Police were on the scene. Another twenty minutes after that a dog handler turned up. After they'd given their statements, Lorraine tried to persuade Jo that they should go: she was concerned about leaving Stella alone and bored in a house she didn't know very well – she couldn't be sure of Freddie's attentiveness – and they could always come back later.

'I can't exactly desert Sonia, can I?' Jo whispered. 'She's still shaking, look.'

Lorraine could see that Sonia's shoulders were indeed juddering with every breath she took. She and one of the PCs were sitting on the ends of two adjacent bunks. The young female constable was taking down notes while Sonia alternated between cradling her head in her hands and staring upwards into the cavernous ceiling.

'Is she always like this?' Lorraine asked quietly.

Jo looked sympathetically at Sonia. 'As long as I've known her, which is a year or so now. We've only really become good friends in the last few months.' She cleared her throat and moved in a distracted semi-circle around the bunks. Then she sat down on one of them and looked up at her sister. 'Look, Lorraine,' she continued quietly, 'the motorbike suicide I told you about, Dean Watts? He was a regular here at the shelter. Sonia knew him well. His death gutted her, brought back horrific memories of Simon.'

'Oh, that's terrible,' Lorraine said, understanding completely.

'It's been awful. She felt responsible somehow, as if she'd failed Dean as well as her son.'

Lorraine took a moment to think about this. Then the other PC, a young chap with fiery red hair, came over to speak to them again.

'The dog has picked something up,' he informed them. 'Straight from the kitchen window, down the street and into the back entrance of the supermarket car park. We're trying to get hold of the manager so we can view their CCTV footage. We lost the trail after that. Meantime, we'll get a forensics officer on scene to see if we can get anything.'

Lorraine was about to reply when she spotted a man coming into the shelter. He was tall and sturdy with a crumpled, weathered face set beneath wiry grey hair. It looked greasy.

'What's going on?' he said.

The way he stood, his shoulders broad, hands on hips, bearded chin jutting forward, was commanding, and also slightly intimidating. He was probably in his early sixties but looked fit and strong.

'Oh, Frank, thank God you're here,' Sonia said, getting up from the bed and making her way over. 'There's been a break-in. The dinner was stolen.'

'And Tony's computer,' Jo added quietly.

Frank took a moment before speaking. Pale blue eyes peered out from behind rimless glasses, scanning the scene. 'What do you mean, a break-in?' His voice was deep and gravelly, and seemed somehow to pull Sonia closer, as if he was coaxing her to explain what had happened.

'Someone smashed a window in the kitchen,' Lorraine said, approaching the man. She noticed the jeans he was wearing had oily streaks down the front, and she caught a whiff of sweat as she drew near. Heavy tattoos spread out over his forearms beneath the rolled-up sleeves of his check shirt, making it look as if he had greeny-black bruises. 'But no one was hurt.'

'I see,' he said, looking Lorraine up and down. Then he switched his gaze to Jo and sized her up too.

Sonia's shaking was intermittent now, although she was still very pale. Her eyes were red and inflamed, and two small trails of black mascara crawled down her cheeks. Lorraine dug in her bag for a packet of tissues and handed them over.

'We're taking this very seriously,' the young red-haired officer stated. 'There's been a spate of similar burglaries in the area recently.'

Sonia stiffened noticeably. 'Spate?' she whispered.

'It's been a tough few weeks for her,' Frank said slowly to the officer, his tone slightly less gruff, as if he was making an effort not to sound menacing. 'Don't worry, I'll look after her. She'll be fine now I'm here.'

Lorraine watched as Sonia relaxed, allowing Frank to take control. Jo, on the other hand, now seemed more shaken than Sonia.

Lorraine frowned, staring at her sister. 'Shall we go then?' she suggested.

It was a moment before Jo spoke. 'Yes, sorry,' she replied.

When she still didn't make a move, Lorraine took her by the hands, pulled her upright and guided her towards the door, wondering what on earth had upset her sister.

5

The walls of his bedroom seemed to be closing in on him, pressing down on his life, making everything seem unbearable. The room was a mess, he knew that, but he couldn't be bothered to sort it out. There were other things on his mind.

Freddie went over to his bed and swept the pile of clothes and wet towels on to the floor with his arm. He lifted the corner of the mattress and pulled out his laptop from underneath. He'd started hiding it a few months ago, when things got really bad. His mum was always moaning about the state of his room, using it as an excuse to nose about, he reckoned, prying into his phone, his diary – except he'd given up writing that long ago. He'd hate it if she somehow managed to get on his computer, if he'd accidentally left it logged on.

He shoved a stack of dirty plates and mugs aside on his desk, clearing a space for the laptop. His heart began to thump as he waited for it to start up. It was like a drug – he had to know, had to get his fix, even though it was slowly, surely destroying him. His palms became sweaty, his fists balled up and tense. Why him? he wondered. Why wasn't he allowed to enjoy life like everyone else?

A lump filled his throat, but he swallowed it down. He was beyond crying about it now.

First he checked his emails, laughing when he saw one from a gap year company trying to sell him some working holiday in South America. Losers like him didn't do things like that. What had he been thinking, signing up for information when they'd had that stupid talk at school? Some kids in his year had already gone off on their adventures – teaching English in China, kayaking stretches of the world's longest rivers, helping to build schools in poor African countries. What was he doing with his life?

Freddie stared around his room again. He hadn't even bothered to open the curtains in weeks.

His fist came down on the desk, sending a plate to the floor. It cracked in half.

He deleted all the spam emails and hovered the cursor over the only important one in his inbox. It was from Malcolm Wade, his stepdad, the only man who'd ever been a father to him. Except he wasn't in his life any more. What was the point of even reading it?

He still couldn't believe he'd left. When it happened, his mum told him that they'd just grown apart, that it was best for all concerned if Malc lived in London near his work.

All concerned. He'd thought about that.

Did his mum think he was stupid? He'd known something was up for a long time, seen the signs, the little changes in them both – his mum always in a cheerful mood (except when Malc was home at the weekends) and Malc increasingly anxious, turning up unannounced, drinking too much. But with everything else going on in his life – exams; this *shit* – he'd not been able to do anything about it. He wished now that he could take time back, help them sort it out. Malc might still be here then, perhaps notice something was wrong, maybe give him some advice.

Freddie stared at the computer screen, idly drifting on to eBay to see if that hard drive he'd had his eye on was still there, then going to check what was on telly later. He didn't take any of it in.

Finally, there was nothing for it. He had to know. Had to know what had been going on. That's what they thrived on, he realised. The certainty that wherever he was, whatever he was doing, he'd never be able to ignore it, walk away from it, act like he didn't care. Sure, he was eighteen; he could leave home, struggle to establish a new life somewhere. But one thing was for certain: wherever he went, cyberspace would go with him.

He logged into his profile, his shoulders slumping forward as he realised what was going to happen.

The little red alert showed he'd got fourteen new messages and twenty-seven other notifications. He suddenly felt sick. Whatever he'd mindlessly shoved down his throat for breakfast churned and curdled in his belly. He dashed into the bathroom across the landing and threw up.

'Hi, love,' his mum said when he went into the kitchen to fetch a glass of water.

He felt dizzy, dry-mouthed, not real. For a second, he stared at her, wondering if he could tell her.

No way, he thought.

'We saved you some lunch,' his Aunt Lorraine said. Her voice was crisper than his mum's, more to the point.

He stared at her for a moment too, wondering if he could confide in her. But she was a cop and would just make it worse. Everything would get out of hand if he told her. He was coping OK, wasn't he?

'Not hungry,' he replied, not meaning to sound so ungrateful. He saw Lorraine shrug as he walked out again, retreating to his room.

He passed Stella on the landing. She said something to him in an excited voice but he just slammed his bedroom door. Whatever it was, he didn't want to hear it.

Malc had given him the framed photograph years ago, the one he'd always kept on his bedside table. For the past few weeks it had been face down in a drawer, but now he took it out, held it under the light.

He'd thought it was silly at first, to have it on display, but then he'd grown to love staring at it, remembering all the good times they'd had. The three of them on holiday in Spain, the waiter snapping the picture of them at the table, the huge paella in the foreground.

Freddie stared at himself. He'd been about fourteen, he reckoned. He had a tan, too, just enough to highlight his hair, and he'd been excited about going back to school, to see if that girl Lana would notice him.

He traced his finger over his mum and Malc, joining them up with an invisible line. Surely he could get them back together again? How would he ever escape Radcote otherwise? How would he get away from all the crap? He could hardly leave his mum alone as things stood.

You have been tagged in two photos.

Shithead loser gonna die 2nite . . . was the caption beneath the latest picture. It was of a rack of pig carcasses hanging in an abattoir.

Why r u not dead yet? put yrself out of yr misery fuckhead. This one was linked to an actual picture of him getting on a bus. He was wearing his new trainers, he noticed, so it had been taken after term ended. His stomach churned again. Would they follow him to university, if he ever got there, and through the rest of his life?

Freddie read a couple of the messages. Occasionally he laughed at them, to see if that helped. It didn't.

After enough time, he'd begun to believe what was written. He was a loser, useless; he was ugly and he stank; he shouldn't even exist. They were right. Everyone in his year hated him; they all wished him dead. He was a waste of space.

The underlying message was always the same: why don't you just kill yourself?

They'd set up a page for him, dedicated to him as if he'd already done the deed – already hanged himself, taken an overdose, slit his wrists in the bath. Sometimes they made suggestions about how he should do it, sent him links to suicide websites or pictures of corpses. There were fake messages of condolence put up every day, vile pictures either of him or something gory sent to his inbox. He was tagged in everything, just to make sure he knew.

And then there were the text messages. Day and night, anonymous, malicious . . . and they were getting worse.

Of course, he'd considered telling someone – a teacher, his mum, Malc, or the authorities, like you were supposed to – but that would make them hate him even more. He'd thought about telling Lenny, reckoned he might understand. Lenny had been through a load of shit himself and was always getting out of one scrape or another. He was the only friend Freddie had these days, and even then they'd only got to know each other as mates because Lenny had been on the scrounge – food, money, beer, whatever.

Sometimes he disappeared for days, turning up at New Hope when he needed a hot meal, a bed.

He rubbed his eyes. What was he thinking? He couldn't tell anyone, not after what had happened to Dean. His mum couldn't handle it, and neither could Lana's mum, Sonia. If he just kept quiet, he reckoned, stayed strong and resolute, it would probably, eventually, go away.

He opened his desk drawer, reached to the back and felt around among the mess of pens and exercise books. The blade was still there, encrusted brown with the dried blood. But it was still sharp; it would work well enough.

Then his phone vibrated on his desk. He read the message and closed his eyes for a moment.

The old hut, Blackdown Woods, 2morrow, midnight.

Freddie made sure the door was shut tight and rolled up his sleeve.

6

They don't know I'm here. It's what I do – hiding, watching, spying. It gives me a funny feeling inside, but I have to take care of them. It's dark outside; light in there. Invisibility for me. The window is open a sliver, just enough for me to get a whiff of the end of their chicken meal. I made my own food tonight because Sonia says women like an independent man. It was pizza from the freezer and some parts of it were still hard and cold when I bit into it.

My hands are itching to write my name on the dusty glass. *Gil*. But I won't. I don't want them to know I was here. It's my secret. Taking care of things.

'Lana,' Sonia says, 'aren't you going to eat that? You'll waste away.'

Sonia is collecting up the plates, slotting them into the dishwasher. I could help, I think. I'm good at washing up. I know how to do it. She slices her way about the kitchen as if she's on roller skates. I've been roller skating before. With my friend.

'I'm not hungry,' Lana says. She sounds sad tonight. She has crescents under her eyes the same colour as a sepia photograph. I wonder if any boys at the shelter are being mean to her.

They all want her. I've seen it in their eyes when she's peeling potatoes or shaking out their beds.

Lana stands up and goes to the refrigerator. I see her take a bottle of beer when her mother's back is turned. Then her father comes into the kitchen and she stares sadly at the pair of them. Sonia is bending down to the dishwasher and doesn't notice. I'm watching all this and they don't even know. Tony doesn't say anything until his daughter slides past and leaves the room.

'What's wrong with her?' he says.

I duck down. They've come close to the window. There's a tap running and then the smell of warm lavender handwash comes wafting up from the drain at my feet. I always wash my hands because you can catch germs otherwise.

'She's been acting really odd this last month,' Sonia says. 'I'm worried for her.'

'It's probably stress,' Tony replies. Tony is a doctor in the hospital. 'She'll be OK once she gets her exam results.'

Then there's a kissing sound and a little moan from Sonia. To me, it sounds as if she wants to get away, but I don't do kissing as I've never had a girlfriend. I cover my eyes even though I'm staring at the ground and it's all black and earthy and I'm standing in a flowerbed and it's not my fault and I don't like these noises because it's revolting.

It stops. There are more low voices.

'I got angry earlier and I shouldn't have, it's just a computer,' I hear Tony say. 'I shouldn't have shouted at you in front of Lana.'

'It's my fault for borrowing it. I was going to ask but you weren't here and I didn't know what to do.'

Then there's more kissing so I creep away. Spying on people doing those things isn't right. But sometimes I can't help it.

It's a nice evening for a walk. I walk and walk lots, all through the night if I can't sleep. I know my way around every inch of everywhere. Probably the whole planet. Tonight is a very good night for a walk. The security light flashes on when I go round the side of the house, but that's OK. I know where they all are, how not to set them off if I don't want to. No one will notice this one.

I look up. Lana's bedroom light is on. I imagine her sitting cross-legged on the duvet, her computer open in front of her, beer bottle in her hand, her long hair spilling over her eyes, tapping stuff into Facebook. I've seen her do this many times before. My mouth starts watering so I swallow it back down. I'm getting a stiff neck from staring up at the window.

The flat roof just below it is a good place to watch, peek inside Lana's bedroom. I look at the trellis and the drainpipe. They are waiting to be climbed, urging me up. I know where all the footholds are. But what if I get told off again? What if Tony catches me doing it? He might send me away once and for all like he said last time.

Gil, I do my best for you. Honestly I do. But this can't carry on. The authorities have places for people like you.

I hear a noise. Something rustling nearby, under the bushes and close to the wall.

'Smudge?'

Smudge comes stalking out of the undergrowth and I pick him up. His paws rest on my shoulder and his claws sink a tiny bit into my skin as I walk off with him.

'We'll look after her, won't we Smudge?' I whisper into his fur.

He purrs back, and we both know there'll be no more watching tonight.

7

Lana frowned. It wasn't like her mum to miss a shift. Her first thought was that she was trying to scupper her plans, that she didn't want her to hang out with her mates. It was clear she disapproved of them. But when she saw the way her mum's eyes had become small and pebbly, pressed into the soft dough of their puffy sockets, she knew she'd been crying.

'Of course I'll take your shift for you, Mum,' she said, putting a hand on her shoulder. 'Are you ill?'

She watched her mum tip a couple of pills into her hand, take them with a glass of water. She hated that she was using them to mask her grief. She'd always been so fit and healthy, filled with a zest for life. Ever since Simon, things hadn't been the same.

Her mum nodded, mustering a smile. 'Will you give this to Frank?' she said, handing Lana a file. 'It's the fundraising plans.'

Frank was good with the hands-on side of things but useless when it came to keeping the charity's paperwork in order. He'd be lost without her mum. She was the treasurer and one of his most dedicated helpers.

'Tell him I'm under the weather today,' she finished.

Lana imagined her mother trapped flat under a snow drift, washed away by the rain, shielding herself from the desert sun, or beaten to the ground by a great wind. It wasn't far from the truth.

Before she left, Lana texted Milly and Dan. She wouldn't be coming bowling with them today. She knew they would understand. She was always cancelling plans.

When she started her car, Smudge shot out from between the front wheels. 'One of these days . . .' she called out to him. The cat leapt on to a brick wall but his back legs didn't quite make it and he flopped on to the gravel. He gave himself a few brisk licks.

Lately, Lana had taken to driving the slightly longer route into Wellesbury, wanting to avoid the spot where she knew the crisp, sun-dried blooms were still tied to the tree at the end of Devil's Mile. She'd known Dean well and it was still too upsetting. She couldn't understand why he'd take his own life. Last time she'd seen him he was telling her about his plans, his ambitions, and how he'd been applying for jobs. He'd told her he'd got a girlfriend.

She recalled the funeral – a small affair, with no family members present, just a handful of friends from New Hope. The local paper hadn't run anything about his death, not after what had happened last time, but her mum inserted a few words in the obituaries section of the *Tribune*. No one else would have bothered otherwise.

Five minutes later, Lana drew up outside New Hope. Parking wasn't always easy, especially if there were a few local residents home, their cars shoe-horned into the available spaces outside the terraced houses. She eyed the double yellow lines, not wanting to risk it, so all she was left with was an awkward slice of tarmac behind Frank's white pick-up, blocking him in. She hoped he wouldn't be cross with her.

Suddenly, the parking sensor on her Ka changed to a continuous tone and she felt a crunch. When she got out to look, she saw that Frank's tow bar had left a dimple in her bumper.

'Bugger,' she said, just as Frank appeared through the back gate. He was holding a bag of rubbish and she didn't think he'd seen what had happened.

'Language,' he growled, almost playfully, even though it didn't sound right coming from a man like him. Lana had been scared of him at first, told her mum he was the kind of man she'd cross the road to avoid.

'Hello, Frank,' she said, locking her car. 'This is from Mum.' She held out the file.

His eyes were ice-cold blue and his mouth puckered open through the thicket of his wiry grey beard. What she thought might be a smile set Lana's heart pumping.

Frank had once said he hadn't been to a dentist in decades – hence the blackened teeth – and claimed never to have been to a doctor in his entire life. With his check shirt, tattered jeans tucked into black Doc Martens, and the old oily cap he usually wore, Lana thought he wouldn't look out of place playing the part of a redneck in a hillbilly movie. She decided not to tell him about bumping his tow bar.

'Mum can't make it today,' she explained. 'She's . . .'

Frank squinted at her. A group of kids charged past on scooters, spitting and yelling obscenities. He roared at them to clear off.

'She's busy.'

'Always doing something, your ma,' he responded, with the same open-mouthed expression. 'There's a lot of spuds to be peeled if you're offering.'

He disappeared into the small courtyard, and Lana followed him through the back door into the kitchen, where she saw that he'd already made a start on the meal. The chipped Formica worktop was strewn with cuts of unidentifiable meat and a load of out-of-date vegetables they were often given free by the supermarket.

'Get this on then,' he said, tossing an apron at Lana.

It was dirty but she put it on anyway.

'Who stayed last night?' she asked tentatively, grabbing a potato.

'The usual crowd. One or two haven't gone out since this morning. They're ill, so they say.'

76

Frank grabbed hold of a large piece of red meat with a bone poking out of one end and thumped it down on a wooden block. He then took an old cleaver and brought it down hard, cracking the bone in two. He did this over and over until it was hacked into stew-sized pieces.

Lana swallowed and looked away.

'Did Lenny come in?' she asked after a short while, taking another potato. She knew her mum had been concerned about him recently, had been worried about his cough. She'd wanted to keep him in, but New Hope had a policy of turfing out its guests by nine a.m. sharp so the volunteers could clean up as well as giving everyone a fair chance of getting a bed later. The queue began to form about three in the afternoon, earlier on winter nights.

'No sign of him,' Frank replied. 'Oddly,' he added slowly.

He threw the meat into a huge pot and wiped his hands across his face. He looked as if he'd been in a fight, had a nosebleed.

Lana instantly heard her mother's voice: *Consider deficiencies, trauma, blood-thinning medications . . . Check blood pressure, platelet count, Vitamin K . . .*

Frank took the meat scraps out to the dustbins and Lana sighed, getting on with the peeling. But a moment later she heard sobbing coming from the main hall. She went to investigate and, on one of the nearer bunks, she found someone cocooned and writhing in a sleeping bag. Whoever was in there was caught in a jet of sunlight streaming in through the tall arched window opposite.

'Are you OK?' she asked, tentatively touching their shoulder and catching a whiff of sickness and despair.

Always get involved with the guests, her mother had told her. *Find out their stories, see what makes them tick. It's good for your CV. You'll get interviewed about your work experience!* Actually, she'd been wrong. Her CV, honed to perfection by her mother – eighteen years broken down into eleven straight A stars at GCSE, the same superlatives predicted four times over at A level, Grade 8 piano with distinction, Gold Duke of Edinburgh Award, and enough work experience for Lana to qualify as a doctor without even going to medical school – hadn't prompted any of the four university interview panels to ask one single question about her work at New Hope.

Lana tried again. 'Are you OK? Do you need help?'

The thing was, even though the interviews were over, even though she'd got an offer to study Medicine at Imperial College London if she got the A grades in her exams, Lana still kept coming back to New Hope. Sometimes she wondered whether she was trying to assuage some of the guilt she still felt over Simon's death. She wondered if her mother felt this way too.

She patted the shoulder of the pupa-like wrapping. A mass of sweaty hair emerged.

'No.'

Lana recognised her voice. 'Cup of tea?'

More wriggling, and then a hand came out of the sleeping bag, followed by a face.

'Abby, you don't look well. Do you want some water?'

Another shake. In fact, all of her was shaking.

'I'll get you some.'

When Lana returned from the kitchen, Abby was sitting up in bed scanning the jobs section of the local paper. She took the drink and shoved something into her mouth from the palm of her hand. It got washed down.

'Are you staying for lunch?' Lana thought she could do with a good meal.

'Dean would have loved that job,' she said instead of replying.

Lana could hear Frank in the kitchen, grumbling that he'd been left alone to prepare the meal.

'What job?'

'Vet's assistant. He liked animals.'

Lana turned her head sideways and read the job description. She fought the curl of pain in her stomach. 'It's the kind of job that vet sci students might apply for in the holidays.' For a second, she heard her mother's once-keen voice sounding within her own.

'What's vet sci?' Abby said, turning her dark eyes on Lana. Her voice was thin and bitter, like the rest of her. Apart from her expanded pupils, she was barely there.

'It's short for veterinary science,' Lana said. She didn't want to say that Dean would have had no chance of securing a job like that, that you needed qualifications, ambition. 'Simon was going to be a vet.'

She froze for a second as she realised what she'd just said, then turned and rushed back into the kitchen.

'Who's Simon?' Abby's thin voice somehow filled the entire hall.

But Lana was peeling potatoes again, fighting back the tears, incapable of an answer.

*

Gil appeared at the window, making her jump as she washed her hands at the sink. One side of the kitchen window still had chipboard nailed to it, waiting for the glazier to fix it; Gil was peering in through the unbroken side, his face looming like a large moon.

Lana put her hand on her heart. 'Jesus, you scared me. Where's Dad? Did he bring you?'

Gil held up two black dustbin sacks stuffed full of clothes. 'He's waiting in the car and he said I have to bring these to you.'

Lana snapped off the rubber gloves and opened the back door.

'Has Mum been having a sort out?' she asked, but Gil was already shaking his head.

'Mum's nowhere to be found,' he said.

Lana smiled, guessing she was tending to the horses.

Gil often got muddled, sometimes even forgetting that he was her uncle or that Tony was his elder brother.

He handed the bags to Lana just as one split open. An assortment of male clothing puddled at her feet, as if their wearer had magically disappeared from inside them. And when Lana saw the rugby shirt with the stitched-on name label at the breast, she realised that was kind of true.

'Bye then,' said Gil, and headed for the door.

'Wait.' Lana bent down to retrieve the rugby shirt and ran her finger over the embroidered name. *Simon Hawkeswell*. It was the second time in five minutes that she'd been faced with her dead brother. 'Whose idea was it to get rid of this stuff?'

'Tony said to bring them he said they were in the way. I tripped over.' Gil rolled up the leg of his long shorts to expose his kneecap. It had the red crown of a fresh bruise.

Think patella, her mother said in her head. *Consider X-rays. Cartilage. Hair-line fractures. Reduce the swelling. Immobilise and ice . . .*

'Ouchy,' Lana commented.

She knew the tack room had been used for all sorts of dumping over the years, not least for Gil. He'd been moved out there not long after Simon died, when his artwork took over the house. Her dad had got fed up of all his mess and converted the little outbuilding into a place for his brother to enjoy some independence. Lana had felt bad for him at first, as if he was an unwanted possession, like Simon's things – stuff that no one had the heart to get rid of completely but didn't want in the house.

'He likes it out there,' her father had said.

'He's perfectly happy,' her mum had agreed.

And Gil did seem content living in the tack room. It had a wood-burner, a kitchenette with a couple of cupboards from Ikea, an old sofa and an ancient boxy television rigged up to receive all the channels. There was no bathroom so Gil used the gardener's toilet and washed standing up by the kitchen sink. Lana always knew when he'd sneaked into the house for a bath because of the earthy scent he left behind.

'Thanks for bringing the stuff, Gil.' She tried to sound grateful. She'd had no idea Simon's things had been bagged up to be given away. She'd not been in his bedroom since it happened.

'Dad said you have to give them to the homeless people,' Gil said.

Lana felt a pang of sadness. She smiled and nodded, placing the bags on the table. When she looked round, Gil had gone.

✳

Simon had been big and healthy, sprouting out of himself for as long as Lana could remember. Abby was twig-like and drugged, her head poking out of the wide neck hole like a dried-up autumn berry. Simon's shirt was massive on her.

'How do I look?'

She was lying on her bunk, smoothing the bloated curve of her belly, the only large thing about her. Lana thought she looked like a famine victim.

Think mineral and protein deficiencies, her mother shrieked in her head. *Electrolyte imbalances, dehydration and muscle atrophy.*

Her stomach clenched at the thought of the exam results. She remembered her papers being collected up and whisked off to an unknown marker who would decide the rest of her life with a few quick flicks of a pen. She felt sick. The pressure was on now Simon was gone.

'You look great,' she said quietly.

Sometimes she hated Simon for what he'd done to them all. He'd played in the first fifteen. He was fit. He was the best-looking lad in his school – *the jock*, Dad used to tease proudly. He'd gained a scholarship to university for that autumn, won essay-writing competitions. Got straight As and played the violin. Everyone was his friend. The girls adored him. He was going to be a vet. Then he hanged himself.

'What else you got in the bags?' Abby had finally got up off her bunk after the effort of digesting a sparrow's portion of lunch had worn her out.

Think enzymes, peristalsis, Crohn's disease or coeliac sprue, her mother's voice suggested.

'There are a couple of T-shirts. They might be good as nightshirts.' Lana pulled out some more clothes, trying to stay dry-eyed and pragmatic about her brother's possessions. 'What about this one? The colour will suit you.'

'Really?' Abby queried, as if she'd never had a gift in her life.

'Really,' Lana said, pressing it into her hands, noticing the skull ring hanging on a chain around Abby's neck, the one that Dean had always worn.

There was a sudden bang as Frank came into the hall, his heavy boots echoing on the floor.

'I need a word,' he boomed, his voice causing Abby to shrink back on to her bed.

Lana swallowed. 'Yes, of course,' she called back, wondering if she'd not peeled enough potatoes.

She walked quickly to the kitchen and Frank closed the door, shutting them in together.

'It's about the burglary,' he said in a much quieter voice. He came up close to Lana and she reckoned she could smell something sweet and boozy on his breath. 'The police were in touch.'

'Do they know who took the computer?' She couldn't help the quiver in her voice.

'Indeed they do,' he replied, his voice now barely there, ghosting out from between his rotten teeth. Frank's hands reached out to her shoulders, his fingers sinking into her skin. 'Indeed they do.'

8

Lorraine wanted nothing more than to give her nephew a big hug. He looked surrounded, defeated, and utterly miserable.

'So not even the beer-battered fish and chips would tempt you?'

Lorraine's hands twitched, wanting to take hold of him, show him that however much he was hurting she would try to help.

Freddie shrugged. 'Not hungry.'

Jo stood opposite them, unintentionally blocking his exit from the kitchen. The three of them – Jo, Lorraine and Stella – were all ready to head down to the village pub for a meal. It was renowned for its good food and no visit to Jo's house was complete without a meal at the Old Dog and Fox. It wouldn't be the same without Freddie.

Lorraine looked at his clothes. His tracksuit bottoms were grubby and frayed, and the long-sleeved top he wore seemed out of place for such a humid evening.

His face appeared so gaunt today that she couldn't help consider the possibility he'd been taking drugs. The idea filled her with dread. She'd have to speak to Jo about it, see if there was any chance.

'We can have chocolate mud cake, Freddie, like we did last time.'

Stella's attempt to get Freddie to change his mind went unnoticed.

'For God's sake, what the hell's got into you?' Jo suddenly snapped. Her cheeks reddened and she glanced at Lorraine. 'I . . .'

'Go and grab a sweater, Stella,' Lorraine said. 'It might be cold later.'

Stella went upstairs, and Freddie turned and followed her. They heard his bedroom door slam, and Jo sighed. It was all too obvious that he wouldn't be joining them.

*

From the moment they walked into the Old Dog and Fox, Lorraine sensed that Jo regretted coming out. It could have been because of the upset with Freddie, of course, but as they entered the beery, low-beamed pub, her sister fell into an even stranger mood.

'This place gets more and more popular,' Lorraine said, sending Stella off to save a table for them.

She watched as Jo's eyes flicked around the cosy lounge area.

'Mmm,' Jo replied slowly, thoughtfully.

She turned back to the bar, a faraway look in her eyes. Lorraine tracked where she'd been looking, her own gaze settling on a commotion in the corner. Voices briefly became raised, sparking the attention of the other diners and drinkers. 'Will you just sit down? Good. You're doing really well. Drink your beer. There's a good chap.' The voice was loud and superior and seemed to be dealing with another man's behaviour.

'Oh look, it's Sonia and her family,' Lorraine said in surprise.

'Stop gawping,' Jo said sharply. 'They'll see us.'

'Don't you want to say hello?'

'Not really. I don't feel sociable.'

Lorraine tried to catch Sonia's eye, and wondered whether she should go over. She could find out if there had been developments with the stolen laptop. But Jo had hold of her sleeve and was staring at the exit.

'Maybe we should get a takeaway from the Indian in Wellesbury. I can tell the service here is going to be slow tonight.'

'Are you trying to avoid them?' Lorraine waved her hand at the barmaid, who came straight over. 'A diet Coke, please, half a cider and . . . what are you having, Jo?'

'An orange juice, please.' She sighed. 'I'm not avoiding anyone. I'm just feeling a bit antisocial. I'm upset about Freddie.'

Lorraine nodded, patted her sister's arm. Even as kids she'd always been the one to take control, the one to bail Jo out of impossible scrapes or provide a shoulder to cry on. Perhaps it was knowing that she was only a step or two behind, waiting, watching, that had given Jo confidence. The overall effect was that she'd grown up rather reckless, though she still had a ton of friends, and was the one their mother had always favoured. Why, Lorraine didn't know to this day. It felt to her as if she'd been born her sister's minder.

She took the first tangy mouthful of cider, enjoying the summery taste. They found where Stella was sitting, joined her and began to relax, although Jo was still subdued.

Stella offered her crisps around then put several in her mouth. 'It's nice here,' she said between chews. 'The menu looks delicious.'

'Did you see the specials board over there?' Lorraine said, pointing.

Stella looked across the crowded room then froze. Her eyes widened and she sucked in a gasp. 'It's that nasty man, Gil,' she whispered, putting the crisps on the table and hugging her arms around her body.

Lorraine twisted in her chair. Stella was staring right at Sonia's table.

'You know,' Stella pressed on when no one responded, 'the one who shoved me. Just before Freddie told me about the kids who'd been killing themselves.'

'Ki*d*,' Jo said, stressing the singular of the word. 'Look, Stell, one local lad took his own life last month, on a motorbike. It was really sad. But it's got nothing to do with what happened eighteen months ago, which is what Freddie's probably talking about.' She swirled her drink around, clinking the ice cubes.

Lorraine was heartened by Jo's sensible statement.

'What do we all fancy to eat then?'

'Freddie said that man isn't all there,' Stella said, ignoring her mother's question and tapping her head. 'He's the one who lives in that old tact room. It looks haunted if you ask me.'

'Tack room, I think you'll find.' Lorraine tried not to laugh. 'And no one is asking you, are they, sweetheart?' She pointed at the menu. 'Look, steak and ale pie. Your favourite.'

While Jo and Stella studied the menu, she couldn't help another look at Sonia's family, and more especially her husband. Lorraine had spotted his good looks when they were at the bar, although he'd got his back to her now. His sandy-coloured hair was endearing, the way it brushed at the collar of his blue Oxford shirt, and she'd already noticed the way it flopped down over one of his strikingly green eyes, and how he kept brushing it aside. His broad shoulders, straight and square, stretched beneath his slightly crumpled shirt, making him seem as if he'd had a hard day at work. He didn't turn round.

There was a girl with them too, about the same age

as Freddie – Lana, Lorraine guessed. She was also very attractive, the kind of looks that would garner a second glance even if she wasn't a beauty. It was her vitality that made her striking rather than the thick dark hair, the wide-set velvet eyes, the full lips. The energy she seemed to exude was the antithesis of Freddie.

Oh Freddie, Lorraine thought sadly. She would talk to Jo when they got back.

There was a sudden peal of laughter, which rose above the dull bass tones that constituted the general noise of the pub. When Lorraine looked to the corner again, she saw Lana dabbing at the corner of her eyes with a napkin, laughing and looking at her father adoringly.

But Sonia wasn't laughing with the rest of her family. She was slowly turning the beer mat over and over between her long, slim fingers. Lorraine thought she looked even more gaunt in the dim light of the pub. For a second, she looked up and caught her eye, but before Lorraine could wave or smile in return, she looked down again.

'Right,' Lorraine said with conviction. 'I hereby raise my glass to fine food, good weather and my lovely family.'

'And to steak and ale pie,' Stella added, 'because that's what I'm having.'

They chinked glasses.

Then Lorraine suddenly became aware of someone behind her. The man was standing close, looming over her. He was round-faced and staring.

'Hello, Gil,' Jo said, giving Lorraine a quick look. 'Are you having a nice night out?'

'Yes thank you I am having a nice time.'

Even in those few syllables, Lorraine detected something unusual about him. She shifted her chair around so she could see him properly. His proximity made her feel slightly uncomfortable.

'I heard lots of noise and laughter at your table,' Jo said, and took a mouthful of her drink.

'Lana is going away soon she is my friend and I am sad.' Gil pulled an overly expressive face, like a child or a clown might do to indicate sadness.

Lorraine felt Stella's hand creep under the table and clutch at her fingers. She gave them a squeeze.

'How will I look after her when she has gone away?' he continued.

'Where is she going?' Lorraine said, interjecting. She couldn't completely ignore what Stella had said. 'I'm Lorraine, Jo's sister.' She held out her hand, but Gil just stared at the floor.

'Lana is going away to university to be a doctor and then she will make me better.' Gil crossed his arms over his broad chest.

Lorraine could understand why Stella had been intimidated by him. His mannerisms were unchecked and literal, slightly erratic, and could be misconstrued as aggressive.

'You don't need to be made better, Gil,' came a clear voice from behind.

Lorraine saw two hands slip over Gil's shoulders.

'Hello,' said the sandy-haired man. 'I hope my brother's not making a nuisance of himself.' He was charming and well spoken, and sounded like the kind of person who would take control in a crisis.

Lorraine thought of Adam.

'Oh, not at all,' said Jo, bringing her hair forward over her shoulders. 'He was just telling us about Lana becoming a doctor.'

'Like you didn't know already,' he said with an overstated laugh.

'When Lana's a doctor she will make me better and then girls will like me and I can get a girlfriend and get married.' Gil shifted nervously from one foot to the other.

'That all depends on her exam results, of course. I'm Dr Hawkeswell by the way – Tony,' he said to Lorraine.

This time a handshake was exchanged.

'This is my sister, Detective Inspector Lorraine Fisher,' Jo said, smiling up at him.

Tony was as striking at close range as he had been from across the room. Lorraine noticed his strong jawline, the clean-shaven yet slightly stubbly skin tanned from the good weather they'd had. When he moved, she caught a spicy whiff of cologne.

'You are the police,' Gil stated flatly.

Lorraine folded the menu, unable to help another smile. 'Yes, I am. But I'm on holiday right now.'

'Glad to hear Radcote's tourist industry is thriving.' Tony laughed, still holding on to his brother's shoulders.

He certainly seemed pleasant and caring towards his brother, Lorraine thought, but she wanted to get on with her evening now the two parties had acknowledged each other. Just for an hour or two she'd like to put aside her worries about Freddie and Jo, enjoy a couple of glasses of cider and a good meal. She was starving.

'Are you here to find out who killed Dean?' Gil said earnestly. 'He was my friend but he's dead and so she's my friend now aren't you?' He pointed directly at Stella with a jabbing finger.

Stella slid down in her seat and squeezed her mother's hand again, her eyes wide with embarrassment and something else. Fear, Lorraine thought, giving her a smile that only she would notice.

'Come on, Gil,' Tony said, trying to guide him away.

But Gil was a big man and remained in his place.

'Why do you ask that, Gil?' Lorraine said, curious.

'Dean was my friend,' Gil repeated, rocking from one foot to the other. 'He's dead now but he didn't mean to be.' He stared straight ahead, his hands scratching inside his pockets.

'Gil hasn't quite got over the shock of what happened to Dean,' Tony explained sympathetically. 'Sonia often takes him to New Hope when she works there. That's how they met. You two were always hatching crazy plans, weren't you? What was it last time – a road trip across America on a Harley?' He laughed, but then his face became sombre, his eyes heavy.

Lorraine wondered if he'd been reminded of his own son.

But Gil was nodding, beaming a smile that made his cheeks apple-like. His arm lifted slowly and pointed at the wall opposite. The pub was an eclectic mix of low beams, mismatched pine furniture, and half-panelled walls painted in various muted shades of grey and mushroom and covered with a large collection of framed cartoons and posters. Gil was jabbing his finger at a pen and ink drawing opposite.

'Well spotted,' Tony said, trying to steer him away again. 'You wouldn't get far on that motorbike though.'

Lorraine looked at the framed cartoon. A caveman was riding a motorbike made of stone and there was a dinosaur in the sidecar beside him. The bike's wheels were square and also chiselled out of stone.

'That man in the picture isn't wearing a helmet and he could die like Dean.' Gil was frowning, showing off the deep furrows between his eyes and heavy brows. 'The other person on Dean's bike was wearing a helmet. Why didn't Dean have one?'

He was looking at Lorraine.

Lorraine felt herself tense. Was he expecting her to provide an answer?

'Don't worry. I'll talk it over with him later.' This time Tony was firm with his brother, one arm wrapped around his waist and the other gripping his elbow. 'Goodnight, ladies,' he said. 'Enjoy your meal.'

'Goodnight ladies,' Gil kept repeating as he was led away.

'He's well-meaning,' Jo said. 'Quite a character in the village. Everyone's very fond of him. We all watch out for him as he likes to wander from home and sometimes forgets his way back.'

'Autism?'

Jo nodded. 'And other complications at birth, apparently.' She stared into her glass, swirling it, chinking the ice cubes. 'OK, I'm ready to order. Fish and chips for me.'

'I wonder what Gil meant by "the other person on Dean's bike"?' Lorraine said. 'If he killed himself, surely he would have been alone?' She sighed, feeling the beginnings of her mind forming a mental map of what she knew so far. She couldn't help it.

'The police said it was suicide,' Jo reiterated matter-of-factly. When Stella tipped the last of the crisps into her mouth, she mouthed *They found a note*.

Lorraine's curiosity was still not sated. 'Gil said the other person on Dean's bike was wearing a helmet. I want to know what he meant by that. And anyone planning a road trip across America on a Harley doesn't sound very suicidal to me.'

When no one bothered to reply, Lorraine went up to the bar to order their food. As she stood and waited in line, she couldn't help a final look at the Hawkeswell table as they tucked into dessert. Gil was sitting down again, but this time he was on the bench seat next to Sonia. He had a plate of untouched apple pie in front of him.

Sonia looked up, and this time she gave a fragile smile. Lorraine offered a quick flick of a wave in return, and watched as Gil shifted closer, taking hold of Sonia's hand and pressing it under his chin for comfort. He was rocking gently, oblivious to being observed, as he put his head down on her slender shoulder. Sonia stroked his hair.

On the other side of the table, Tony and Lana tucked into their puddings. Lana showed her father something on her phone, causing Tony to play-punch her arm. Then they each laughed loudly.

A normal family, Lorraine thought, drumming her fingers on the menu she was holding. Just a normal family out for dinner.

9

Lana is crying. It makes me want to smash the window and burst into her room and chase away her sadness and everything that's horrid. But I can't. They would tell me off. So I watch her from the flat roof, peeking in through her window, sending her bits of my heart as she lies on her bed, staring at the wall. Her shoulders bounce up and down. Mine do that when I laugh but she has snot and tears collecting at her mouth so I know she's sad. I've seen her cry before, although she keeps it a secret.

I like secrets.

Her room is like a princess's. Pink and cream and tidy. Not like mine. If I get a girlfriend, I'd like her room to be like this. Not that I would go into it, because that would be wrong. Tony keeps reminding me that it's bad to go in ladies' bedrooms and I have put it on my list of things not to do. There is a big list of those.

So clambering up the trellis and on to the flat roof

and looking through the window of Lana's room isn't actually breaking the rules because I'm not inside. All the same, Tony would be really cross if he found me again. It makes my heart go funny to think about it.

Then I hear Lana's telephone ringing through the slightly open window.

'Hello?'

I have a phone. It's Lana's old one and is really special and even though the screen is cracked it still works. I keep it in my pocket. My hand dives in there. It's safe. Tony would be cross if I lost it.

'Tonight?' Lana says, turning away to sniff. She holds a tissue to her nose. 'For fuck's sake, be careful.' Then she is silent, listening to the other person.

I wonder if I should phone Lana and talk to her. Sometimes I do. Hello, I say to her. How are you today? And she replies that she's OK, thanks, even though I know she's not. We like to chat on the phone. I like phoning people but I didn't call the police when Dean died because Tony had taken my phone away for a whole week as punishment for spying through the windows. He said next time I did something bad he would take my pencils away too so I just keep it all in my head now.

'OK,' Lana says. 'I already told you a thousand times, I don't know for certain. It was really quick. I just feel so wretched and miserable. Let me know. Yeah, OK. Bye.'

It's hard to see things very well with only one eye peeking above the sill, but when Lana is finished on the phone she stands up and pulls her T-shirt off over her head. She is wearing a white bra and her skin looks butter-icing soft. I bite my teeth together as my one eye lets me have a little look. It's OK to do this, I think, because it's Lana and it's only the one eye and I'm not actually in her room. She turns round just as her bra falls to the floor and then she disappears into her bathroom. I clap my hands together a little bit, not too loudly, and when I hear the shower begin to flow I climb down off the roof.

I go back to the tack room. I like it in here. It's my house. When Tony and I were little we used to play in here and get scared. Tony says it will do me good to live in here and then he made it nice for me with a kitchen and a sofa and a bed upstairs. I try to keep it clean and tidy, but sometimes Sonia has to help me sort it out.

'What you need,' she tells me, 'is a wife, young Gil.'

That makes me grin. I would like a wife but have to get a girlfriend before I can do that. I would like to go on a date with someone. I can't ask people like Lana out on a date because she is my niece. Tony says her friends are too young to go on a date with me, even though they are nice and pretty like Lana. I have to find someone my own age because that is the right way to do things. We could go for a picnic or go to the cinema. I wouldn't hold hands on the first date. I have looked for a girlfriend in the New Hope shelter. There are sometimes nice ones staying there.

I put the television on and decide to do some drawing. I like drawing and keep my art things in a huge plastic storage box under the steps that lead up to my loft. Things don't always want to be tidy in it. Sometimes it's in a jumble, like now. When I open the lid of the tub, I see the plastic thing that I found after the crash happened. I had to keep it secret so I hid it in here. No one knows I've got it. I don't know what to do with it. I'm scared it was stealing and Tony says that stealing's wrong.

Then I have a special idea.

10

Freddie listened to their happy banter, the thoughtless clattering as they came in through the front door, and the slightly tipsy laughs of his mother and aunt as they reminisced about sneaking in late as teenagers. He felt the burning in his gut, the familiar rush of his heart.

Soon it would be him sneaking out.

He stared at his computer screen – all he seemed to do these days. The vitriol blurred into a mash of hatred, today's new comments blending in with the old. He reckoned part of him was going numb, not caring what they did any more. How could he feel any worse?

He allowed his head to drop forward on to the desk, letting out a sigh he felt he'd been holding all his life.

Someone was coming. He heard fast footsteps on the old wooden stairs, followed by slightly slower ones. 'Night, night,' he heard his mum say to Stella. Then there was a tap on his door, before it opened. Freddie sat up and switched screens to a music website. He casually looked up from his computer, forcing a half-hearted smile.

'Hi, darling,' she said. 'You missed a great meal at the pub.'

Freddie shrugged. 'Oh,' he said. He managed a glance at her, noticed the sideways tip of her head, the little frown at the top of her nose.

'Lana was there,' she said hopefully.

Freddie nodded. Once, he would have been interested to know the details. Now, he was just relieved that he'd got out of going to the stupid pub.

'Freddie . . .' His mum let out a little sigh.

'Yeah?' Freddie tapped a pen on his desk.

'Nothing. Night.' She shut the door quietly.

He heard her footsteps retreat, slower now, mirroring the ache he knew she carried inside. The low mumbles of his aunt's and mum's voices in the kitchen below filled his head as he went back to the other website, tormenting himself, going over and over all the crap.

He glanced at his watch. Not long now.

*

Cursing every stair, every floorboard, every door handle and hinge, he crept from his bedroom. After each seemingly deafening sound he paused, held his breath in the darkness to see if anyone had stirred. He guided himself through the house he knew so well by memory and the faint silver haze of moonlight coming through the small windows. Everyone stayed asleep.

One cautious step after another led him to the kitchen back door. The gravel in the yard seemed to crunch louder than ever, making him think he'd wake the whole village. He'd put on his dark sweatshirt, even though he knew it was a sticky night, and pulled up the hood to hide his distinctive hair.

He'd had the good sense to get his bike out of the garage earlier, leave it propped in the gap behind the shed. The lanes seemed silvery, ghostly, as he pedalled hard, leaving Radcote behind him. He panted along the deserted road, his heart feeling as if it might stop completely from fear. What if someone saw him? What if he got caught and had to explain everything? But he kept going, the empty pack on his back slapping against his ribs as he cycled onward.

Blackdown Woods was about fifteen minutes away on a bike, but he'd forgotten the couple of hills that could delay him. Sweat began to soak into his top as he struggled up the inclines. What if Lenny grew impatient and didn't wait? He might get twitchy, think it was a set-up and scarper. Freddie pedalled harder, wishing he'd brought some water.

He passed the remains of the small floral shrine at the site where Dean had killed himself. He'd not really known him, just seen him around at the shelter when Lana was working there. Lenny had been mates with him, though, each of them sharing the same desolate future with New Hope being their *only* hope.

It scared him that he understood why Dean had done it.

The woods spanned a broad crescent of countryside south of Radcote, bordering the mainline railway to London. His mum had often told him stories of how she and Aunty Lorraine had played down there, taken picnics to the woods, made dens and campfires right next to the tracks, even though they'd been warned not to. He'd always kept out of the woods when he was younger. He knew the bad kids from school went down there, threw stuff on to the tracks, daubed graffiti on the metal fence the other side of the line. There was an old workers' hut, long since disused, where they went to smoke pot, take drugs, get pissed. He'd discovered it a couple of years ago, when he was out walking their old Airedale, Ringo. He wondered if that had been the start, when he'd spotted them at it, beating that other kid. He'd turned a blind eye, never said a word, but it was soon after that the shit had started.

It was where Lenny had said they should meet. The old hut in the woods.

✳

Freddie hid his bike behind some bushes, sinking it into the bracken. He hoped he'd remember where he'd left it later, having decided to take the field entrance into the woods. It was further on, but he preferred to clamber over the fence rather than enter from the road. He couldn't risk being seen. Several cars had already gone past, and he'd seen one parked up in the lay-by a hundred metres or so back. Probably a couple making out, he guessed, deciding not to look.

He skirted the perimeter of the wheat field, the tall, nearly-ripe ears of corn whipping at his thighs. The woods cast a thick shadow, protecting him from the pale moonlight, which was conveniently dimming as clouds gathered. He took one look back to where he'd hidden his bike before leaping over the fence and disappearing into darkness. It was as if the trees had swallowed him up.

He was pretty sure of the route to the hut, having walked it many times with Ringo. He felt determined to get what he'd come for. He was doing this for Lana. They'd scraped together the fifty quid Lenny was demanding, knowing he'd spend it all on weed. But that was up to him. He'd taken the risk, after all. He must be scared, Freddie reckoned, wanting to meet all the way out here. The money Lenny wanted was safe in his back pocket and it suddenly seemed a small price to pay.

Freddie froze.

A twig had cracked. Somewhere behind him. He looked back the way he'd come but the field wasn't visible any more. The trees and undergrowth were too thick. This place was more disorientating than he remembered, especially at night. He suddenly felt a chill.

'Len?' he called out, hating that his voice wavered.

No reply. No sounds now at all.

He crept forward a few more paces, his mouth dry and his head pounding from worry. 'Stop being stupid,' he whispered to himself. He held on to the straps of the empty pack on his back.

Then the noise again. There was definitely someone there.

Freddie darted sideways and hid down behind a tree stump, listening to his own breathing rasping in and out of his tight throat. After a few more minutes of silence, when his watch showed five past midnight, he decided to press on towards the hut. He didn't want to miss Lenny. It must have just been a fox. He still kept glancing over his shoulder, though, squinting back at the route he'd take if he had to run for it.

The hut was smaller than he remembered, dilapidated, the wooden door hanging off its hinges and half the roof missing. It was barely visible here in the thickest part of the woods. It was only a short distance from the railway line but hadn't been used by railway workers in decades. He couldn't see Lenny, although he supposed he could be inside, so he went closer to take a look. An owl hooted directly overhead, making him jump sideways. He stubbed his foot on a jutting rock and grunted in pain.

The owl hooted again.

Taking hold of the old door, Freddie creaked it open. 'Lenny, mate. You here?' he whispered loudly into the hut. If anyone else had been in there, lads hanging out, smoking, drinking, they'd surely have answered by now.

But no one was there. Not even Lenny.

A sound. *Fuck!* Someone *was* there.

Freddie ran through the dry undergrowth and hurled himself down behind a bush, thirty feet or so away from the hut. He cursed his loud panting. What the hell was Lenny thinking, meeting out here at this time of night? He could virtually taste his own heart, it was leaping so far up his throat.

'Oi, Freddie, is that you? I got what you wanted.'

The familiar sound of Lenny's voice approaching caused Freddie almost to laugh out loud with relief. It had been him all along. Thank *God*. Slowly, he stood up from his hiding place and waited for him to catch up so he could do the deal and get the hell out of there. He'd had enough of this bloody wood for one night.

Lenny came into view. Freddie was about to reveal himself, maybe give him a bit of a fright in return by grabbing him, when a figure leapt out of nowhere on to Lenny's back and pulled him to the ground.

It happened so quickly. Freddie heard angry grunts from Lenny as he fought off his attacker. A second later and Lenny was upright again, scrambling for balance, arms flailing, taking off in the direction where

Freddie was hiding. He was fast. The other person chased after him, yelling out in a fearsome, unintelligible growl, as Lenny streaked past, his assailant only a few seconds behind.

Freddie didn't know what to do. His fingers danced over the screen of his phone in his pocket, but he was too terrified to use it in case the other man heard the beeps or spotted the glow. Turning slightly, shaking, he watched as Lenny was tackled to the ground again. The other man was on top of him now, thumping him with all his strength. 'Oyyy!' came Lenny's agonised cry as his head smacked against the ground. Freddie could almost feel the vibrations as the man pounded him with his right fist, over and over again, sending Lenny's skull thumping to the ground every time he tried to get up.

He had to do something! It was his fault they were here after all, his fault for telling Lenny to nick the computer.

Freddie crept forward, praying that Lenny's attacker wouldn't hear his advance. But then he saw the man grab a rock and smash it down on Lenny's face until it was bloody. Even in the dim moonlight he could see that Lenny had no chance of escape now, and if he went to help, he'd get beaten to a pulp too. The man was big and broad, would easily overpower him. Freddie couldn't make out the features on his face, and he suddenly realised why – he was wearing a balaclava. Apart from black and white stripy cuffs poking out from the sleeves of his dark top, the man was shrouded in darkness. Unidentifiable.

Freddie wanted to throw up, and pressed his hand over his mouth to quash the gagging sounds, even though there was little chance of being heard over Lenny's shrieks. The man just sat on him, pinning him down, thrashing the rock at him – on his head, neck, chest, everywhere. It wasn't long before Lenny's desperate attempts to free himself lessened, and his body went still.

There was nothing Freddie could do.

The man grunted and stood up, wiping his forearm across his balaclava, shaking out his shoulders. He then stamped around the area, making guttural noises with every step, scuffing the undergrowth with his foot. Seconds later, a beam of light shone out from waist height.

Shit. He's got a torch.

Slowly, quietly, Freddie made his way back to the bush and sank behind it. The man was coming his way. If he ran, he'd be caught, just like Lenny. If he stayed put, the torchlight would pick him out.

He wasn't even aware of throwing the rock, making it smack against a tree trunk the other side of the hut. The beam of light quickly swung round to where the noise had come from, then went down to Lenny, caught the twitch of his leg as he spasmed.

The man grunted again, satisfied, and resumed his search, this time closer to the hut.

After a few moments, when he'd found nothing, he beat his fist hard against the hut door which fell from its hinges and dropped to the ground. Several night animals screeched in the distance.

And then another sound, causing Freddie's heart to leap, his breath to stop. The noise from the phone was shrill and clear, piercing the darkness with an out-of-place jazz piano ringtone.

It wasn't his. Shaking with relief, tears welling in his eyes, he watched the man silence the call before making his way back to Lenny and picking up the pack that had fallen at his side. He tipped the contents out, and swore gruffly again. He gathered up the items, shoved them back in the bag, then paused for a few moments, as if he was thinking.

Freddie couldn't see what the man was doing as he was facing away from him, crouching down, hunched over, the torch beam shielded by his back. After a few more seconds he put something else in the bag and slung it on his back. Then he hefted Lenny's limp body over his shoulder. Stuff came out of Lenny's mouth and Freddie could see that his arms were outstretched, as if he was reaching for help.

The man lumbered off in the direction of the railway embankment.

This was Freddie's chance to escape. Slowly, his knees stiff from crouching, he stood up and took a couple of steps from behind the bush. He could just make out the diminishing torch beam as it disappeared down the slope towards the tracks. It was now or never. He ran for it.

He stifled the shriek as pain seared through his ankle and up his leg. Before he knew it, he was flat on his face, dirt in his mouth.

Fuck!

His foot was caught in something – he'd gone down barely five strides from the bush. He turned, saw the white of a plastic bag handle trapped around his trainer. Reaching to unhook it, he felt something weighty inside. He opened the bag. It was the laptop.

Scrambling upright, clutching the computer to his chest, he spotted a jumping, zigzagging light cutting through the trees at speed. The man must have heard him fall. Freddie reckoned he only had about a five-second lead.

He started to run as fast as he could, but almost immediately his hoodie got tangled in thorns. He wriggled out of it in a flash and was soon leaping over stumps and fallen branches, smashing his way through the undergrowth, tearing back towards where he thought he'd left his bike. But he'd obviously got it wrong. As he turned round and round, trying to get his bearings, the torchlight struck him full on.

The man was just a shadow behind the beam, but he'd seen Freddie. Seen the look of horror on his face as he searched for his bike, then turned and fled for his life.

Lorraine didn't have a clue what it was at first as Stella held out the item, pushing it towards her until she took it. The odd-shaped curve of tinted plastic was scratched and flecked with dried mud. At either side were holes, presumably where fixings had once been. They were both cracked.

'Thanks, love,' Lorraine muttered as Stella went outside.

Jo looked up from the pile of sandwiches she was cutting for their lunchtime picnic. 'What on earth is it?'

'Gil said I had to give it to you,' Stella yelled back from the garden. 'When I saw him in the village earlier.'

Jo squinted at the item. 'Poor Gil. I feel sorry for him sometimes.'

Lorraine was about to ask why, but Stella came running back inside, through to the hallway, returning a moment later. 'He told me to give you this as well,' she said breathlessly. 'It's horrid but amazing.'

Lorraine unrolled the sheet of A4 paper. The lines didn't resolve immediately, but when they did she wasn't sure what to be more shocked by first, the sublime quality of the pencil drawing or its subject matter.

'Good grief,' she said.

'Ah, that must be one of Gil's drawings,' Jo said, casting a quick glance. 'He's bloody talented. I keep telling Sonia they ought to take his work to a gallery or something. He could make a fortune in London.'

'Not with pictures like this he couldn't.'

The drawing was obviously done by someone with an eye for detail and photographic accuracy, but with a very troubled mind. The face of the dead body was actually a rotting skull, flesh peeling away from shattered bone with medical detail, while the rest of him was bent around the metallic form of a crumpled motorbike. Lorraine supposed it was night-time. There was something ethereal about the tones that suggested moonlight – a full moon, she guessed.

Lorraine had seen a lot worse in real life but still, the image made her feel sick. And concerned. She hoped Stella hadn't studied it too closely. She wasn't overly protective when it came to gore and grisly stuff in films, but somehow this was different. Being hand-drawn, it was more personal, more real.

'Take a look,' she said to her sister.

Jo wiped her hands on a tea towel and moved round next to Lorraine to get a better look at the drawing.

113

'Oh God,' she said as she took the paper and pulled it close.

'It's nasty all right.'

Lorraine went back to the bit of plastic she'd placed on the pine table among the typical family detritus that had built up there – a pencil case, letters half out of envelopes, a stack of junk mail and free newspapers. She turned the object over a couple of times, put it down again and returned to where Jo was standing.

'Why would he draw something like this? And why give it to me?'

'What do you think it means?' Jo said, handing the picture back to Lorraine, instinctively washing her hands before touching the food.

'Autistic people sometimes have problems expressing themselves verbally. Given the subject matter – a dead man and a motorbike – it could be he's still very upset about losing his friend.'

Jo was nodding, taking bottles of chilled water from the fridge and loading them into an ice box. 'That sounds plausible.'

'Should we mention it to Sonia? Perhaps call in on the way to the castle.'

'Oh, I don't think that's necessary,' Jo replied. 'I know it might look as though Gil is upset, but he and Dean weren't exactly best mates. Gil would have just latched on to him.'

Lorraine nodded slowly, watching as Jo busied herself. 'Maybe we should tell Tony then.'

Jo looked up from her packing, her face white and tense. 'You have to interfere, don't you? Why don't you just admit it, Lorraine? You're jealous. Jealous because I live in this house and jealous of me having friends. Most of all, though, I think you're jealous because I ditched Malc, and because I have a lover.' She pressed down hard on a packet of cheese and tomato sandwiches. 'Go on, admit it.'

Lorraine folded her arms. 'Bloody hell, Jo.' She couldn't understand the overreaction. 'How did we go from stopping off at the Manor to me being jealous of you in the space of a few seconds?'

She didn't want this to escalate, as it so easily could with Jo, so instead she looked back at the strange drawing. She tracked the fine pencil lines on the cartridge paper, drinking up the detail of the tall stems of the hedgerow grasses, the fading crowns of cow parsley, and the spent stalk of a dandelion clock, the seeds of which might have been blown away by the dead man's last breath.

Was she jealous of Jo?

'I'm just concerned for you,' Lorraine said finally. 'I don't want you to get hurt by . . .' She trailed off, knowing that going any further would cause trouble. Instead, she looked down again at the drawing, spotting the hand in the grass as she did so.

'Whoa,' she said, bringing the picture close. 'Jo, take a look at this.'

The surprise in her voice brought Jo to her side.

Sisters were like that. Grace and Stella did it – at each other's throats one minute, in full-force collaboration the next.

'It's a hand,' Jo said.

'A female hand, by the looks of it.'

Lorraine marvelled at the detail on the fingers, the knuckles, the picked skin around the thumb cuticle, the bitten-down nails as the palm lay splayed out on the grassy verge a few feet away from the dead man. It was woven cleverly into the composition from the bottom right-hand corner, creeping, barely perceptibly, into the scene. The ring, shaped like a skull, subtly harnessed the moonlight, making it look as if it were made of pewter or tin.

Both women stared at the bit of plastic on the table again. It was what the fingers were stretching towards in the picture, except that in the drawing it had context.

'It's the visor off a motorbike helmet,' Lorraine said, picking it up. 'Jo, I really think we should call in at Sonia's house on our way to the castle and let her know what's going on.'

Jo snapped down the lid of the ice box. 'Fine,' she said curtly.

✳

At first, it appeared no one was home. They heard the door chime ring out behind the thick oak door, but it went unanswered. There was a single car parked on the gravel drive, which Jo confirmed was Sonia's, but even with more knocking and a couple of calls through the letterbox, no one came.

'The place is so huge, it's not surprising she can't hear,' Jo said. 'Let's go. It's a waste of time.'

'Hold your horses,' Lorraine said. She was clutching a plastic bag containing the helmet visor and rolled-up drawing. 'This is important.' She glanced at the car again. 'Sonia must be home.'

She walked back towards the small brick building they'd passed on the way in, with Jo following grudgingly. She wondered if this was the tack room Stella had mentioned. Surely Gil didn't live here. It looked too dilapidated for habitation. Ivy strangled an old cast-iron downpipe, reaching right up to a badly pointed chimney stack. A pigeon clapped lazily off the single clay pot. She tried to peer through the window, but it was too inaccessible due to the weeds. The sun flashed off the glass at an annoying angle, making the summer dust cast a haze over whatever was inside.

'Yes, hold your *horses*,' Jo said in a flat voice. 'She'll be down in the paddock.' She seemed resigned to the encounter now.

They walked round the east side of the Manor, signalling to Stella and Freddie in the car that they wouldn't be long, and cut through the gravel paths of a formal rose garden that was in full bloom. Once again Lorraine was reminded of her scraggy patch back home – the antithesis of these grand borders.

117

'Son-i-a!' Jo called out as they approached the field.

The horses heard them before Sonia did, raising their heads with simultaneous flicks of their dark brown tails. Four of them stood in a huddle around her while she worked, as if protecting her. She slowly stood up, her hand rubbing her lower back as she straightened. She'd been shovelling muck into a wheelbarrow.

'Hello,' she said with a small smile. Her hair was bundled back into a thin ponytail with a cloth band and she leant on the shovel. 'Sorry I'm in such a state.' She swept her hands down the front of a pair of khaki cut-off trousers.

Jo put her hand up to shield her eyes from the sun. 'You look as if you're hard at it.'

There was a fond laugh between the two women, showing the bond they clearly shared. Lorraine remembered her sister's change of mood not an hour earlier. She was nothing but pleased that she had good friends and still couldn't understand why she'd accused her of being jealous.

She thought briefly of her own group of friends back in Birmingham. She owed several of them a phone call – most of them actually – but there was always something work-related to take care of, or daughter-related, or just plain exhaustion. In fact, she couldn't remember the last time she'd been out with any of her girlfriends. She'd probably have to reintroduce herself by now. She sighed. Maybe she was envious of Jo.

'Lorraine?' Jo was nudging her. 'I was just explaining why we're here.'

Lorraine held up the plastic bag. 'Yes, it's about that motorbike crash.' When she saw the way Sonia's face paled, she felt as if she should apologise, tell her it wasn't really important.

'How can I help?' Sonia asked in a quiet voice.

'Gil asked my daughter Stella to give me a couple of things. He knows I'm a detective so he's probably just doing his bit to help.' Lorraine smiled, trying to reassure her.

Sonia shifted her slight frame from one foot to the other, still gripping on to the shovel. Her knuckles were white on the wooden handle.

Lorraine took the plastic visor from the bag. 'I think this has come off a helmet.' She passed it to Jo to hold. 'And there was this, too.' She took out the rolled-up drawing.

Sonia stared at the broken visor, frowning.

'Gil did this drawing,' Lorraine continued, rolling the elastic band off the tube of paper and unfurling it, exposing the graphic artwork bit by bit. 'It's a little upsetting, I'm afraid.'

Sonia took it. 'Oh my goodness, it's getting worse.' Her hand went to her flat chest.

'Has he done this kind of thing before?' Lorraine asked. Several years ago she'd been on a course, learning about various developmental disabilities they might encounter on the job. It was all about understanding the person rather than their actions, and not making assumptions. With someone like Gil, Lorraine thought, that would be easy to do.

Sonia sighed. 'What you have to understand about Gil is . . .' She turned to an approaching mare. Her hand went out to its searching nose as it butted against her shoulder. She smiled, steadied herself. 'Well, he's a very special person. And, as you can see, he has an incredible talent for drawing.'

Lorraine nodded, willing her to continue.

'In fact, we like to look at Gil's autism as exactly that, a talent rather than a disability. He's extremely visual in outlook. He might find the washing up a bit of a challenge, but he can draw something like this in an hour or so.' Sonia rolled up the picture, as if it was all neatly explained.

'Does he remember lots of things?' Lorraine asked.

'With minute detail,' Sonia said with a laugh. 'But only visually. Give him a verbal shopping list and he'll have forgotten even a couple of items by the time he gets down to the village shop. But if I show him the empty packets first, it's not a problem.'

'So the pictures Gil draws, are they usually of things he's seen first-hand?'

'Always,' Sonia replied. Then she frowned and looked apologetic. 'Well, that's not entirely true. He often uses his art to express himself if something's really troubling him. It's as if he *sees* his emotions, and then draws them.'

One of the horses came close to Lorraine, nudging against her shoulder. Sonia pulled the mare away by her head-collar, making a clicking sound with her mouth.

'Look,' she continued, 'Dean's suicide upset Gil a lot. It brought back feelings he thought he'd dealt with.' She hesitated. 'Feelings about Simon.'

Lorraine noticed the tears gathering in her pale eyes. 'I understand,' she said, although there were several things she wasn't sure about. She was aware of Jo checking her watch. 'Did you see the hand he drew in the corner of the picture?'

Sonia frowned again and was quick to unfurl the paper. She was silent for a moment then seemed as shocked as Jo and Lorraine had been. 'Oh my goodness. I'd not noticed.'

'Do you recognise the ring on the hand?' Lorraine asked.

'No, sorry,' Sonia replied, glancing up. 'You know, this could be Gil transferring Dean's suicide into an accident. He'd be able to process that. He knows what accidents are, the types of mistakes that cause them, how to be careful and suchlike. He goes to a brilliant group in Wellesbury where he learns all about personal safety and things like that.'

'So you don't think he's reproducing something he actually saw in this case, then?' Lorraine said.

'Oh no, nothing like that. Anyway, Gil couldn't have been there. He was with me that night. I cooked a meal and we watched a couple of films.' Sonia rolled up the drawing again and handed it back to Lorraine. 'But what you must understand is that to draw something like this, in his mind, Gil might as well have been there. He has a vivid imagination.'

'I see,' Lorraine said. 'Can I keep the picture? It's pretty incredible.' She smiled, already popping it back into the plastic bag.

'Of course. Gil wanted you to have it. As for that old thing, Tony's had an old helmet kicking about for ever. Gil must have found it. We're having a big clear-out at the moment, you see. I'll chuck it away for you, if you like.'

'Don't worry, I'll do that.' Lorraine smiled again, took the visor from her sister and dropped that back into the bag too. She had no intention of disposing of any of it.

12

'Does it all add up?' Lana asked her mother, leaning her head on her shoulder. It was midday and they were at New Hope, working together. She'd brought in her laptop for her mum to use, having shown her how to open up the accounts spreadsheet from a memory stick.

'Not quite,' Sonia said glumly. 'We need to make this fundraiser our biggest yet.' She stared at the figures. 'The roof needs fixing before winter and the council tax will clean us out again next quarter. The water bill's gone up and we're still paying for last year's gas.' She ruffled Lana's hair. 'I think I'll buy the new sleeping bags with my own money. These ones are getting a bit old now.'

'I'll see what I've got to sell,' Lana said. She'd already got rid of tons of stuff on eBay to help out, although she knew it was her mum's conscience she was helping just as much as the people at New Hope. These days, Sonia almost seemed to put them above her own family.

'I'll ask around the village for donations, old clothes and bric-a-brac, stuff like that.'

Sonia smiled and nodded in approval. Lana thought she looked exhausted. Her skin was soft but seemed pale and grey as if it hadn't seen the sun in years, even though she spent time outside with the horses. The gentle loosening of it around her eyes, her mouth, on the backs of her hands, suddenly made her seem old, as if she'd stepped into another generation.

'That's a great idea, love,' she said. 'Shame it's too late to go on your CV.'

'Mum . . .' Lana said, but stopped. She'd already had months of honing and shaping, training and chiselling. Nothing would change the outcome now.

Sonia took Lana's hand and guided it to a pile of receipts. 'Can you sort them month by month and put them into categories?'

Lana nodded and set to work. There was something comforting about having her mum tapping away at the keys beside her, making little sighs every so often. She felt a familiar bond between them – a bond she'd worried had been lost since Simon died.

'You ladies busy at it?'

Lana jumped and looked up. Frank was standing there holding two mugs of tea. He put them on the table, sloshing some on the wooden surface.

'Thanks,' Sonia said without looking up.

'Sorry I didn't make it in last night,' he said, looming over them.

Lana's ears pricked up. She'd overheard her parents arguing. Her dad hadn't been happy about Frank demanding her mum take his shift after their meal at the pub.

'It's OK,' Sonia said quietly.

Frank didn't make a move. He stood there, square to the table, hands on hips and a frown set on his face. The tea was obviously some kind of apology.

'Something important came up,' he finally muttered, before heading off to the shower room. A moment later, Lana heard a rush of water as he began his cleaning duties.

'What was all that about?' she asked when she was sure Frank wouldn't hear.

'I don't really know,' Sonia said, pausing to look at her daughter. 'It's weird. He's never missed a shift before.'

Lana watched as Frank came out of the shower room. He returned from the kitchen a moment later with a bucket of steaming hot water and a mop. He gave her a lingering glance as he disappeared back inside the tiled washroom. The scent of disinfectant soon travelled across the hall.

'I heard shouting,' Lana admitted. She hated it when her parents argued. It wasn't often, but with everything else going on, she'd become sensitive. 'Did Dad go and sleep in the spare—' She stopped herself. 'Gil came in yesterday with some bagged-up clothes. They were Simon's things.' She regretted saying that, too.

'Lana, it's fine if you want to talk about him, you know.' But her mum was looking at the ceiling, trying to hold back the tears. 'I'm glad to be rid of all the stuff, to be honest. I've been having a big clear-out. Frank collected a load of things from our place. Clothes, mainly. Your dad's, mine, some of Gil's. I think people have been helping themselves already. No point it going to waste and, really, what use is there in holding on to the past and—'

'Mum,' Lana said gently, 'you don't need to explain.'

'It's just . . . Simon's everywhere at the moment. Do you feel it?'

'Oh, Mum,' Lana said, dragging her chair closer. The noise echoed through the hall, stirring Abby, who was cocooned in her sleeping bag. Lana wrapped her arms round her mum, embracing the warm skin of her shoulders. She smelled faintly of horses and deodorant. 'I've sensed him, too.'

'It's not as if it's even the anniversary or his birthday.'

'Yesterday Abby mentioned a vet's assistant job she'd spotted in the paper. That reminded me of him.'

Lana felt her mother tense in her arms.

'Anyway, Dad and I decided it was the right time to let some of his things go,' she said.

They each took a sip of their tea, and a second later both pulled a face.

'Did Frank put sugar in yours?'

'Yes,' Lana said, trying not to sound ungrateful. 'It's disgusting.'

For a moment they went back to their work, but Sonia was restless.

'I had a visit from Jo Curzon and her sister earlier,' she said with her fingers hovering over the keys. 'It was a bit embarrassing, to be honest.'

'How come?' Lana began sorting the receipts again. She couldn't be sure she'd got them in the correct order.

'Gil did one of his drawings and gave it to Jo's sister. She's a detective.' Sonia turned, stretching her neck because she'd been at the computer too long. 'It was of Dean's crashed motorcycle. It was really gruesome.'

'Oh dear,' Lana said, imagining what Gil would have drawn. She knew his pictures were exceptional and accurate. 'But how did he know what to draw? He wasn't at the crash.'

'You're right, he was with me that evening,' Sonia said quickly. 'And I could have done without them coming round implying things that aren't true. Gil coped in a similar way after Simon died, if you remember.'

Lana didn't. The aftermath of her brother's suicide had gone on around her as if she didn't exist. Of course she recalled the police and the relatives and the doctors and journalists and several weeks off school as if it had all happened yesterday. But she also felt she'd been shielded and protected from the truth, the intricate details, the whys and the hows and the process that had, over the months, turned her parents into strangers.

127

But she nodded in agreement, knowing from experience that this was easier.

'Poor Gil,' she said. 'He'll be suffering no end.'

'I tried to explain to the detective but I'm not sure she understood.' Sonia's hands were shaking now as they hovered over the keyboard. 'If you see Freddie, perhaps you could reiterate what I said about Gil. It might filter back to his aunt.'

'Sure,' Lana said. 'Freddie says she handled a really important murder case last year. I remember it from the news.'

She waited for her mum's reaction. She knew that on the one hand she was in complete awe of people with jobs like Lorraine's (she was surprised they hadn't had Jo and her sister round for dinner yet), but on the other she was now petrified by the sight of a police car, a uniform, an ambulance with its lights flashing. It was no wonder, she thought. The day they lost Simon was filled with all that and more.

They worked silently side by side for another five minutes, then Sonia shut down the laptop.

'I think I'll go to the cemetery,' she announced. 'Would you like to come?'

Lana stared up at her. Her mum had no idea how much she hated going there. She couldn't bear gathering up the rotten flowers or standing talking to the plaque they'd had carved out of expensive marble as if Simon was still alive, as if he might burst up through the earth, shake himself down and carry on as if nothing had happened.

'You go,' she said. 'I'll finish up here and do the shopping on the way home. I'll take care of the horses, too.'

'Are you sure?' Sonia sounded disappointed.

'I'm certain,' she replied.

Then, as her mother collected her bag and keys and put her sunglasses on her head, Lana reached out and took her hand.

'Mum?'

'What is it, love?'

There was a bang followed by swearing as Frank emerged from the shower room.

Lana took a breath to force out the words she'd been desperate to ask for months and months: 'Why did Simon do it?'

Her words rang through the hall, stopping even Frank in his tracks, his bucket clattering. Her mum's hand stiffened within hers.

'Love . . .' Sonia began. 'I . . .' She stopped, her mouth open, her eyes closed. A moment later she was gone, mumbling an apology, promising they'd talk later.

Lana knew they wouldn't.

✤

Frank had the kind of arms that could sweep up a young child effortlessly, haul a catering-sized sack of potatoes on to his shoulder without a thought, break up a pub fight with ease, or, it turned out, offer a tight and comforting hug just at the right moment.

'You don't want to go getting all upset now, do you?' he said.

Lana's cheek was pressed against his chest. She wasn't sure if she should be terrified or grateful. In all the time she'd known him, Frank had never touched her. Certainly not pulled her this close, or rested his mouth against her hair as he was doing now.

She moved her head. He didn't let go. Only when his hands travelled down her back and back up again, his fingers reaching too far around her sides for comfort, did she attempt to pull away. For a second he gripped on to her, making her catch her breath; then he let go and she could breathe again.

'Thanks, Frank,' she said. But he'd made her heart pound.

'Your brother was a good lad and what happened was terrible. No one's seen anything like it around here before. All those kids killing themselves.'

Lana nodded, watching as Frank filled the kettle. His tattoos rippled over his strong, sinewy forearms.

'But asking your mother questions she can't answer isn't going to do anyone any good, is it? You need to move on. Surely that's what your brother would want.'

He stared at her, those silver-blue eyes softening just a little.

'More tea?'

Lana swished her hair back. 'Only if you don't put sugar in this time,' she said with a grin.

They decided to sort out the dustbin sacks of clothes together. Lana wondered if she'd misread Frank over the last couple of years. Maybe he was one of those gentle giants, the kind of man who would silence even the roughest of pubs when he walked in but turn out to be as tender as a lamb. Looks could be deceiving, she told herself.

They put the clothes into piles – winter and summer, male, female, different sizes. There were shoes too, belts, hats, CDs and books, a portable radio and even a couple of old mobile phones.

Frank was incredulous. 'You sure your mum doesn't want these things?'

'I'm pretty certain. She hates hoarding stuff. The only reason we haven't got rid of Simon's things before now is . . . well, you know.'

Lana turned to fetch another bag of clothes from the back hall, taking the opportunity to blow her nose as she did so.

'I'll have to go recruiting again to fill all these clothes,' Frank said when she returned. He was holding up one of her father's sweaters, and smiling.

Lana had to look away from his rotten teeth. 'Recruiting?'

'You know, go and find me some more homeless lads. The rate they keep dropping off, we'll have spare beds.'

Lana didn't like the throaty laugh that followed, which ended in a clogged-up smoker's cough.

'Where do you find them?' she asked, wishing she hadn't. She should go home. Since her mum left half an hour ago it had been just her and Frank at New Hope, apart from Abby, who was still sleeping.

'Everywhere and anywhere,' he replied. He stood and carried a pile of coats over to a large table. When he'd dumped them, he ran his hands down the front of his grimy jeans. Lana hadn't noticed how strong his legs looked until now. 'Parks, public toilets, shop doorways, you name it. Come dusk, there are plenty who appreciate a warm bed for the night.'

'I see,' Lana said, trying not to imagine Frank herding up young lads from public toilets. She couldn't help glancing at his right hand. 'You've hurt yourself.'

'It's nothing,' he said, showing her his grazed and scabbed knuckles. 'You should see the other bloke,' he joked. Then the rotten grin again.

'I'd better go,' Lana said, hunting around anxiously for her bag and keys.

Frank was suddenly close again, dangling her bag by its strap.

'Of course, not all of them deserve a bed, you know. Some of them don't appreciate the work your mum and I do here.' His voice was slow and deep.

'Oh?' Lana said, wishing Frank would hand over her bag. Her hand was on the strap but he wasn't letting go.

'Some of them would steal from their grandmother's grave, given half the chance.'

Finally, Frank let go. She hooked the strap over her shoulder and started to walk off, but he caught her by the arm and pulled her close, making her gasp with fright.

'Between you and me,' he growled, 'one or two of them deserve everything they get.'

His laugh followed her all the way out to her car.

BEFORE YOU DIE

13

The rain had washed them out of the castle grounds before they'd even started their picnic. The sky had quickly yellowed and greyed, transforming the ancient and crumbling buildings into a colour not normally visible to the human eye.

The café was packed with lunchtime trade, so Lorraine and Jo drank cups of tea and hot chocolate, and surreptitiously ate the sandwiches they'd brought, passing them under the table. Stella was reading the Kenilworth Castle guidebook, while Freddie stared at his phone, his knee jiggling beneath the table.

'Why don't we just go home?' Jo said when it was clear the weather had set in.

'How about the cinema instead, kids?' Lorraine suggested.

Kids seemed a ridiculous fit for Freddie these days. He reluctantly agreed, not wanting to upset his younger cousin.

'This gives us a chance to pay a visit,' Lorraine said to Jo on the drive to the cinema.

'A visit? Where? Aren't we watching the film too?'

'I thought we could drop into the local nick and find out how things are progressing with Sonia's stolen computer.'

Jo pulled an incredulous face. 'That computer will be long gone by now and no one apart from you cares. Not even Sonia gives a hoot about the damn thing any more.'

Lorraine grinned. 'OK, I admit I want to mention Gil's drawing and give the visor to the officer in charge.'

Jo sighed. 'Don't, Ray. If the police go to see Gil, it'll upset him no end. Not to mention what it'll do to Sonia.' She stared out of the passenger-side window, shaking her head.

'Actually, I have no choice,' Lorraine said. 'It seems to me that Gil may have witnessed something very important. Besides, there are special procedures in place for dealing with people like him.'

❋

The Warwickshire Justice Centre was a five-minute walk from the cinema, where they'd left Freddie in charge of Stella. They went up the front steps of the modern white building and entered the police department.

'I won't be long,' Lorraine said, guiding Jo to a row of seats.

She went up to the desk to explain who she was and why she was there, and was then taken through the security door and led up several flights of stairs. Moments later she was standing in the office of the detective who'd been in charge of the Dean Watts case. He was sitting at his desk, facing a window that looked out on to the back of a row of terraced houses and drainpipes. Raindrops wiggled down the small square of glass. All Lorraine could see of the detective was the curve of his shoulders and a balding mottled patch on the back of his head. When she knocked lightly on his open door, he swung round, an expectant look on his plum-shaped face.

Lorraine froze, but it was too late to back out.

Fuck.

'Good grief,' he said slowly, heaving himself out of his desk chair. 'If it isn't Lorraine Fisher.' The smirk thinned his lips, as if her name had left a bitter taste on them.

Greg Burnley. His accent was certainly the same, flecked with phlegm and smudged-together words. He had less hair now, and he'd lost weight, though not a lot, Lorraine thought grudgingly.

'Detective Inspector Fisher, in case you've forgotten,' she shot back. 'I wasn't expecting to see you today.' Or ever again, she thought, forcing a smile to hide her shock.

'Apologies, *ma'am*,' Burnley replied sarcastically. His face turned red, the creeping capillaries on his cheeks plumping up as he hitched his trousers higher on his hips. He came out from behind his desk. 'Funny you should say that though.' He edged his backside on to the corner of the desk. 'Me too. Passed my exams. Got the T-shirt. You know.'

Lorraine nodded, trying to hide her incredulity.

'Please, sit down.' He pulled across a chair with his foot.

The main office space was large and open-plan but they were in one of a series of smaller offices that had been partitioned off. On one of Burnley's walls there was a corkboard on which were pinned several photographs of overweight children, a German Shepherd dog, and a plump woman in pink running gear. His family, Lorraine presumed, rather than anything crime-related. Scattered across his small desk were case files and more photographs – this time of crime scenes – three empty coffee mugs and a half-eaten pasty.

'What can I do for you?'

'I've come about the Dean Watts suicide a month ago. You were in charge of the case?' Her tone was businesslike and cool, though not so much that he could accuse her of being unfriendly.

DI Burnley nodded. 'It's put away now, you understand.'

'I have new evidence that may change that.'

Lorraine swiftly explained her connection with the

Hawkeswell family, told him about Gil and mentioned how she'd come to be in possession of the drawing and the visor.

'And that's new evidence?' Burnley said with a discernibly mocking tone.

Lorraine nodded, pulled the rolled-up paper from the plastic bag and unfurled it. She noticed his eyebrows flicker when he saw the drawing.

'Gil says he saw another passenger on the motorbike. And there's a female hand drawn in there.' She pointed to the spread of fingers wearing the ring in the bottom right-hand corner of the drawing. The paper kept rolling up so Lorraine used two of the mugs on the desk to keep it open.

'I think it's worth looking into,' she continued. 'Gil is autistic but you shouldn't discount what he's saying. He's upset and no doubt concerned he'll get into trouble for not speaking up sooner.'

'You think I should reopen the case even though the coroner has ruled suicide just because some autistic chap has drawn a picture?' He scratched his temple.

'I do, yes.'

'There was a suicide note, detective. The case is closed.'

'Then unclose it.'

'I'm afraid I can't do that.'

Burnley slipped on his jacket, stuffed his wallet into the inside pocket and gathered his keys from the clutter on the desk.

'Why not?'

'Lorraine . . . *ma'am*,' he said in a fake voice, 'if you'd come to me with a painting by Leonardo da bloody Vinci showing a homeless lad being murdered by my own grandmother I wouldn't do anything about it.'

Let's get real, Lorraine thought he'd said after this, although she couldn't quite tell because he was holding his car keys in his mouth while gathering up a pile of papers.

'I'm sorry, love.'

That she did hear. He'd called her 'love'. He'd fucking well called her *love*. The moment she'd walked in and recognised him she'd decided not to pull rank, but now she couldn't even do that if she chose. He was, by some bizarre machinations of their superiors, the same as her.

'Look,' she said, struggling to hold on to her businesslike tone, 'I'm presenting you with potentially case-changing evidence. I suggest you take it seriously.' She was tempted to add 'given your track record', but decided against it. 'Do you remember what you said when you left Birmingham?' she asked instead.

Burnley sighed loudly and folded his arms.

'You said "You can't make an omelette without cracking eggs" when you let those scrotes get off scot-free. Do you not think you should crack a few eggs now?'

'That's irrelevant,' Burnley said. He forced a cough.

It sounded as if he still smoked heavily. 'The intel the scrotes traded saved me a load of trouble. Besides, that kid was dead anyway.'

Lorraine felt her neck tense as she shook her head. 'I am on leave,' she stated tersely, pointlessly. She was never on leave. None of them were. 'But I am prepared to pursue this.'

Then he dropped his bombshell.

*

Burnley's car was dirty inside and reeked of meat pies and cigarette smoke, and he was driving too fast. Lorraine opened the window. He pressed the button and put it up again, turning the heater on full blast. 'Doctor's orders,' he stated. 'My back mustn't get cold.'

'Hurt in action?' Lorraine said sourly. When he'd worked for West Midlands, before his enforced transfer, he'd barely left his desk if he could help it. Burnley's style of policing was conducted with a cake in one hand and a pen in the other. He'd probably strained his back reaching across his desk for his coffee.

He ignored her. 'Some parts of the body have been photographed and bagged already. We're tented up because of the earlier rain. I need to get the railway track open again, although they've rerouted where they can. You know what it's like, pressure from Transport.'

Lorraine remained silent as they drove on, heading

south-east out of the spa town. Back in his office Burnley had told her there was a note, had asked if she'd wanted to come along, throw in her twopenn'orth. He made some quip about her disproving another suicide. But that wasn't what had dragged her out with Burnley. It was the homeless bit that had got her. Another lad from New Hope. She wouldn't have wasted a moment of her time with him otherwise.

Before they'd left the Justice Centre, Lorraine had told Jo where she was going, that she'd get a taxi back later. Jo said she'd go and do some shopping and wait for the kids.

As they slowed down, Lorraine's BlackBerry located them at a place called Blackdown Woods. Unnervingly, it wasn't far from Radcote, and equidistant from Wellesbury. Burnley pulled into a lay-by and yanked on the handbrake. He folded his arms and stared across at her. 'What's left isn't nice,' he remarked before they got out of the car.

It was a peaceful and warm spot, the brewing heat hanging over the surrounding fields like a shroud now that the rain had finally stopped. A couple of wood-pigeons hoo-hooed overhead as they crossed the lane and headed down the narrowing track that led into the woods. If someone had particularly wanted death by high-speed train, this was the place to do it, Lorraine thought – private, remote, a serene resting place, even if the aftermath was horrific for those left to clean up.

The trees seemed to swallow them up in darkness,

even in the day. Lorraine didn't relish being alone in the forest with Burnley, and she certainly wasn't dressed for such terrain in her linen trousers and sandals. But they marched on, cut across towards the railway line and scrambled down the leafy bank, Lorraine tearing her cotton top on a bramble bush. Before long they met up with several white-suited forensics officers scouring a patch of ground. A rabbit froze in the bracken fifty feet or so away and watched them before tearing off across the line.

'The others have gone now, boss,' one of the forensics said to Burnley. He gave a cursory glance at Lorraine as if she was his wife who'd come along for a bit of sightseeing. 'We'll be done soon, too.'

DI Burnley nodded and scanned the scene. 'Over here,' he said to Lorraine, beckoning her with his head. She followed him down the edge of the double railway line, crunching over the granite chips. 'A pair of ramblers found him a couple of hours ago.' Burnley stopped. 'Correction. They found his legs. He was spread about.' He thrust his hands in the front pockets of his nylon trousers. 'No reports from any train drivers so it probably happened during darkness. Went unnoticed. Poor fucker.'

Lorraine walked briskly beside him, listening, scanning the scene. Nothing seemed particularly unusual, apart from the deceased being another lad from the homeless shelter. She presumed that's why he'd brought her along. To make a point about the Dean Watts case.

The stench in the small white pop-up tent reminded Lorraine of the butcher's shop she went to with her mother as a child. She stared at the remains that had clearly been flung away from the spot where the train had actually hit him. Shredded blue jeans were black with congealed blood, barely adhering to the legs that had become separated from the torso at the hips. Yellow-orange fat bubbled out of the top of one leg, the remarkably strong tendons showing stretched and white.

Lorraine swallowed. 'White male, possibly late teens, early twenties,' she said automatically. She thought of Freddie.

'Leonard Jackman,' Burnley said. Lorraine noticed that he wasn't looking at the body parts, rather the gently flapping sheeting of the tent. A breeze was getting up. 'Nineteen. There were ID details in a bag found nearby.' He tapped his phone screen and handed it to Lorraine. 'His note,' he said, zooming in on a photograph of a piece of pale blue paper set out on a white sheet.

Lorraine tilted her head and read it. It was badly written and pitiful, almost beautiful in its raw simplicity. The words of a young man who'd had enough. She closed her eyes for a beat and passed the phone back to Burnley.

'That makes it a suicide, does it?' she said, thinking of Dean, of Gil.

'Pretty much,' Burnley replied. 'He was a hopeless fucker. Known to us for years and always in trouble.

Addict: theft, aggravated assault. His file says his last outing was nicking a laptop from the homeless shelter where he stayed.' Burnley covered the body parts with a plastic sheet. 'Biting the hand and all that. Want to see the head?'

Lorraine nodded, absorbing the news.

Burnley removed another sheet to expose it. The eyes were semi-open, giving Lenny an intoxicated expression. The rest of his face was hard to determine because of the blood and matted hair and other detritus that had become embedded in the skin. At first glance it appeared that his head must have tumbled a good distance on impact, such was the bruising on the cheeks and forehead. The neck was severed relatively cleanly compared to some she'd seen. But it was the face, the skin, the direction of the bloody streaks that spread from mouth to chin and mouth to hairline, as well as the swollen bottom lip, that shocked Lorraine most.

'Where was it found?' she asked.

Burnley again referred to a photograph of the marked-up scene on his BlackBerry. He held it out. Yellow marker 3 had toppled over where the head lay after impact, right beside the brown metal of the rail track.

'Where do you think the body was actually hit?'

'Seven,' Burnley replied, switching to another picture. He zoomed in.

'Show me outside,' Lorraine said.

Burnley wrenched up a mouthful of phlegm and left the tent. She followed him to where one of the forensics team was crouching down, snapping shut a metal case. He pulled back his hood.

'The head was about here, wasn't it, Neil?' Burnley asked.

Lorraine noticed a patch of blood on the granite chippings, how it had stained the metal track in a plum-coloured spill.

'Just there,' the forensics officer replied, pointing, before going off to the tent further down the line.

'What do you think caused the facial trauma?' Lorraine asked Burnley.

His shoulders bounced up and down. His laugh was low and ended with a cough. 'He was hit by a fucking night train to London Marylebone.'

Lorraine walked a few paces away, up to the steep bank that led back into the woods. 'Rather a quick clear-up, isn't it?' she said, casting a glance towards the tent and the officers packing away.

Burnley looked at his watch. 'Indeed,' he said proudly. 'Well done, lads.'

One of the forensics team pulled back their hood, revealing a blonde ponytail.

'And ladies,' he added. 'We've already begun allowing the freight through. Another twenty minutes and they can reopen fully. Do you know the costs involved in closing a line for more than—'

'There were cuts and bruises, detective, with distinct dribbles of blood running vertically on the face – not conducive to the position in which the head came to rest.' Lorraine pulled herself up the overgrown bank, casting her eyes over the ground away to the left as she did so. 'I presume you'll be highlighting these initial findings to the pathologist and coroner?' she called down.

Burnley clumsily followed her up the bank, an incredulous expression masking the effort it took him to climb up.

'Stick to my path,' she ordered. She pointed at the grass and bracken. 'Someone's recently scrambled down there.' She indicated an area of flattened undergrowth. It wasn't the mapped-out path they or the other officers had taken.

'Bugger me,' Burnley said nastily. 'Could it have been our Lenny Jackman on his way to kill himself?' He was out of breath by the time he reached the top and stood beside Lorraine.

'So who made those tracks coming back up again then?' she asked, pointing to the clear direction of the disturbed vegetation with a sweep of her hand.

Without waiting for an answer, she walked on towards a hut she'd spotted a hundred feet or so away from the top of the bank. It was old and dilapidated and looked like the sort of place where kids got up to no good. She gave the flattened undergrowth she was following a wide berth, checking that Burnley, who was lagging behind, didn't walk through it either.

'I didn't bring you here to help,' he said, lighting a cigarette.

Lorraine was staring at a faint flattening of the

woodland floor. 'Shame,' she replied. 'Because I'm going to.' Nearby, the ends of several twigs on a low thorny bush had been snapped. The exposed wood was fresh and green. She spotted fibres caught on one of them. 'For starters, you might want to get one of your team to harvest that and get it analysed.'

Next she went over to an area closer to the hut. It was clear the ground had recently seen a scuffle. Freshly stirred leaf mould showed dark and damp beneath the drier surface covering where the rain hadn't penetrated the thick canopy above. Several areas had been gouged and disturbed more deeply, revealing the rich earth of the forest floor.

Lorraine bent down to look carefully at a rock on the ground. There were several in a cluster, as if there'd once been a fire lit there, but one was dislodged and separated from the half-buried circle. It was fist-sized and, while mostly dark grey in colour, the underside showed dark reddish-brown stains when she flipped it over with a stick.

'Likewise this rock,' she said, straightening up.

She stared around the woody clearing, then focused her attention back on Burnley who was blowing a column of smoke up into the branches as if he'd made his point by simply bringing her here.

Lorraine rested her hands on her hips. Pitiful note or not, she didn't believe for one moment that this was a straightforward suicide.

14

Lorraine called out to Jo as she crossed the Parade in the town centre. Burnley had dropped her off on the way back to the Justice Centre, offering a scathing departing comment about nuisance evidence and never seeing her again. She waved at her sister, finally catching her attention.

'Sorry to abandon you,' she said, putting a hand on Jo's shoulder.

'You never could keep home and work separate,' Jo said, holding up a couple of shopping bags. 'Anyway, as you can see, I spent the afternoon wisely.' She grinned.

'Jo . . .' Lorraine linked her arm with her sister's as they walked. 'There's something I need to tell you.'

She felt giddy suddenly, perhaps from the glare of the sun that had broken through the clouds again, but mostly because of where she'd just been. It often hit later, once the personal details of the deceased married up with the images burnt on her mind.

'Sounds important,' Jo said, stopping outside Boots.

The pavements steamed around them and the air smelled sweet and musty as they stepped out of the way of shoppers. Lorraine wasn't sure how to tell her so she just said it, plain and simple, keeping the details to a minimum.

Jo paled and stood still for a moment, stunned. Then the frown came, the flush on her cheeks. She blinked several times, and Lorraine could almost see the rush of thoughts sweep through her mind.

'Does anyone else know?' Jo asked. Her voice was brittle.

'Only the police and the people held up on the trains,' Lorraine said.

She gave Jo a little hug.

'I should tell Sonia before she hears it from someone else. She'll go to pieces if she finds out from the local news.'

'Are *you* OK?'

'I think so. Just . . .' She hesitated, brushing her hair from her eyes. 'Just tell me it's not all kicking off again.'

Lorraine took Jo's hand and squeezed it. There was nothing she could say, no way to make what had happened better.

✦

'Since Simon died, she's tried to make everything perfect, to please everyone, as if she's atoning for something or trying to put up a great façade. I've dropped hints but she shuts me out,' Jo explained.

They were walking along the main road through Radcote, although it hardly warranted the description. Only two cars came past during the five minutes it took to get to the Manor. They'd already dropped Freddie and Stella back at Jo's place.

'That must be very hard for Lana and her dad,' Lorraine said.

'They tolerate a lot, believe me. Sonia's very protective of Lana and she leans on Tony for everything.'

'It's understandable though, after losing a son like that.'

'I only hope Lana gets the exam grades she needs or her life will be over.'

'Lana's life will be over?' Lorraine said. Grace had a friend who was obsessed with results, too.

Jo was shaking her head. 'No, I meant Sonia's life, actually.'

They turned down the drive of the Manor, discussing how they would break the news.

'Are you saying Lenny might have been murdered then?' Jo asked when Lorraine mentioned Burnley's unwillingness to investigate properly.

'That's not what I'm saying. But with any death we always begin by assuming the worst. Start with murder then work down.' Lorraine couldn't be sure that Burnley believed the same.

'I'm just so worried, you know, with Freddie being down all the time.'

Lorraine drew her sister to a halt. 'Look, Jo, let's be realistic. These two homeless lads are entirely different to Freddie and the group of youngsters who killed themselves eighteen months ago.'

'But—'

'I know he's miserable about something but he's not homeless and he's not desperate. Nothing bad is going to happen to him. He has far too much sense to copy Dean or Lenny.' Lorraine looked Jo in the eye, praying she was right. 'OK?'

✴

As they approached the house, Jo told Lorraine how the gothic-style manor had been bought by the Hawkeswell family a decade ago, and how they were still in the process of renovating it. Twisted chimney stacks rose into the sky, with symmetrical bay windows either side of an arched and ornate porch that shouted out grandeur: over the years, since Lorraine had first seen it, the house had been transformed from a relatively humble farmhouse into an imposing home. At the back, the cobbled yard, the small multi-paned windows and the proximity of the stables gave clues to its working provenance.

They stepped aside as a car came speeding into the yard.

'Let's keep it calm and brief,' Lorraine said quietly as Sonia got out of the car.

Tony unlocked the back door of the house and a couple of Labradors burst into the yard, running straight up to Lorraine, tails thumping against her legs, noses trailing across her trousers.

'Jo, what a lovely surprise,' Sonia said. 'Come in. I'll put the kettle on.'

Lorraine glanced at Jo and gave a little nod.

'Perfect. We're parched. Our trip to Kenilworth Castle got rained off.'

The kitchen was cool and smelled vaguely of over-ripe fruit and a day beset by damp and humidity. Sonia went to open the windows.

'Son, I'm afraid there's been a bit of bad news,' Jo began.

Lorraine watched Sonia's expression, which transformed into a tight grimace.

'What?'

'I wanted to tell you myself because I know how it's going to make you feel.'

Jo took Sonia's hands in her own. Lorraine busied herself filling the kettle.

'What is it, Jo?'

'I'm afraid there's been another suicide.' Jo paused. 'I'm really sorry, but it was another boy from New Hope.'

'Oh my God, *no*.' Sonia's shoulders started to shake and she began to sob.

'I'm so sorry, Sonia.' Jo wrapped her up in a hug.

Lorraine plucked a tissue from a box and handed

it over. 'I'm really sorry too, Sonia,' she said. 'It must be very upsetting for you.'

'Are they certain it was a suicide?' Tony had come in from the yard with the dogs weaving round his legs. He'd overheard what had been said and had gone over to his wife. His voice and presence seemed to soothe her: she left Jo's embrace and went to him.

'I can't release too many details at present,' Lorraine said. 'The local police are dealing with it. I was . . .' She hesitated. 'I was visiting them about another matter when I learnt the news from an old colleague. Of course, every case gets treated as suspicious, but I can tell you that a suicide note was found at the scene.'

Sonia was nodding, sniffing, blowing her nose. 'How did it happen?'

'Details are vague at present,' Lorraine replied. She knew the importance of not allowing suicides to be visually recreated in other people's minds, especially those vulnerable or close to the victims.

Sonia pulled away from Tony for a minute. 'You haven't told me who it was.' She took another tissue, blew her nose, and scrunched it up in her hand.

'It was Lenny Jackman, I'm afraid.' Lorraine let the news sink in. 'It was also Lenny who stole your laptop.'

'Yes, Frank told Sonia the police knew it was him from the CCTV,' Tony said. 'They couldn't find evidence to actually pin it on him, though.'

'What did the note say?' Sonia asked.

'Love, don't torture yourself,' Tony said, passing

153

over a cup of tea from Jo. 'I don't care a jot about the computer. You know that, don't you?'

Sonia nodded. 'I'd have given him the money if only he'd asked. Anything. *Any*thing to stop this nightmare happening again.'

'Apart from the New Hope connection, there's nothing to indicate Lenny's death was linked to Dean Watts in any way,' Lorraine said, wondering whether this was in fact the case, but not wishing to upset Sonia any more.

'You can't rule out the possibility, though, can you?' Tony asked as Sonia sank back against him.

'That's up to Detective Inspector Greg Burnley and his team to decide. He's the officer in charge. I'm sure he'll be in touch soon,' she added, wondering if Burnley would bother. If it was up to her she'd be all over New Hope by now.

'We can't allow another suicide spate to happen again,' Tony said, allowing himself to fold down into a kitchen chair. Sonia sat in the one beside him. 'The community hasn't recovered.'

The confident man Lorraine had met in the pub only the night before seemed changed, as if he'd been successfully concealing his grief until this moment.

'I understand,' she said. 'I'll see if I can get DI Burnley to arrange a liaison officer to keep you informed.'

Then, suddenly, Jo announced it was time to go. 'You know where I am if you need me, Son,' she said, giving her friend a hug. She glanced briefly at Tony and offered him a small smile.

'One last thing,' Lorraine said, stopping in the doorway. 'It's about Gil.' She felt a prod in the ribs from Jo but ignored it. 'He seems rather preoccupied with the night Dean died. After what's happened today, I'd keep a close eye on him.'

✳

As Lorraine and Jo walked off down the drive, they saw Gil standing with his arms outstretched, staring up at the roof of his little cottage. There was a tile missing from the patchwork of clay squares and a white and grey cat was stalking along the ridge. It emitted a pitiful mew every few paces.

'Hello where is your daughter?' Gil said, staring at Lorraine, unnerving her slightly. His blinks were deliberate and slow, almost as if he was counting them.

'She's back at Jo's house, Gil,' Lorraine replied, wishing she hadn't. 'Is your cat stuck?'

'No,' said Gil. 'I am watching to see if he jumps and dies.'

Jo shot Lorraine a look. They didn't think the cat would leap to its death but both were unnerved by Gil's lack of concern if it did.

'Would you like to see my drawings?' he asked. A grin spread across his face.

'We need to get going,' Jo said under her breath.

'I've got lots and lots,' he said, walking off towards the tack room.

The door to the little building was open and Lorraine could see that it looked quite cosy inside, if not rather dark because of the ivy that had partially obscured the window. Gil stopped and turned, framed by the doorway.

'The motorbike helmet visor was in the grass where Dean's girlfriend fell off the bike but now the helmet's broken and nothing can be fixed any more not anything not even Dean.' Gil was looking at Lorraine again, and she noticed how his pale blue eyes were transformed to navy in the shadow of a cedar tree.

'I'd love to see your drawings, Gil,' she said, ignoring Jo's heavy sigh and following him inside.

It was nicer than Lorraine was expecting. Someone, no doubt Sonia, had gone to some trouble furnishing the place and making sure Gil had everything he needed to live comfortably. It reminded her of a place she'd once rented years ago.

'I draw everything,' Gil said.

He held out a glass of water to Lorraine, then poured another for Jo. They each drank some so as not to offend him.

'You have an amazing talent,' Lorraine said.

The table was covered in his work, ranging in size from small scraps of paper with minute drawings to poster-sized creations and half-finished works that seemed almost life-size.

'Do you only draw things that you've seen?'

For a moment, Gil appeared puzzled, but then a grin spread across his face. 'Yes, but I see everything,' he said, shuffling through the stack of papers. He pulled out a drawing and handed it to Lorraine.

She gasped. Stella was staring back at her from a large sheet of cartridge paper, peeking coyly out from behind a big tree. There were other trees and bushes all around her. If Lorraine hadn't been slightly disturbed by this man having such an interest in her daughter, she'd have asked to keep it – or buy it. It was certainly worthy of framing and hanging on the wall.

'Why did you draw this?' Lorraine asked.

'Because she is my friend,' Gil said honestly. 'Do you like the woods?' he asked. 'I have drawn Stella in the woods because I like the woods and I'd like to take Stella there to play hide and seek but I would let her win so don't worry.' He laughed before gulping down half a glass of water.

'What else do you like to draw?' Lorraine asked, aware that Jo was looking out of the window as a car went off down the drive.

'I like drawing cars and trains and aeroplanes.' Gil knocked some of his drawings on to the floor before plucking out several others. 'I go walking and I see things,' he said proudly.

In one of the sketches the train was modern and flashed diagonally across the page, as if it would burst from the paper with a blare of its horn. There were several other precise drawings of trains, all speeding through the countryside as if they'd been photographed from above.

'Oh, that's my car,' Lorraine said in surprise, looking at another picture. 'You can even see my registration number.'

'I like to draw cars but trains are my favourite,' Gil said, clapping his hands and snatching the pictures back from Lorraine. 'But it's a secret right? Just like Dean's girlfriend and the helmet.' His face was suddenly swept with a concerned expression. 'You won't tell, will you?'

Lorraine stared at him. Tiny beads of sweat had erupted on his forehead.

'No, Gil,' she said thoughtfully. 'I won't tell.'

15

Freddie was sweating. An uncomfortable layer of moisture coated his face as he helped Lana make the beds at New Hope. His muscles felt weak and his legs and back ached. He'd come to talk to her, not change sheets.

Lana stopped what she was doing, put her hands on her hips. 'Have you heard a word I've said, Freddie?' She shoved a pillowcase at him.

He nodded weakly.

'Mum said to me, "You are not going and that's final", as if I'm a little kid. We were grooming the horses first thing and she just put her foot down. It's getting worse. She never lets me do anything any more. Apart from work here.'

'I'm sorry to hear that.' And he was. Lana deserved better.

He stared at her through aching eyes.

Two nights had passed since Lenny's attack, and he'd not slept a wink. Instead he'd lain, fully clothed, on top of his bed, haunted by the memory of the *thud-thud* of footsteps behind him, the rasping breath of his assailant ringing in his ears as he'd run in terror, not caring where he ended up. Somehow, several hours later, he'd got back to Radcote, still clutching the laptop, but he hadn't since dared go back to find his bike. It could rot wherever he'd left it for all he cared.

'So I guess I have to resign myself to a life of solitude,' Lana said, snapping out a fresh-smelling sheet.

'You'll be off to uni in September,' Freddie said. He'd no doubt still be stuck in Radcote, the void of his life stretching before him. 'You'll have a great time.'

Lana stared at him – Freddie couldn't read the odd look she gave him – and then chucked a pillow at his chest.

'Mum thinks I'm going to die of a drug overdose if I go to Tammy's party,' she continued. '*Any* party. She thinks all my friends are bad influences and will convert me into a crack addict before I know it. She's completely paranoid about me falling in with the wrong people, getting myself a police record, making it impossible to go to med school when they CRB-check me.'

Freddie noticed a glint of tears in Lana's eyes. He recognised her frustration, understood it completely. He suffered the same emotion every waking moment, even more so now. For a second he wondered if she would understand if he told her – told her everything, from the horror he'd seen the other night to the creeps that made every day of his life unbearable. There was a chance it would bring them closer.

His mouth opened, and Lana glanced at him expectantly, but he quickly closed it again. What was he thinking?

'I've got the computer,' he said instead. It was what he'd come to tell her, after all.

He looked around the big hall furtively.

Lana stopped tucking in the sheet, straightened up and came round to his side of the bed. 'You have?'

He could smell the zesty scent of her shampoo as she pulled back her hair.

'So now what do we do?'

Freddie shrugged. 'I don't know,' he whispered. It was the truth. Whatever else was going on in his life, however much he needed to tell someone about the wretched texts and shit online, he mustn't tell her what he'd seen on Monday night. He could hardly bring himself to even think about it, let alone involve Lana. He'd texted Lenny just in case he was still alive somewhere, but there'd been no reply.

'Have you had a chance to look at it?'

Freddie shook his head. He'd stared at the laptop, certainly. Spent hours staring at its shiny lid, wondering what secrets it contained. Lana's claims weren't to be taken lightly – both their lives would be affected by this. It's why they'd decided to take it in the first place. The only good thing, as far as Freddie could see, was that they'd been brought closer because of it.

'I will soon,' Freddie said quietly. 'But you know, it's going to be hard. I'll have to do a bit of techie stuff. It takes time.'

Lana nodded. That was the thing about her. She was always so understanding, so accommodating.

Freddie felt the buzz of his phone in his back pocket. He slipped it out, read the message, shoved it away again.

'Are you OK?' Lana asked.

'Yeah,' he retorted, instantly regretting his tone. It was hardly her fault, the light-headedness the texts gave him, the feelings of sheer terror.

'I've been worried about you recently. You've not been yourself. I know what I told you about the computer is hard to swallow, but there's something else. I feel—'

'Look, just shut up, will you?' Freddie wiped the sweat off his face with the back of his hand. 'I did what you wanted, got the laptop, so just, like, forget it, will you? I'll call you if I find anything.'

Lana folded her arms. She stared at him, the camp bed like a mountain between them. 'I don't get you, Freddie Curzon. Not one bit.' She shook her head, waited a moment for him to say something, and when he didn't, she gathered up an armful of dirty laundry and went off to the kitchen, leaving Freddie with an empty, sinking feeling deep in his chest.

He was a loser. Just like they'd said.

He slumped down on to the bunk and dropped his head into his hands.

Someone came out of the kitchen and walked up to him. He was going to apologise, tell her he was sorry, that there was loads of stuff on his mind, but when he looked up Frank was standing there. Freddie's spine stiffened.

'You two planning on coming to Tammy's gathering later?'

Freddie wasn't sure if he was about to get a warning or if Frank was trying to be nice. He'd heard Lana speak about him once or twice in uncertain terms, as if she never knew which way to take him. He reckoned he'd be wary, stay on the safe side.

'I don't know,' he replied. He hated that his voice sounded lame next to Frank's. 'I don't think Lana's allowed, and I'm pretty tired.'

Frank stared down at him. He was holding a tool-box in one hand, a metal one like Freddie had seen plumbers use. 'Just saying, you know, lad. Tammy's a good girl.' He stared at Freddie for a moment longer, then walked away down the hall. A quick glance back over his shoulder unnerved Freddie even more.

'What was that about?' Lana said, returning to the bunk. She looked pale.

Freddie shook his head. 'Nothing much. Just about Tammy's party.'

'It would freak me out to have a dad like him.' She sat down on the bunk next to Freddie. 'Anyway, forget that. Frank just told me something terrible when I was in the kitchen.'

Freddie wondered whether he should put his arm round her shoulders.

'There's been another suicide.' She gave a little choke, looked directly at him. 'Oh my God, Freddie, I don't believe it.'

'Who? When?' He was conscious of his voice squeaking.

'Lenny. They're saying that Lenny killed himself. The story's been going around since yesterday.' Lana leant in closer. 'You don't think we . . . you don't think it's our fault, do you?'

Then her head was bowed, pressing against his shoulder. He felt the electric shock of her touch in every part of his body.

'Jesus fucking Christ,' he said, although it felt as if his mouth wasn't working. He bit his tongue until he tasted blood. 'Lenny *killed* himself?' He didn't know what to say. Nothing made sense.

'That's what Frank just told me.' Lana pulled a tissue from her pocket. 'He says it probably won't be reported in the papers much because of what happened round here before.'

'Bloody hell.'

'And with Dean killing himself so recently, they don't want it kicking off again. Oh God, what's going on, Freddie? Was it because we got him to steal the computer? I really wish we hadn't now. We could have got it another way.'

Freddie put his hand on Lana's head and stroked

her hair. It was soft and shiny, but he hardly felt it, barely appreciated it.

'No, no, it's not our fault,' he said, trying to sound as soothing as he could. He needed time to work this out. 'Lenny was always after money, ducking and diving. He said I'd done him a favour, asking him to nick it.'

He stared around New Hope in a daze. He'd seen Lenny's head being pulped with a rock. He had to confess what had happened. Something this big couldn't sit inside him. He'd witnessed a *murder*, and he'd run away like a coward. Why hadn't he gone back and helped his mate?

Then the enormous rotten hole those bastards had carved out over the months opened up inside him and swallowed the secret back down. No, he thought, he had to hold on to this shit. How could he possibly tell anyone what he'd seen? He was as guilty as Lenny's killer. They were right: he was a loser and deserved to rot in hell.

Freddie's eyes filled with tears as Frank stared at him through the kitchen hatch.

✳

That evening, his mum, all cheery and excited, dragged him downstairs to greet his Uncle Adam, who'd just arrived from Birmingham. He'd taken the first opportunity to slope back up to his room once the chit-chat was out of the way. It wasn't that he didn't like his uncle, far from it, but the thought of making small talk – lying about how he was, how he thought he'd done in his exams, what he was up to this summer with his mates – was frankly nauseating. Adam was another cop, after all, and he knew from the stories Lorraine had told him that cops had a way of sniffing things out – things like the nature of Lenny's death in particular.

Anyway, they were all chattering away about some stupid canal boat trip and other stuff that he wanted nothing to do with. How could he get excited about anything ever again when he felt like this?

He sat down at his desk and folded his arms, rocking slightly in his chair. His head ached and his eyes throbbed. He stared at his bed, knowing what was underneath the mattress. It wasn't a very good hiding place, he knew that, but he didn't want to keep the laptop for long. He wanted shot of it. Since he had learnt that Lenny was dead, it suddenly seemed tainted, dangerous even.

He couldn't put it off any longer. Everyone downstairs was preoccupied, and he doubted they would disturb him until it was time to go out. They'd been invited to the Hawkeswells' for a barbecue, but he couldn't face an evening of socialising, even if it did mean a couple of hours in Lana's company.

He lifted up the corner of his mattress, stuck in his hand, and pulled out the silver laptop. He put it on the desk, opened up the lid and turned it on. His stomach churned as he checked his door was firmly closed. A peal of laughter wound up the stairs, making him feel even more wretched about being miserable and alone.

A moment later and the screen was glowing in front of him. Once he'd hacked through the password, he saw loads of icons displayed on the desktop, some familiar, some not. What he was looking for wouldn't be obvious, cleverly tucked away in a hidden file or emailed to a secret address no doubt. Lana had described what she'd glimpsed; apart from the unpleasant details, she'd said there were many windows open within some kind of photo-viewing software. It wasn't much to go on, but Freddie set to work, beginning by trawling through recently opened files.

Fifteen fruitless minutes later there was a knock at his bedroom door. He slammed the laptop shut and threw his dressing gown over the top of it. When he opened the door, Stella was standing there, a grin cutting across her rosy-cheeked face.

'Are you coming then or what?' she said. 'Mum sent me to get you.'

Freddie felt drunk from staring at all the files, from delving into the private workings of someone else's life. He actually quite liked Lana's dad and felt bad, as if he'd crept into his bedroom in the middle of the night and rifled through his personal possessions. But he quickly reminded himself that he was doing it for

Lana's sake as well as his, and he just had to get it over with. They needed the truth. So far, he'd found nothing out of the ordinary.

'Sorry Stell,' he replied. He didn't want to be mean to his cousin. 'I really don't feel like coming.'

He heard his mother's voice ring up the stairs, echoing what Stella had said. She shrugged, looking at him imploringly.

'Wouldn't it be easier if you just came along?' she whispered.

'No,' Freddie said quietly.

He knew he couldn't lump all his troubles on her, but he reckoned she'd been astute and picked up on something because she nodded obligingly and walked off, leaving him with a gentle pat on the arm. To keep his mother off his back, he yelled down the stairs that he would be along later, that he was just chatting to a mate online.

Another ten minutes after that he heard them all go out and the house fell silent. Freddie turned back to the computer, but the power was getting low and he didn't have a charger to fit it. Anyway, he wasn't in the mood any more. Searching through someone else's private stuff just felt wrong, even if there was good reason. All he'd found were innocent family photographs, some personal letters, and a few medical articles.

He shoved the computer back under the mattress and grabbed the A4 pad from his bedside drawer. He'd started the letter a couple of weeks ago and never got round to finishing it. But it had made him feel a tiny bit better, writing down all his troubles, his worries, his fears and anxieties. It was addressed to his mum, but that didn't mean she was ever going to get it. God, no. It was just something he'd seen on a bullying forum, about how writing a letter to someone you love could, eventually, help you speak up or feel better. Freddie thought he would give it a go. He was desperate, after all.

The text woke him. The pad was lying on his chest and the pen had fallen from his hand. Instantly the sick feeling lurched in the pit of his belly. He pulled his phone from his back pocket, sat up, blinked several times to clear his sight, and read it.

'Shit, *no*,' he said out loud, his heart hammering in his chest.

He got up from his bed and stood in the middle of the room, not knowing what to do. It was the worst message yet. As far as he could see, there was only one way out for him now.

16

Lorraine had called Adam as soon as she'd got back from telling Sonia about Lenny's death. Although she wasn't certain of his plans for the next few days, she hoped he could come to Radcote. She missed him.

'Thanks a lot,' she'd said good-naturedly as she lay on her bed, phone pinned to her ear. He'd just said she'd sounded stressed.

She'd told him about her encounter with Greg Burnley at the Justice Centre, and brought Adam up to speed about Gil and his claims regarding Dean Watts' death. She was intrigued, and she knew that Adam's curiosity would also get the better of him, especially with Burnley involved.

'He hasn't changed much,' she'd said after describing the second suicide, almost hearing Adam's mind ticking over on the other end of the phone: *two lads dead from the same homeless shelter . . . a witness who saw a second person on the motorbike . . .* 'We went to the scene, but Burnley had his blinkers on as ever.

I had to push him to get some basic SOC forensics he was going to overlook, and I've also asked to see some reports on the case from a month ago. He's being rather difficult.'

'*We* went to the scene?' Adam said. 'As in you and Greg Burnley? You've taken it upon yourself to *work* with him?'

'No, Adam, of course not. Anyway, he made it quite clear that he wasn't interested in reopening the Dean Watts case, whatever information I had. He basically told me to get lost so he could get on with mopping up the railway suicide. This area gets special consideration after the previous suicides.'

Lorraine had gone on to explain about Jo's friend, Sonia, and how they'd lost their son over a year ago, how he was the second last in a spate of suicides in the area. It was, in the end, enough for Adam to say he was coming to Radcote. Besides, he'd said, it was too quiet at home alone.

Lorraine had smiled after hanging up. Taking time out of the office was one of the perks of being a detective inspector. They managed their own workloads, and as long as they got the job done, questions were rarely asked. Besides, Adam had a special interest in cases like this, having led a similar investigation in the past and written a well-respected paper on the subject. He'd been a keynote speaker at a conference aimed at community police and the risk of copycat and cluster suicides.

The next morning, she'd told Jo that Adam was coming to stay.

'I'd better call Sonia and let her know then. She's just asked us all round for a barbecue at the Manor tonight.'

✳

When he arrived, Lorraine had had to prise his arms from her waist. 'We're due in half an hour, Adam,' she reminded him. She hadn't had a chance to change yet. Jo had emphasised that it was just a casual arrangement, nothing to make a fuss about, especially as Sonia was unlikely to go to a huge amount of trouble under the circumstances, but Lorraine felt she ought to make an effort.

'This old place has certainly changed,' Adam had remarked, looking around the spare bedroom. It wasn't like him to notice interior decor, wallpaper or furniture, Lorraine thought, but he was gazing approvingly at the makeover – probably thinking what it would have been like to live there had Lorraine's mother given the place to them instead.

'Jo spent a fortune on it just before Malc left.'

'Those two were a divorce waiting to happen.' She'd filled him in on her sister's news as soon as they were alone. 'Jo will never stay with one man for ever. She's just not like that.' He hadn't been surprised when he'd learnt that it was Jo who'd met someone else.

Lorraine had shaken her head. 'It's so sad. Some of

Malc's stuff is still lying about as if he's just popped down to the pub. Jo says that he comes from time to time to see Freddie, but not often. I have no idea who the other man is. I'm not sure I want to know, either.'

Adam had pulled a face. He'd caught the sun in the last couple of days, Lorraine thought, and looked good.

'How's Freddie taking it?'

Again, Lorraine had shaken her head. 'Not well. You know how he adored Malc as if he was his real dad. To be honest, he's been in a really low mood since we arrived. Jo says he's been like it for months. She's really worried about him.'

'He just needs a good dose of his Uncle Adam,' Adam had said, wrapping his arms around Lorraine again. He'd lifted her up until only her toes were left on the carpet.

'You think that'll sort him out?'

There was no answer, just the soft spread of her husband's mouth against hers. She was glad she'd tempted him to Radcote, even if it was with something that was bothering her increasingly the more she thought about it. But for now she would just enjoy being with Adam again, away from the pressures of work.

✳

They'd been greeted at the Manor with unexpected joviality, Prosecco, and several platefuls of intricately constructed canapés. Sonia had set everything out in a balmy spot under a stripy awning near the spread of the cedar tree that was almost as imposing as the house itself.

'I thought you said she wouldn't go to too much trouble,' Lorraine whispered to Jo.

She watched as Adam chatted amiably with Tony over the spitting barbecue. After introductions had been made they seemed to hit it off straight away, with golf as a common link. Not that Adam knew much about the game or was any kind of expert, having spent a number of troubled weekends trying to master his technique back in Birmingham. The friends he played were high-ranking officers he needed to keep on-side. Golf, much to Adam's dismay, seemed to be the way these things worked. He'd have much preferred a ten-mile run.

Jo and Lorraine chinked glasses, enjoying the sun before it sank behind the yew and laurel thicket. Even though she was smiling and chatting, Lorraine sensed that Jo was still troubled. Freddie hadn't joined them yet, as he'd promised he would, and her concern for him was growing.

'You wait, he'll be here soon,' she said kindly, giving Jo's hand a squeeze.

Jo nodded and forced another smile.

The Manor gardens were stunning, ranging from formal rose beds and hedges clipped into fantastic-looking beasts to vast expanses of mossy lawn edged by rampant azalea bushes twenty feet high. Lorraine felt slightly guilty knowing that Sonia, who was no doubt still upset about Lenny's death, was doing all the work. But she'd refused their offer of help.

She watched as she dashed between kitchen and garden carrying trays of salmon-covered blinis topped with rusty-coloured drops of caviar, tiny stuffed baked tomatoes bubbling out a white cheese, miniature fish-cakes crammed with herbs slid fresh from the Aga, and, of course, the regular top-ups of Prosecco. She was so thin she appeared birdlike, and Lorraine couldn't help noticing the pale, set expression on her face.

'You have such a beautiful home,' Lorraine commented when Sonia halted near her for a moment. 'You could hire it out for weddings. It's the perfect setting for a marquee.'

Sonia's eyes grew wide. She looked stunned for a moment, then managed a weak smile before going back inside. It was a while before she returned.

'Just before Simon . . . well, right before he died, we learnt that he'd become engaged,' Tony said, giving the briquettes another quick squirt of lighter fluid. Flames briefly leapt out of the Weber drum. 'He told us he wanted to get married here, at home, with a marquee, the works. Sonia still finds it hard to talk about weddings.'

He drew a deep breath as if he was going to explain further but Lorraine halted him almost immediately with an apology. 'I'm so sorry. Jo told us what happened. It must be incredibly hard for you both, especially with the recent news.'

The mood was suddenly lifted by a change of expression on Tony's face. 'Ah, here comes trouble.' He was beckoning to someone behind Lorraine. 'Come on, come on!' he called out.

Lorraine hoped it was Freddie, though she knew he'd be mortified by such a welcome.

'Gil, just the man,' Tony boomed in a friendly voice.

Lorraine managed to take Adam's arm and give it a little squeeze, conveying that this was the man she'd mentioned on the phone to him.

'You're quite an artist, I hear,' Adam said, but he may just as well have remarked that the sky was blue or they were standing on the ground. In Gil's eyes it didn't warrant comment or further exploration. It was affirming the obvious.

He blinked several times, staring somewhere around his feet.

'I'd like to see some of your work,' Adam continued, not put off. 'Do you draw often?'

'I draw at my table,' Gil mumbled. He was looking at his phone now, his finger tapping the touchscreen.

'Lorraine tells me you're extremely talented.'

Adam reached for a plate of canapés and offered them to Gil. He stared at them for a good few seconds before slipping his phone into his pocket and putting at least half a dozen blinis on to the palm of his left hand. Then he walked off.

'Some days he's more talkative than others,' Tony said good-naturedly, poking the coals. 'It's no good disappearing, mate,' he called after Gil. 'I need you to help me with the barbecue.'

Lorraine noticed how Gil briefly halted and nodded his head, tipping it off his round shoulders for a moment like a planet losing its centre of gravity, before continuing his trudge.

'He'll be back soon enough,' Tony explained. 'We just let Gil be Gil, and as independent as possible, although we have to keep a watch over him. He wanders off quite a bit.'

'He seems keen to get a girlfriend,' Lorraine said, remembering how he'd looked at Stella, how it had made her feel uncomfortable.

'Ah, yes.' Tony smiled. 'Gil has one aim in life and that's to settle down with a nice lady and have a big family. The tack room's perfect for him now it's converted. He has his independence but is still close by.'

'I just tried to phone Freddie,' Jo said quietly to Lorraine. She'd come out of the house carrying two platters, one of meat and one of fish. Lorraine eyed the selection of butcher's sausages, steak, home-made kebabs, huge scallops and fresh mackerel. 'He didn't pick up.'

Tony glanced at Jo as she put the platters on a fold-out table beside the barbecue. Her face was creased with worry.

'When's the rest of the party coming?' Lorraine laughed, eyeing the quantity of food. 'We need Freddie here to eat all this lot.' She gave a reassuring smile to her sister.

'Aunty Jo, did you remember to ask Freddie to pick up my phone and bring it with him when he comes?' Stella called out from her spot beneath the tree where she was reclining in a stripy hammock chair Tony had set up especially for her.

Jo nodded. 'I left a message for him.'

'Is he not joining us?' Tony asked. He sounded disappointed. 'Lana will be here shortly.'

Jo laughed, but Lorraine could hear the strain behind it. 'You know what kids are like,' she said.

Tony nodded in agreement.

Right on cue, Lana came outside carrying another bottle of Prosecco. She topped up everyone's glasses, smiling and chatting – again, it struck Lorraine, the antithesis of Freddie.

'Is Freddie coming tonight?' she asked. 'I've been trying to get in touch with him all afternoon.'

Jo glanced at her watch for the hundredth time, and took a large sip of her drink.

'Relax, Jo,' Lorraine said. 'It's not a disaster if he stays home, is it?'

As Tony concluded a discussion with Adam on the cooking order of the meat, Jo took Lorraine aside and said, 'Ray, I suggested this afternoon that he go to the doctor about how he's feeling, but he refused. He said there was nothing wrong with him.'

'Mmm, smells good already.' Sonia had finally stopped running around. She was standing beside Tony, who was putting the sausages and kebabs on the grill, resting her head against his shoulder. 'Any sign of Gil?'

'I'll go and look for him,' Jo offered before anyone could reply. Lorraine knew she just wanted an excuse to go and find Freddie.

Tony nodded his approval. 'That's fine, you've got a good twenty minutes before this lot's done.'

Jo nodded, striding off down the drive, taking her glass of Prosecco with her.

'Jo's a bit worried about Freddie,' Lorraine said. 'He's been rather glum recently.'

There was silence while the meat sizzled.

'Poor Jo,' Sonia said. 'I could talk to her.'

'Did you have any inkling about Simon's state of mind?' Adam asked out of the blue.

'None at all,' Tony replied calmly, as if he was quite used to talking about it. 'It was the biggest shock of our lives.'

'Simon was studying to be a vet at the Royal Veterinary College,' Sonia explained, still pressed against Tony's side, a smile on her face. 'He loved animals. It was his dream.'

'*Your* dream, Mum,' Lana piped up. 'He hated it, if you remember.'

She walked over to sit with Stella. Her feet were bare, and Lorraine noticed how her painted toenails clawed the ground.

'Lana's right actually,' Sonia continued with a remorseful expression and a sigh. 'He was thinking of quitting, taking time out to go travelling and reconsider his options. He'd met someone and . . .' She paused, flicking a fly away from her face, and took a sip of her drink. 'Well, it never worked out, did it? There was one more suicide after him. Jason Rees.'

'I'm very sorry,' Lorraine said, making a mental note of this new name, knowing she probably shouldn't dig up old files but at the same time wondering what harm could come from it.

Tony was turning the sausages over with a large pair of wooden-handled tongs. Some were stuck and had burst open. 'I hope Jo-Jo manages to find Gil and Freddie,' he said, taking a quick look in the direction she'd left.

Jo-Jo? Lorraine thought. No one apart from their mother had ever called her that.

'I'll go after her,' she volunteered, suddenly feeling strangely concerned for her sister.

✻

Lorraine walked briskly down the drive. There was no sign of anyone in the little cottage, but she decided to knock anyway. When there was no reply, she turned the handle and pushed the old door inwards.

'Gil? Hello? It's Lorraine. Dinner won't be long.'

Nothing. She ventured inside and, when her eyes grew accustomed to the dimness, she could see there was even more artwork strewn about than last time.

'Good grief,' she whispered to herself, scanning the

drawings. They were everywhere and very different from the pictures Gil had shown her before. 'This stuff is . . .' She couldn't find the words to describe them. She placed a hand on the back of a chair to steady herself, allowing her eyes to settle.

While many of the pictures were of everyday scenes, each had a horrific element – a child on a swing but with one leg half amputated and bloody; a mother holding a baby, unaware of a masked man about to stab her from behind; a still-life of a vase with the reflection of a hanged body in the glass. She wondered if Tony and Sonia knew.

Lorraine turned and left the building, striding quickly down the drive and out on to the lane towards Glebe House. She got halfway there when she saw Jo running at speed towards her.

'What's wrong, Jo? You look as if you've seen a ghost.'

'It's Freddie. He's gone.' Jo was panting, her chest heaving in and out. She leant forward, placing her hands on her knees, her hair falling over her face. 'He's not anywhere in the house and the back door was wide open. It's not like Freddie. He never goes anywhere unless I force him to.'

'Maybe he thought it was about time he did go somewhere,' Lorraine said calmly. 'Freddie's eighteen. He'll be absolutely fine. Come on, let's get back to the barbecue.' She hooked her arm through Jo's and eased her upright. 'Did you find Gil?'

'You don't understand.' Jo pushed her fingers through

her hair. 'His backpack's gone, and some of his belongings, too.'

'Jo, you need to calm down.' Lorraine felt the first surge of worry creep through her. 'Let's give him a call, shall we?'

'You think I haven't tried that already?'

Jo slid her phone from her back pocket and dialled Freddie's number again, biting her lip as it went straight to voicemail.

Lorraine put her hands squarely on each of Jo's shoulders. 'I need you to calm down,' she repeated. 'You're no good to anyone in this state.'

To her surprise, Jo nodded.

'Freddie will be absolutely fine. If he has gone off somewhere, it's probably to stay with a friend. Maybe he left you a note and you missed it.'

Lorraine had learnt many years ago that you could never say anything with certainty, that people rarely behaved the way you would expect, even the people you thought you knew.

'Come on,' she continued, coaxing Jo back to the Manor. 'He's probably just doing it to annoy you.'

'Why would he do that?' Jo asked.

'Why? To get back at you for leaving Malc, of course.'

❋

Surprisingly, the rest of the evening was enjoyable. Lorraine managed to convince Jo that Freddie would come to no harm and would more than likely be home by the time they got back. Even so, Jo couldn't resist calling him a couple more times, leaving another message on the last attempt. Gil had at last materialised and was tucking into several sausages stuck into a long bun, which left a ring of tomato sauce around his mouth.

'We came looking for you,' Lorraine said to Gil with a grin. She decided not to mention the drawings she'd seen.

'I'm good at hiding,' Gil said through a mouth full of food. He laughed and a small piece of bread fell out of his mouth, sticking to his T-shirt.

'Please,' Sonia said to her guests, 'have seconds. We can't have any leftovers.'

Adam had already piled his plate with kebabs and scallops and was making quick work of the home-made accompaniments. The salads Sonia had made were delicious and were being devoured by everyone.

'Freddie had better not lose my phone,' Stella said.

'That's a good point,' Jo said. 'I should have looked to see if he'd taken it. Where was it, Stell?'

She thought for a moment. 'I left it on your coffee table.'

Lorraine could see that Jo was itching to get back to the house to check.

'I saw Freddie before dinner,' Gil said, wiping at his mouth with a napkin. His face shone out earnestly. 'He was in a hurry and I said "Hello Freddie would you like to come to our barbecue?" but he told me to fuck off that's a rude thing to say and if I had a girlfriend I would never say that to her.'

Jo stood up. 'Oh dear,' she said, swiping at the hair that had blown across her face. 'I'm really sorry, Gil.' She looked anguished. 'That's not like Freddie at all.'

'Jo, it's OK,' Lorraine said. 'I'm sure he'll be home by the time we get back.'

✳

It was a quarter to eleven when they left the Manor. Stella was tired and begged for a piggyback, so Adam hoisted her on to his back and galloped off, making silly noises. Even at her age she still loved messing about with her dad, Lorraine thought. Jo had already raced off ahead. When they finally caught up with her she was standing outside the front door in the light of the porch.

'He's not here. And Stella's phone isn't here either. What the hell do we do now?'

'You should probably phone Malc,' Lorraine suggested, watching her sister's face transform from worry to anguish. 'He might have gone to see him.'

Jo lunged for the phone and made the call.

At midnight they were all still awake, sipping coffee around the kitchen table, waiting for news. Malc hadn't answered and several messages had been left, as well as a few more for Freddie, and even some for friends of his.

'I'm so worried, Lorraine, *really* worried,' Jo said for about the tenth time that evening.

Lorraine sighed and looked at Adam. 'We know how you feel. Grace took leave of her senses last year and decided to move out. It was all over a boy.'

'I didn't know that. I'm sorry.' For a moment, considering someone else's troubles seemed to calm Jo, and she almost managed a smile. 'Kids, eh? What did you do?'

'In the end, absolutely nothing. We were lucky. She came back.'

Jo's phone beeped as a text came in. She read the message eagerly, then her shoulders dropped a couple of inches. 'It's James, Freddie's mate. He hasn't seen Freddie since Tuesday last week. Oh God, what if he's going to sleep rough or has been in an accident or got in a fight?'

'In our experience, that's unlikely,' Adam reassured her. 'Most teenagers turn up soon enough. He might well spend the night in a farmer's barn or a neighbour's shed, yes, but that's character-building.'

'I can't stand the thought,' Jo said, her eyes filling with tears. 'And it's all my fault.' She turned to Lorraine. 'You know it. And I do too.'

17

It is messy so I gather up all but one of the drawings and pack them away in a box. I don't want anyone to see them. They are my secrets. I like secrets. I'm good at keeping them, although sometimes they burn the inside of my head until there's nothing left to hold them in.

Tonight my pockets have secrets, too, so I turn out the contents, laying both things next to each other. The iPhone is better than mine, white and shiny with a pretty pink sparkly cover. I won't steal it. That would be wrong, even though it's the latest model, but I can't help reading through all her texts, looking at her pictures, taking one of myself looking handsome for her. Stella is my friend now. I know she likes me.

Then I pick up the little pebble, turning it over and over between my fingers. It's shiny and has special green bits on it. Stella gave it to me. She was playing with it at the barbecue tonight, chucking it from one hand to the other, looking bored. When she saw me watching her, she threw it at me. She was smiling and her hair was hanging down, looking all pretty. I said thank you for the stone and now that must mean she is my good friend because she gave me a present.

I kiss the pebble in case it's like one of those fairy tales where something amazing happens. I close my eyes and wait, but when I open them again everything is still the same. There is no beanstalk or fairy godmother or golden carriage, or even Stella standing in front of me. I put the stone on the table beside the phone.

I make a cup of tea and put the television on but I can't concentrate. My legs are everywhere tonight, jiggling and annoying me, so I decide to go for a walk. I put on a lightweight jacket. Sonia says it's best to do that, even in the summer, so I don't catch my death, she said. If anyone threw my death at me, I told her, I would let go of it, not catch it. Sonia laughed for ages, but that was before Simon died. She doesn't laugh now.

Thinking about Simon makes me feel cold so I zip up my jacket right up to the neck. I don't feel any warmer. Poor Simon. I am alive and he isn't. I can do my drawings but he can't. He can't do anything any more.

Before I leave, I stare at my new picture, the one I left out on the table. I squint at it. It's making me cross. It won't go the way I want. Stella is riding one of Lana's ponies, but the pony has collapsed beneath her and is dead and Stella is screaming from the swarm of flies that is on her face. Then I think: if I just put Freddie in the picture, if I draw him being angry and running away, if I draw snakes coming out of his mouth, then it will be better and it will be finished.

✳

The lane is bright from the moon. I like walking at night. People don't come up to me and say 'How are you today, Gil?' as if I am ill. If I had a girlfriend, she wouldn't think I was ill and ask me questions all the time. She would watch television with me and hold my hand. That is why I need to get one although I probably won't find one tonight.

I go down into the village and stop when I get to the crossroads. I look right then left then right again. If you go out of the village for about a mile it takes you to where Dean died. But you can also go over the fields if you want to get to Devil's Mile. It's quicker that way. I sometimes go and watch the kids on their skateboards or scooters down there. I don't have a skateboard or a scooter. I'm shivering again.

The lights are still on in Jo's house even though it's late. I creep up to the front hedge and watch them all sitting at the kitchen table. Jo has her head resting in her hands and her hair has fallen over her face. I glance at the upstairs windows but they are all dark. Stella will be asleep now. I would like it if she came for a walk with me. I would take care of her. She is my friend and now Jo is standing up and sitting down again. Her sister and that other man are the police. I am not scared of the police even though Sonia is because of what happened to Simon. She gets upset every time she hears a siren.

I go round the back of Jo's house, stepping carefully over the gravel because it makes a noise like that beach we went to. People sometimes get cross if you go into their gardens at night.

I stop. I hear voices. A man and a woman. The police detectives have come outside. I recognise their voices. Then I smell cigarette smoke.

Shouldn't do that . . . don't be stupid . . . she's panicking for nothing . . . I'm not so sure. Listen, Adam . . .

Then it goes fuzzy like a radio going out of tune. Someone coughs.

. . . concerned about what Gil said . . . someone else on that bike . . . How would he know? . . . Not your problem . . . No, I know that . . . that dick Burnley . . . not a murder inquiry for heaven's sake . . .

Then I just hear bits about a girl called Grace and an athletics camp and then they're talking about next week and the man says *Let's talk to Gil then, if you like. We'll keep it secret for now.*

I'm good at keeping secrets.

18

When Freddie woke on Thursday morning, he had no idea where he was. Had he drunk too much the night before? But then he remembered and his heart began to quicken as he sank further down inside the sleeping bag.

Last night it had seemed like a good idea to come here when the only other option had been sleeping under a hedge. He'd been certain that Frank wasn't on duty – the shift manager's timetable had been pinned to the wall when he'd called by to see Lana – and of course he knew that Sonia and Lana were at home entertaining. None of the other volunteers had any idea who he was, and as for the people who stayed here, it was only Lenny who'd known him. And he was dead.

The other cocooned bodies were waking and shuffling from their bunks. The smell of bacon and toast tantalised Freddie – he hadn't eaten for ages. But the tang of cigarette smoke from the open doorway where some of the stay-overs were standing, inhaling their first fag of the day, made him feel nauseous.

He pulled the sleeping bag over his face, wondering if everyone was out looking for him. He thought of his mum. She'd be desperately worried. How long would it be before anyone searched here at New Hope? He needed to get up and out, in case Frank or Sonia arrived. But where could he go?

'Come and get it!' Freddie heard a voice yell out of the kitchen hatch. 'Breakfast's ready!'

Shit.

He couldn't sink any deeper inside the sleeping bag. He'd just have to wait, hide inside the bedding until Lana left, then he could sneak away quietly.

'Come on, you lot. Anyone would think you didn't want it.' Lana was rounding everyone up.

A few minutes later, Freddie peeked out of his bag. It seemed he was the only one still in bed. Everyone else was perched on their beds with a plate on their knees, shoving piles of toast and eggs and bacon into their mouths. The youth on the next bunk caught his eye, pulled his plate closer to his mouth, and gave him a friendly nod as he chewed.

'I'll go over and see who it is.' Lana's voice rang out from the kitchen, causing Freddie to dive back inside his bag.

He heard her approaching, humming her favourite song. A moment later there was a hand on his shoulder, gently shaking him.

'Morning,' she said, patting him on the back. 'It'll be time to leave for the day soon. Don't you want any breakfast?'

A pause.

'Are you awake?'

Freddie stirred, pretending to be asleep. 'Leave me alone,' he grunted in a low voice.

He'd wait for her to go back in the kitchen, then grab his stuff and run for it. He could get dressed properly down the road.

But Lana gave his shoulder another shake. 'How about some egg and bacon?' she said kindly. 'There's still some left.'

Freddie curled himself into a ball. 'I'll get up in a bit,' he growled. 'Just leave me, right?'

'Up now, please, or we won't be able to guarantee you a bed later,' she said, more sternly this time. 'Don't you know the rules?'

Freddie had no idea about the rules. Since that text last night, any rules he'd ever lived by had been blown apart.

'Are you new here?' she persisted. 'There's tea and coffee too. You don't have to eat.'

Knowing now that Lana was not going to go away, Freddie turned over and blinked up at her, praying he could trust her.

'Oh my God, Freddie!' she said.

'Shhh,' he hissed back. 'For fuck's sake, shut up.'

'What the hell are you doing here? Everyone's out looking for you.'

'Just go away, will you?' he whispered back. 'Pretend you didn't see me, right? I'm serious, Lana.'

She knelt down beside him, their faces close, her voice quieter now. 'Freddie, what on earth is the matter? Is it to do with the computer? Did you find the pictures? I'm not going until you tell me.'

'I can't tell you. I just had to get away from home, that's all, and I didn't know where else to go.'

'Everyone was expecting you at my house last night for the barbecue. When you didn't come, your mum got really worried. We all did.'

Lana's cheeks coloured briefly, and Freddie knew that he should take this as a good sign, that she'd wanted to spend time with him last night. He tried not to think about it. They'd never have the chance now. His life here was over.

'I hitched a lift here and some old boy took pity on me and gave me a bed.'

'That'll be Derek,' Lana replied, glancing over her shoulder. 'He does Wednesday nights. Has something happened between you and your mum?' She grabbed his hand. 'Just tell me. Were there any pictures on the computer?'

Freddie's head dropped down on to the pillow. What was he supposed to say? That a crazy psycho-killer had anonymously texted him from a number he didn't recognise; that he'd witnessed Lenny being beaten to death, he now realised; and that he was on the run because the killer was after him too?

'It's complicated, Lana,' Freddie mumbled, wishing he could confide in her, do anything to release some of the pressure in his chest.

'So you did find something then,' she said defiantly. 'I can help, Freddie, if you'll only let me.'

Freddie lifted his head and glanced furtively around. No one was paying him any attention. 'Lana, if you want to help, then get me out of here without being spotted.' He looked at his watch. 'Is your mum working here today? Or Frank?' If they saw him, they'd tell his mum for sure.

It hurt deeply to know that he'd never see any of his family again.

'I'm covering Mum's shift this morning because, ironically, she wanted to help search for you.' Lana gave Freddie a dig in the ribs with her fist. She was angry at him. 'Just tell me what's going on will you?'

Freddie sighed. He couldn't possibly tell her about Lenny. Not after the threat. Her life would be in danger, too.

He pulled her closer, enjoying her sweet scent. He'd probably never see her again either.

'Some kids are giving me stick, that's all. I need to lie low for a while.'

Lana's face crumpled into a sympathetic look.

'And I don't mean just a bit of banter. I mean sustained, soul-destroying harassment. It's been going on for months, online and while we were at school. I never get any peace. They're on my back day and night. Don't ask me why because I don't know. Probably because I'm the loser they tell me I am. They won't be happy until I'm dead.'

Freddie looked down, not wanting her to see the tears welling in his eyes.

'Oh Freddie.' Her hand reached into the folds of the sleeping bag and sought out his fingers. 'Have you told anyone else?'

He shook his head. 'No point. It would just make it worse.' He looked around the hall. People were packing up their belongings. 'Just help me get out, right?'

'But—'

Freddie dived down into his sleeping bag.

'Freddie? What is it?'

'Frank's just arrived,' came the muffled reply.

'He might be able to help you,' Lana offered.

'*No one* must know I'm here,' he said as clearly as he could without raising his voice. He was shaking.

'But Derek will have logged you in the book last night.'

'I used a fake name.'

'Freddie, I—'

'Just shut up, right? I need to leave. It was a mistake to come here.'

'OK, OK, I'll help,' Lana replied, squeezing his fingers.

For a moment Freddie felt soothed, as if none of this was happening, as if this was the beginning of the connection between them that he'd dreamed of.

'But where are you going to go? What will you do?'

There was genuine concern in Lana's voice.

Freddie hadn't thought this through. He didn't even know which way to turn when he left New Hope. Up the hill or down the hill? Left or right?

'I think you should go back home,' Lana said. 'I'll help you work everything out, I promise. We'll sort out this computer mess once and for all and get help about the idiots who are bullying you.'

Freddie was tempted, so tempted, to take her advice, to crawl out of his sleeping bag, stretch back into his life, allow her to work through things with him. But how could he? He couldn't go to the police about what had happened in the woods – he was as guilty as the bastard who killed Lenny – and he couldn't stick around and wait for the murderer to catch up with him. He felt more desperate than ever.

I know who you are and what you saw. You're dead next.

The text had burnt through his fitful sleep. He couldn't tell Lana.

'I can't go back,' he stated.

'Look, why don't you say you went to a mate's for the night, had a few beers and your phone battery was dead. Your mum will just be relieved to see you, Freddie. She's been really worried about you.'

'You don't understand. Please, Lana, cover me while I leave.'

She dropped her head. 'Oh God, I'm so sorry, Freddie. This is all about the laptop and my paranoia, isn't it? It's my fault you're in this mess. And now Lenny's dead and everyone's worried the suicides are happening again and . . .'

For a moment, Freddie couldn't believe what he was hearing or work out where it was coming from. 'Fuck,' he whispered, squirming out of the sleeping bag, throwing on his top and pulling up the hood.

Lana lifted her head. 'Freddie?'

'That noise,' he said, sitting on the floor and pulling on his trousers. 'Where's it coming from?'

'That ringtone?' Lana said, looking around. 'Er . . . sounds like Frank's phone. Yes, it is – look, he's just answered it.'

'You certain?' Freddie asked, shoving a couple of things into his bag, making sure the laptop was still inside. He fumbled with his trainers, not bothering to lace them. 'You're sure it was Frank's phone that just rang?'

'Yes,' Lana said, almost laughing. 'What's so awful about that?'

Freddie could barely speak. It was, note for note, exactly the same as the ringtone he'd heard in the woods. The killer's phone. He'd had nightmares about it ever since watching Lenny get beaten up.

Ever since watching *Frank* kill Lenny.

Freddie grabbed his bag. 'Cover me while I get to the door,' he ordered.

'Freddie, no, wait. This is madness.'

Before he could protest or stop her, Lana was striding off to the kitchen where Frank was on the phone. Freddie, realising he was in full view of the kitchen hatch, ducked down behind his bunk, pretending to search for something in his bag. A moment later, she returned.

'Here's the cable for my dad's computer,' she said hopefully. 'It's been in the kitchen since poor Lenny snatched it.' Her imploring eyes said it all: *please prove me wrong*.

Freddie stuffed it in his bag. 'Thanks,' he said.

She went back to the kitchen and stood by the hatch so no one could see him as he crossed to the door. Then she made her way over to the porch, where Freddie leant forward and gave her a kiss. Her skin felt even softer than it looked.

'Thank you again,' he said.

'I got this for you,' she said, handing him a foil-wrapped packet. 'To keep you going.' There were tears in her eyes. 'Call me later, right?'

Freddie nodded, knowing he couldn't promise anything. He had to get away from Frank. Once he'd found somewhere safe he would think what to do next. He offered a quick wave as he stepped out into the sunlight.

It was only after he'd left the building, as he was walking down the street, drifting into the long expanse of day with some of the other homeless people, that he realised Lana, the only true friend he'd ever had, would soon be all alone with a murderer.

19

Most of the homeless had left for the day; just one or two stragglers remained. Frank was whistling a tuneless song while hanging up the last of the pans above the stove following the breakfast wash-up.

'Do you like going to those music festival things?' Frank asked Lana, who was wiping down the surfaces. 'My Tammy's got a spare ticket for Reading. She was wondering if you'd like it. There's a group of them going.'

Lana laughed bitterly. 'I can't, sorry.'

She could already hear her mum's voice if she mentioned it, especially if it was with Tammy. For some reason, she didn't think much of her and her mates.

Think of the germs, Lana, the poor sanitation and lack of nutrition. Glandular fever and STDs, not to mention the risk of dehydration and alcohol poisoning, drugs and syringes . . .

Frank made a noise as he straightened his back. He'd said he'd hurt it a few days ago. 'If I were younger,

I'd be up for it. Camping, beer, music and friends.' He nodded at the thought. 'I saw the Beatles and the Rolling Stones back in the day.'

'When was *the day*, Frank?' Lana asked idly, searching through the cans of food in the cupboard.

She felt Frank's eyes on her back so she turned, and noticed the chill in them.

'It's *now*, pet,' he replied with a wink. 'The day is always *now*.'

Lana turned back to the cupboard and thought about Freddie and the bullying he'd confided to her. She was desperately worried about him and wished she'd never let him go. What would his mother say if she knew she hadn't stopped him? There must have been something she could have done to help.

She thought of Dean, too, and Lenny, and, finally, Simon. None of them would ever again be having their 'day'. It had been stolen from each of them.

She took a can of soup from the cupboard, opened it and tipped its contents into a saucepan.

'Not making lunch already?' Frank said, coming back in from taking out the rubbish. He was behind her, standing close. Lana felt unsettled. She could sense the warmth of his body as he peered over her shoulder, watching as she stirred the soup.

'It's for Abby to take with her. She looks so thin these days.'

Frank grunted his approval. 'That girl needs to sort herself out,' he said coldly.

'She's had a tough time recently, what with losing Dean. And now Lenny.'

Frank hadn't really talked about the latest suicide. No one had. Rather he'd just carried on the last few days, busier than ever, as if by keeping the shelter in tip-top order it would make the tragedy go away.

'I had your mum on the phone earlier,' Frank said. He swung round, leaning back against the worktop.

Once again Lana felt his eyes boring into her.

'Is she OK?' she asked, staring at the soup. It was already bubbling furiously, sticking around the edges. She turned off the hob.

'She was asking about Freddie, if we'd seen him here.'

Lana swallowed. Her mouth was dry. 'Yes, they're worried because he was out all night.'

'I should help look for him,' Frank said earnestly. 'I know how easy it is for these young lads to run away, thinking they're doing the right thing. Then they fall in with a bad crowd, turn to petty crime, and end up sleeping in the park or a shop doorway.' He coughed loudly and reached into the front pocket of his jeans, which Lana reckoned had never been washed. He pulled out a grimy handkerchief and blew his nose. 'It happens more than you'd think.'

Lana looked round at him as he shoved the handkerchief back in his pocket. Did he know? she wondered.

'Freddie's not stupid,' she said. 'If he's gone off for a bit, it'll be for a good reason.'

'Oh? And what might that be?'

Lana looked at him again and saw something pained behind his small, watery blue eyes.

'I had a son once,' he said. Then he shook his head as if he'd decided he didn't want to talk about it.

'Really?' Tammy had never mentioned she had a brother.

Frank nodded, and pulled out a chair. Lana dug about in the cupboard for the old Thermos flask.

'He ran away when he was fourteen. Never heard a word from him. That was twenty years ago.'

'He'd be thirty-four now, then.' Somehow, it didn't seem plausible. Tammy was only eighteen. Lana poured the soup into the flask. Some of it splashed down her front. 'I'm sorry to hear that, Frank,' she added. 'I had no idea.'

'I don't broadcast it,' he said quickly. 'It's private, so don't you go telling everyone, right?' He made a guttural sound, which Lana took to be grief stuck in his throat. 'That's why I'd like to help find Freddie. If you tell me when and where you last saw him, that'd be a start, right? If we found him, it would help your mum, not to mention his poor family. I know how they must be feeling, see?'

Lana nodded. 'You're right. Mum's not been great these last few weeks. What with Dean's suicide, and Lenny, and now Freddie going missing . . .' She trailed off. 'I'm really worried about her.'

Frank was nodding sympathetically, and before she knew it he was out of the chair and hugging her again.

Up close, he smelled stale and unloved. She didn't like the way it made her feel.

'It must bring it all back for your poor mum,' Frank said. 'I could tell she's been upset these last few weeks, with everything going on.' His voice was clearer now, as if having a mission had given him purpose, clarity. 'She's a good woman.'

If what he'd said about his son was true, Lana could understand why he'd made the shelter his life's work. It was the same for her mum. New Hope meant much more to them than simply helping the homeless.

'So, tell me about the last communication you had from Freddie,' Frank continued.

Lana wriggled out of his hug and pulled her phone from her pocket. She play-acted to see if there were any texts, knowing there wouldn't be.

'No messages,' she said.

Frank continued to look at her expectantly.

'I think he phoned me yesterday afternoon, saying he wouldn't be coming to our barbecue last night,' Lana lied. 'Yes, that was it.'

Suddenly she wanted to tell Frank about Freddie's troubles, about the bullying and the stress he'd suffered for so long, how he felt he couldn't confide in anyone, and now this horrid thing with her dad and his mum and the laptop and Lenny and, oh . . .

Lana covered her face. 'Sorry, sorry,' she said. 'I'm just being silly.' She sniffed, and when she spotted Abby standing in the doorway she rallied and handed her the warm flask. Abby, dark-eyed and sullen, took the soup and disappeared slowly as if her legs would barely carry her.

'Listen, my love,' Frank said kindly, pulling out another chair. 'I want you to sit down next to me and tell me everything. We're going to find this young man.'

He sat down, and clasped his hands beneath his chin, meshing them in the nest of his beard. He smiled at Lana, exposing his rotten front teeth, and tilted his head sideways.

Cautiously, Lana sat down too. 'You think we can find him?'

'I promise on my life,' Frank replied kindly.

*

Lana felt better when she left New Hope half an hour later. Frank was staying on to get on with some jobs, he'd said, citing a blocked drain and leaky gutter as first on his list to tackle. She wondered if she'd misunderstood him all this time, been afraid and wary of him needlessly. He genuinely seemed to want to help. She would, her mother often told her, be expected to deal with all kinds of characters when she was a doctor. Her stomach lurched at the thought as she pulled the big front door of New Hope shut.

She walked across the street to her car. As she was about to get in, someone called out her name. Lana put her hand up to her forehead, shielding her eyes from the glare of the sun. She saw a woman approaching from over the road. She was wearing a knee-length denim skirt and sparkly sandals that hindered her attempt to run.

'Wait, Lana!'

For a moment, as Lana recognised her, all she could think about was whether her dad had remembered to pay her insurance and whether her tax disc was displayed properly.

'I'm glad I caught you,' Lorraine said, panting.

Lana bit her lip. She wanted to tell her to go away, that she was in a hurry, that she didn't know anything, but nothing came out except a few words that were meant to mean 'How are you?'

'I'm fine, thanks, love.' Lorraine pushed her sunglasses on to the top of her head. 'Can we have a quick chat?'

'What about?'

'Is there a café or somewhere around here where we can sit for ten minutes?'

'There's the chippy over there.' Lana pointed to the corner opposite New Hope. Al was just opening up. He waved at Lana and turned the closed sign to open.

'It won't take long.'

Lorraine smiled and took Lana's elbow, escorting her across the road. Lana felt a bit as though she was being frogmarched off to the police station.

Al eyed Lana when they went in. Probably wondering why she wasn't with her mates, Lana thought. Occasionally she'd pop over after a late shift and get a cone of chips.

'A coffee and a . . .' Lorraine looked at Lana.

'A Coke, please,' she said. It was too hot for tea.

'It's Freddie,' Lorraine said after they'd taken their drinks over to an orange Formica table in the window. 'As you probably know, he didn't come home last night.'

Lana nodded. 'Mum told me. I've just done her shift.' She pointed across the road to New Hope, noticing a group of men hanging around outside. One was drinking from a plastic bottle of cider.

'We're very worried about him, Lana. I know you two are good friends. I wanted to check if you'd heard anything or know anything that might help us find him.'

Lana cracked the can and drew in a large swig. The bubbles burned her throat and nose. 'Maybe he just went to a friend's place and forgot to call. I've done that before. Mum went mad with worry.'

'She did?'

Lana gave a half smile. 'I was a couple of hours late and forgot to call home. Mum rang the police and reported me missing. She said I'd been gone for hours and that it was out of character, just to make them take notice. They told her I'd probably be fine, but she went crazy apparently.' Lana leant forward across the table. 'It wasn't that long after Simon, so the police understood.'

Lorraine nodded thoughtfully.

'I was upset too, you see,' Lana found herself explaining. 'Don't tell Mum, but I'd gone and got pissed at a mate's house and passed out. I *never* do that, just so you know.' Lana managed a grin. 'But, you know, at the time it helped.'

'I know,' Lorraine said kindly, stirring her coffee. 'Freddie's mum is concerned because he's been a bit depressed recently.'

'He seems fine to me,' Lana said, far too quickly. She gulped more Coke.

'Seems? That sounds very much in the here and now. When did you last see him?'

Lana stared out of the window, noticing small greasy handprints on the sheet glass, as if a child had been trying to escape. She felt as if she'd quite like to escape. She raised her eyebrows, pretending to think.

'That would be just a day or so ago. Maybe yesterday? Stella wanted to ride one of my ponies. He seemed fine then.' Lana swallowed down the lump in her throat. She knew Freddie was far from fine, and hated herself for lying – lying to a cop, for Christ's sake.

Lorraine smiled at the mention of her daughter. 'It's just that you actually said *seems* fine, as if you'd been with him more recently.'

She was a detective, Lana reminded herself. What else was she reading from the subliminal messages she was sending out? Had she noticed the way her voice quivered as she spoke, or how her feet were jittering under the table? Had she spotted the thin layer of sweat she could feel on her top lip, or the way she couldn't quite look her in the eye?

Lana wondered if she should mention the bullying. That wouldn't hurt Freddie, would it?

'The thing is, Lana, Jo thinks Freddie's been cutting himself. Do you know anything about this?' Lorraine paused, her forehead creased with worry. 'We're concerned what else he might do if he's feeling so low.'

'Oh God.' Lana shut her eyes. She'd had no idea about this. 'You don't think he might . . .'

'That's why I need you to tell me everything, love. Even if you think it's not helpful.'

Lana nodded. A film reel of the stuff that had happened in the last few days flashed through her mind. If only she hadn't seen those damned photographs, she wouldn't have felt obliged to tell Freddie – after all, he was involved too – and they wouldn't have cooked up the hare-brained plan to steal the computer. They'd thought they were doing Lenny a favour, asking him to take it for them, but he'd ended up killing himself anyway. It was such a mess, and they had made it worse.

Lana opened her eyes. 'We never thought Simon would do it,' she said quietly, linking her fingers around the wet can. 'It was like a bomb went off in our lives. We were going away on a trip that day.'

'I'm so sorry.'

'They wouldn't let me see him, but he was hanging, I know that much. Gil saw him. He's told me what it was like. Apparently one of his eyes was open and staring.' Lana had no idea why she was telling Lorraine this. Perhaps to deflect attention from Freddie. 'I was in the car, waiting. My suitcase was in the boot.'

'I can't imagine what it must have been like for you all.' Lorraine sipped more coffee.

'Mum will never get over it. She doesn't want to.'

'And your dad?'

Lana laughed bitterly. 'He's gone off the rails—' She stopped herself. She shouldn't have said that. Her dad was coping in his own way, even if it was wrong.

'How, love?'

Lana shrugged. 'You know.'

'I don't, I'm afraid.'

'It's nothing. Really.'

Lorraine allowed a moment's silence, and Lana realised that was tactics, to make her spill her guts. But she was going to try not to.

'Just something that upset me on his computer, really. But, like I said, it's nothing.' Lana slowed her breathing, told herself to calm down. She had to change the subject. 'You do know that Freddie is being bullied, don't you?'

Lorraine sat up. 'No. Tell me.'

'Some kids were giving him a hard time at school, and online too. Freddie says they never let up.'

'Why didn't he tell someone? Why didn't *you* tell someone?'

'I only found out—' She stopped herself again. She could hardly say *this morning*. 'He didn't want anyone to know. I think it was pretty bad.'

'Did he give you any names?'

Lana shook her head. 'I reckon he felt ashamed about it, as if people would think badly of him if he admitted it. He said they wanted him dead.'

Lorraine was nodding, as if it was all familiar to her. 'You've done the right thing by telling me.'

She looked steadily at Lana, and Lana noticed how alike she was to Jo. Their eyes and hair were similar, yet their personalities quite different.

'Do you have any idea where he might have gone?' Lorraine pressed. 'Even if Freddie told you not to tell anyone, it's really important that you do. You won't get into trouble.'

'No, sorry,' Lana said, shaking her head. It was the truth at least.

Lorraine seemed disappointed. 'Maybe you have some phone numbers of friends we haven't already called.' She pulled a notepad and pen from her bag and handed them to Lana.

Without saying anything, Lana took her phone from her pocket and wrote down the numbers of three friends she thought might be useful.

'Thanks,' Lorraine said, staring at Lana for longer than necessary. 'If you do hear from him, you must let us know, OK?'

✳

The day was heating up. Residual overnight dew was steaming off the pavements, making the town seem oddly tropical. As she and Lorraine crossed the road together the humid air wrapped around Lana's throat and face so closely she thought she might suffocate.

Lorraine waited while Lana got into her car and started the engine.

'We'll be calling the local police soon,' she said when Lana wound down the window. 'It's been long enough.'

Lana nodded and put the car into gear. As she drove off, all she could hear were Lorraine's words ringing inside her head.

She took a left turn at the mini roundabout then a right at the T-junction, driving without really concentrating. She went straight ahead at the by-pass roundabout, and continued on for several miles. She had no idea where she was going, but as the town turned into leafy countryside and the road petered out into a single-track lane punctuated with cattle grids and passing places, it dawned on her where she was heading.

With a quick glance in her rear-view mirror, she turned on to Devil's Mile. She thought of Dean, of Lenny, of Simon. But mostly she thought about Freddie and where he'd gone.

Another glance behind told her that the old white pick-up was still on her tail, as it had been since she'd left town.

20

It was Lorraine who had decided to organise a proper search for Freddie. Jo had telephoned the Hawkeswells at seven a.m., frantic, hoping and praying that he'd gone to the Manor during the night, been in touch with Lana – *anything*, she'd said, that might give them a clue about where he was.

'We've not seen or heard from him,' Sonia had assured her after checking with Tony. 'I'll come up later and help search.'

'Let's leave it a bit longer before we call the local police,' Lorraine had urged her sister when she got off the phone. They were grouped around the kitchen table. It looked as if Jo had aged about ten years overnight.

'Most of them come back, you know,' Adam had reminded her. He'd made coffee for everyone, having already been out for a run. He'd hoped to encounter Freddie, perhaps curled up in a gateway or lying on a bus stop bench, but there'd been no sign of him.

'Most?' Jo had responded, pulling her dressing gown around her tightly.

*

'We don't have a great deal to go on,' Lorraine said when Sonia arrived, noticing again how frail she seemed. She was stooping and her arms appeared wisp-like, protruding from a sleeveless vest that was the same grey colour as her skin. Her wet hair was combed back, showing tufts of grey at the temples. 'Based on experience, this will almost certainly turn out to be nothing more than a hacked-off teenager teaching someone, probably his parents, a lesson.'

Adam glanced at Jo. She looked away.

'A lesson for what?' Sonia whispered.

'We have to take this seriously and form a plan for the next couple of hours,' Lorraine continued. 'This isn't our patch so we can only do so much. I'm still certain, though, that before we even get started Freddie will have skulked back with an apology.'

'Well let's hope so,' Jo said, just as Stella came into the room.

'Mum, where's my phone? Did Freddie bring it back yet?' She was bleary-eyed, most likely having been woken by their voices in the kitchen, even though it wasn't early any more.

'No, darling,' Lorraine replied. 'I'm afraid he didn't come home last night.'

Stella pulled the oversized hoodie she was wearing – Freddie's, by the look of it – around her body. 'Has he run away?' she asked. Her eyes were huge.

'That's what we're trying to find out,' Lorraine said. 'Did he say anything to you? Even if it didn't seem like much?'

Stella pulled a face. 'Not really. He was always getting loads of texts then going quiet. He seemed a bit . . .'

'A bit what?' Jo said, sitting forward.

'Am I allowed to say pissed off?' Stella asked, glancing at her dad.

Jo slumped back. 'Tell me something new.'

'Someone needs to get in touch with Freddie's friends,' Lorraine said, looking at her daughter. 'Close mates first, followed by acquaintances.'

'Yeah, I can do that,' Stella offered. 'I can contact his friends on Facebook. They'd probably be more willing to talk to someone their own sort of age.'

'Thanks, love,' Lorraine said.

'But I'm going to need to borrow a laptop because Freddie's gone off with my phone, hasn't he.'

'We'll sort something out, darling,' Adam said.

'I've already paid a visit to Lana at New Hope,' Lorraine continued. 'She gave me some of Freddie's friends' names and numbers. We could go and see them after we've done a local search.'

'Yes,' Adam said with authority, 'a local search. I'll tackle the surrounding area in the car, question people

214

in shops, bus drivers, the ticket office at the station and suchlike. Jo and Sonia, seeing as you know the villagers best, you should do a door-knock search. Lorraine will go with you. Ask memory-jogging questions relating to last night – anyone taking dogs for a walk, going to the pub, collecting in the washing, that kind of thing. Someone must have seen Freddie.'

'I think that's enough to be going on with,' Lorraine said, giving Jo a hug. 'Don't worry. He's my nephew and I'm not going to let anything happen to him.'

✳

As she walked along the deserted lane running through the centre of Radcote, it hardly seemed possible to Lorraine that Freddie was missing. She fought down her fears. What Stella had mentioned about texts and Freddie seeming upset fitted perfectly with Lana's revelation about the bullying. She had no idea how to break the news to Jo.

They'd decided to start with the outermost houses in the village and work inwards, Sonia from one side, Lorraine and Jo from the other.

'Excuse me,' Jo said, going up to a woman coming out of her house. 'I'm looking for my son.' Her voice was thin and anxious.

The woman stared at her, her hand on the car door handle, a frown on her face, as if they were about to make her late for something. Jo pushed her phone at her and showed her the picture of Freddie she'd taken only days before at Kenilworth Castle. His face was stretched into a fake smile, his disgust at being out on such a trip easily visible.

'Sorry, not seen him,' the woman said after a cursory glance, opening the car door and chucking her bag on to the passenger seat.

Jo continued to hold the phone out. 'Take a proper look. Please.'

'No, don't know him,' the woman insisted, having barely taken another glance. She got into her car and Jo and Lorraine had to move out of the way as she backed out and drove off.

The next house also proved fruitless. No one was home in the next one, so they moved on to the adjacent property in the row of terraced council houses. Most were now privately owned though they still bore the telltale classic grey stucco so popular in the fifties.

'Hello,' Lorraine said, giving Jo a break. 'We were wondering if you've seen this lad. His name's Freddie. He lives in the village. He didn't come home last night. We're very worried.'

The man, in his mid-forties, stared at Lorraine scornfully, probably wondering what kind of mother allowed that sort of thing to happen.

'I know you, don't I?' he said, turning to Jo. 'Your other half, he play darts?'

'He used to,' Jo stated meekly. 'In the Old Dog on a Thursday night. Have you seen my son?'

She held her phone up to his face and the man squinted at the screen, shielding his eyes.

'Nah, it's no use without my reading glasses,' he said. He glanced back at his front door. 'The missus'll be mad if I don't get a move on. She wanted milk from the shop. But hang on, let me get them and see if I can help. Any boy of Malc's . . .'

He went inside and returned a moment later with his glasses.

'Just like his dad, eh?' he said after taking a good look at the photo. 'Handsome lad. You must be very proud.'

Jo turned her head away. Only Lorraine could see the tear on her cheek.

'Did you see him last night?' Lorraine said. 'Maybe walking through the village, getting a lift, catching a bus, anything?'

The man's eyes flicked to the sky. He squinted again. 'Can't say I did. Although . . .'

'Yes?' Jo's gasp of hope was palpable.

'I'm sure Jan said there was a group of lads hanging around the lane last night, down where she walks the dog. She said they were, well, you know . . . a bit nasty-looking. She felt rather intimidated. I'll get her to look at your photo.'

Less than a minute later a woman wearing a dressing gown with her hair wrapped up in a towel was studying Freddie's face. 'Yes,' she said. 'Yes, he was definitely down the lane last night, about nine-thirty. He was with some other lads, about three or four of them.' She tapped Jo's phone screen. 'I've seen him around the village, but I didn't recognise the others. They were a bit unsavoury. I gave 'em a wide berth.'

'Where was he exactly? Did he seem OK? Did he seem sad?' Jo was gabbling. 'What were the other boys like? Can you describe them? Where did he go?'

Lorraine placed a hand on Jo's arm to calm her. 'Anything you can tell us will be very useful.' She took out her warrant card and showed it to the woman.

'They looked a bit intimidating, if I'm honest. They were gathered around your lad. At first I thought they were all hanging out together, but then it became clear they were giving him a hard time. They were smoking and had bottles of beer.'

'Can you describe them?' Lorraine said.

The woman sighed and shook her head. 'A couple were white but they had their hoods up. Another was black, I think. He was tall and skinny. They made some comment about my dog as I went past. He only has three legs, you see.'

The towel slipped off her head, revealing damp, dark blonde hair. It fell on to her shoulders.

'Were they hurting Freddie?' Jo asked in a croaky voice.

'I got the impression there'd been an argument and that by walking past I'd stopped it. They were clustered in a field gateway, the one I usually climb over to take a short cut to the canal towpath. Midge likes to swim.'

Lorraine tried not to think about the feasibility of a three-legged dog swimming in a canal. 'What made you think there'd been an argument?'

'I heard raised voices and yelling as I approached the gateway from round the corner. They were in a tight huddle, your lad in the middle, but when they spotted me they broke up. One of them shoved him.'

Jo let out a little whimper. 'Why didn't you call the police?' she said. 'Or help him?'

'What, and have them turn on me? Anyway, I saw your boy again later.' She seemed confident about this. 'I was half a mile along the canal, where it runs close to the road, and he was walking along it. He'd got some speed on.'

'Are you sure it was him?' Lorraine asked.

'Yes. He was carrying the same backpack as before. Orange and green. It was bright, that's why I noticed it.'

Jo was nodding. 'Freddie has a pack like that.'

'So he was heading north-ish,' Lorraine noted, although she knew the road forked soon after that, one way leading back towards Radcote, the other towards Wellesbury.

'I suppose he was,' the woman said. She rubbed at her head with the towel. 'Look, I got to do my hair. I hope you find him, OK?'

'Yes, of course,' Lorraine said. 'And thanks for your help.'

The woman turned and went back inside. Her

husband, without them noticing, had already left for the shop.

※

Lorraine reported their findings to Adam, who told them he'd not had any joy with his wider search, which made them believe – *hope* – that Freddie was still in the vicinity.

Jo needed to sit down so they paused at the bus stop. 'What if they hurt him?' she said. 'They might have followed him and—'

'Jo, don't let your thoughts run away with you.' Lorraine didn't know what else to say. Were these boys the bullies who had been harassing Freddie? All she could think of was Freddie's expressionless face the last time she'd seen him. 'Adam's going to phone the local police now.'

Jo's face crumpled, and she began to cry openly. 'You'll be involved, won't you?' she asked Lorraine through her tears. 'I want you working on it.'

Lorraine nodded. 'Of course,' she said, knowing that wouldn't necessarily be the case.

※

The heat was really building now as the sun swept higher into the sky above the row of houses lining Back Lane. The forecast of a scorching few days was proving correct.

Lorraine and Jo spoke to the postman, who wobbled to a halt on his bicycle. They soon discovered he knew nothing. They called at six more houses, accosted numerous people on their morning errands, spoke with the village shopkeeper, a lad working at the Old Dog and Fox as he stacked barrels in the pub's car park, as well as several passers-by. Only one was able to help.

'Yes, I saw Freddie. He always gives me a wave and a nod.' The old man's fond chuckle ended in a tight smoker's cough. A cigarette smouldered between his fingers. 'I was just going in for my pint last night and he was off for a stiff walk. I think he'd just been given a bit of a fright by our Gil.' He laughed again.

'Gil?' Jo said weakly.

'I had to give him a warning, I'm afraid. He was yelling and dancing about, waving his fists at Freddie like a savage. I couldn't hear what he was saying as I'm a bit deaf these days, but it sounded threatening.'

'Oh dear,' Jo whispered.

'Then Freddie walked off with them things in his ears they all wear nowadays.'

'Earphones,' Lorraine said, and thanked the old man. She wanted to get on, knock on a few more doors before returning to Jo's house to see if Sonia had come up with anything.

✤

Adam had already called the local nick by the time they got back. Sonia hadn't run into a single person who'd seen Freddie, he told Lorraine, so he'd already sent her home.

'How do you fancy a trip to the Justice Centre?' Adam said quietly to Lorraine.

'You read my mind,' she said. Her shoulders felt warm, almost burning, from the heat of the sun. 'Did you speak to Burnley?'

Adam nodded. 'They're sending a couple of uniforms out though couldn't say when. Then I spoke to the great man himself. Just for old times' sake.'

'I hope you didn't forget to call him *DI* Burnley,' Lorraine quipped.

She gathered up her bag and keys. They could go in her car and he could fill her in on the way.

✳

Lorraine had become involved with Greg Burnley in 2005. It was just after the weekend of the Lozells riots and she'd been working non-stop for days when her boss dumped the internal investigation on her.

Weeks of work revealed that Burnley had written off a young girl and her family as if they were nothing more than rubbish. She remembered the look on Burnley's face as he slammed his office door, leaving Lorraine to sort out the mess.

'Botched, sir,' she recalled telling the super after only half a day on the job.

His face remained blank as he'd instructed her to assemble a team to 'un-botch' it.

It had all started with Farida, a fourteen-year-old in the wrong place at the wrong time – a purse full of birthday cash and a shopping trip to the Bullring with her best friend. Her attackers, two nineteen-year-olds, one of whom slipped a blade into the small space between two of Farida's cat-like ribs to get her money, got off thanks to Burnley's deliberately inept policing – lost CCTV footage, unfiled witness statements, time-wasting arrests, and lack of what was obvious forensic detail.

In exchange for his calculated blunders, Burnley got the names of the trafficking gang the youths occasionally worked for, while they walked free with total anonymity and a press blackout. Burnley made sure no one cared about the dead girl. She was small fry by then. He made two dozen arrests, ripped down the UK division of a Europe-wide network that dealt in drugs, young female sex workers and, more recently, foreign slaves. He got all the glory.

Lorraine worked relentlessly on the case after Farida's mother came to see her, begging for justice. She spent weeks trawling through files, going over fabricated statements, sifting out the truth, picking apart the non-existent forensics reporting, the lack of protocol – all of it overseen by Burnley.

'You deserve a fucking medal,' Lorraine had told him as he cleared out his desk. His suspension was routine.

She remembered how he'd stared back at her.

In the end there was no retribution for the girl or her family. Their only compensation was Burnley's swift and silent transfer to the neighbouring force. Not far enough away, as far as Lorraine was concerned.

✳

'Just watch you don't make an . . .' Adam said, as they strode up the steps of the Justice Centre. He paused, thinking better of it.

'Watch I don't make an idiot of myself, you mean?' Lorraine shook her head.

'Burnley mentioned the files you wanted, but Freddie should be our main focus now. All this stuff about someone else being on the bike and that visor, well, don't read too much into it, Ray. I've met Gil now. I wouldn't give too much weight to his story.'

Lorraine shook her head as they entered the air-conditioned building. If it wasn't for the worry of Freddie pressing down on her shoulders, she'd have defended Gil and his claims. As things stood, she just wanted to make sure everything was being done to find her nephew.

✳

'Nothing better to do?' Lorraine said as she eyed all the paperwork laid out on the table in the corner of Burnley's office. She hadn't bothered to introduce Adam, or to greet him.

'Sorry to hear about the lad.' The whites of Burnley's eyes were tinged with yellow, and he had an aubergine-coloured blister on his lower lip, probably where he'd been biting it.

'The lad,' Lorraine said, leaning forward across Burnley's desk, 'is my nephew. I want him found.'

'I have people going out, as you already know,' Burnley said, holding up his hands in defence. 'Are you after special treatment?'

Lorraine breathed in sharply. 'I want the techies taking a look at Freddie's online activity and phone usage. And while you're at it, get Finance to look into his bank movements.'

'Bit premature, aren't we?' Burnley slumped into his office chair. 'Let's give the lad a chance to come back when he's hungry or runs out of money.' He glanced at his watch. 'What do you reckon, eight or nine o'clock tonight?'

Lorraine gave an imperceptible shake of her head. She knew Adam would have noticed. 'Freddie's been depressed,' she said. 'He's got a history of self-harm and his mood is currently low. His disappearance is out of character. I learnt earlier this morning that he's being badly bullied, both at school and online. A witness saw him being intimidated by a group of

225

youths last night as he was leaving the village.' Lorraine decided not to mention the old man's statement about Gil. 'You, of all people, should be particularly concerned about a missing young person's state of mind, detective. One more suicide around here and I'd call it another spate.'

'Ah, so they *are* suicides now, are they?' Burnley shook his head, and Lorraine noticed his jowls wobbling. 'Everything you wanted to see is over there, by the way.' He gestured to the table. 'Help yourself.'

Lorraine knew he was making a point, that by having her go through his case files and finding nothing wrong it would somehow scratch out the past. 'Thank you,' was all she could manage after requesting somewhere private to go.

*

The room was small and stifling, but at least it didn't have Greg Burnley in it. Adam fetched them a couple of coffees from the machine and settled down to join her. There wasn't much to look through, but since they'd set things in motion with Freddie and were assured that all the appropriate alerts had been put out, Lorraine valued a second opinion.

'Traffic or autopsy?' she asked.

They opted for Traffic first and scoured the usual scene evidence from photographic and hand-drawn plans to analysis of the wrecked bike and the officer's scene report. Dean Watts' body was ethereal in the floodlights, the blood a bronze colour pooling on the road. Everything appeared thorough and in order.

Then they skimmed over the scant bike theft details until Lorraine noticed the name of the pub from where the bike was stolen. 'The Old Dog and Fox. There's a camera in the car park,' she said to Adam. 'I spotted it the other night when we went for a meal. It's just one of those home-security jobs, but it's worth a shot.' She flipped through the file. 'I can't see any mention of it here.'

'It's probably not even connected up,' Adam said. 'Even if it is, the recordings will have been long overwritten.'

Lorraine photographed the relevant details anyway and proceeded to the post-mortem report. It was as she was reading those routine details that her phone rang.

'Hi, Jo, what is it?'

Lorraine frowned as she listened, hardly able to believe what she was hearing.

'Jo, are you there?' The line had gone dead.

She stood up, beckoning to Adam to do the same, and grabbed her bag, leaving the files spread out on the table. 'We've got to get back. Gil has hanged himself.'

21

By the time Lorraine and Adam reached the tack room, Gil had been cut down. Between them, Tony, Sonia and Jo had wrestled his body to the ground.

'It was because of Stella we found him,' Jo said.

They were still in the tack room. Tony and Sonia were huddled around Gil. Lorraine surveyed the scene, picking apart the tumbling chatter and trying to make sense of what had happened.

'I just wanted my phone back,' Stella said. 'I asked Aunty Jo to call it. If Freddie had it, I thought he might answer. He didn't.' She was talking at speed. 'Then I had the idea of tracking it.'

'What do you mean?' Lorraine said.

'God,' Stella replied, as if they were all stupid. 'A bit like you do at work, Mum. You just log into your iTunes account and do "Find My iPhone". It's easy.'

'I can't believe we didn't think of it sooner,' Jo said with a shaky voice. She was standing behind Stella, who was sitting in one of the chairs at Gil's pine table.

Lorraine didn't bother to comment that they'd already requested a ping on Freddie's phone in order to find him, but it had proved fruitless so far. Either he'd switched it off or the battery had run out.

'I borrowed Aunty Jo's laptop and, eventually, I located my phone here, in Gil's house.' Stella shifted in her chair, looking very upset. 'I lost it once before and tracked it this way. It turned out it was in someone else's locker at school.'

Lorraine focused on Stella. 'So the phone led you to the tack room,' she repeated. Stella nodded. 'But Freddie wasn't here when you arrived?'

Everyone confirmed that he wasn't, that it had just been Gil hanging from the beam.

Sonia let out a whimper. 'I couldn't believe it when Jo called me,' she said. 'I charged round here right away, hoping to find Freddie, but found him instead.'

She gestured at Gil, who was now sitting up on the floor. He squirmed, covering his face in shame.

Lorraine felt a sudden chill. She could only begin to imagine how Sonia must have felt when she saw Gil dangling by a rope. She imagined the scene, all of them bursting through the doorway, stopping abruptly at the sight of him, no one quite knowing what to do.

'I'm afraid I screamed rather loudly,' Sonia admitted.

Lorraine and Adam listened as Tony and Sonia explained how Gil's body had been suspended from the gnarled beam that stretched the width of the room.

'I wondered what the hell had happened,' Tony said, red-faced still. 'Thankfully I was in the garden and heard Sonia's cry. I came straight away.' He went on to tell them how the rope had been attached to an old meat hook sunk into the wood.

Lorraine noticed the tipped-over chair that Gil had clearly used on the table to reach the beam. The table's surface was littered with a jumble of pencils and photographs and half-finished drawings, right beneath where Gil must have been dangling. Stella's iPhone in its pink sparkly case lay right in the middle.

'You did the right thing,' Adam said as Tony explained how they'd cut him down. Luckily there'd been a serrated knife on the draining board.

'I was only doing my exercises,' Gil said, removing his hands from his face. He was clearly ashamed at all the fuss he'd caused. 'I need big muscles so I can get a girlfriend.'

Lorraine shook her head in disbelief, relieved it hadn't been a lot worse. When they'd arrived, skidding the car to a stop on the gravel drive, they'd expected to be greeted by an ambulance at least.

'It's not my fault I got stuck,' he continued.

'From what I can make out, you're lucky not to have—'

Adam stopped there, and Lorraine released her breath. Surely even he wouldn't be that insensitive.

But Tony picked up where Adam had left off. 'A few more minutes and he'd have lost his hold and dropped from the beam. The way you'd got that rope tied round your waist, Gil . . .' He took a deep breath. 'Your liver and kidneys wouldn't have thanked you much if your hands had lost their hold, put it that way.'

'I'm not very good at pull-ups yet,' Gil confessed. 'The internet said you should take precautions when exercising so I put this rope on and then I got stuck when the chair fell off the table and then you all came to save me and I am hungry now.'

'Let's get you into the house, shall we?' Tony said, slinging an arm around his brother's shoulder. Sonia followed them, telling the others to come too.

'You needn't worry,' Gil said to Lorraine and Adam as he passed them. 'It's not like what happened to Simon. That was because he was bad.'

✳

As they made their way to the house, Lorraine caught Jo's arm. 'Wait,' she mouthed. She and Adam gathered round while Stella checked her messages on her newly found phone.

'What did Gil mean by that?' Lorraine asked. Then, when all she'd got by way of response was a shrug, she continued, 'Everything's being done to find Freddie,

231

Jo. The local nick's got all the usual stuff covered, I promise. Someone will be out to see you shortly.' She glanced at her watch and hoped it was soon. 'I'm sorry Stella's phone didn't lead you to him,' she added, giving her sister a hug. She couldn't stand to see her looking so dejected.

'We need to question Gil,' Adam commented.

'Agreed,' Lorraine added. 'He got hold of Stella's phone somehow. That old chap we spoke to earlier was convinced he met Freddie last night. We need to know more.'

'Did you find anything out at the Justice Centre?' Jo asked quietly.

'Burnley obliged and let us see the Dean Watts case files.'

'I meant about Freddie, for Christ's sake,' Jo said bitterly. 'Why are you still so obsessed with that suicide when my son's missing?'

'Lorraine thinks there could be a link,' Adam responded, almost patronisingly. He took Jo by the shoulders. 'Freddie's an adult. He will be fine.'

'I have one more enquiry I want to make regarding Dean Watts,' Lorraine told her. 'If that proves fruitless, then I promise to let it go.'

Jo nodded, although Lorraine could see she was trying not to cry again.

But if I'm right, Lorraine thought, then I'm more concerned for Freddie than ever.

✳

Adam agreed to stay with Jo and the others at the Manor while Lorraine made the short walk to the Old Dog and Fox. It was early afternoon, she hadn't eaten, and the smell of real ale and chips doused in salt and vinegar made her mouth water.

She went up to the bar. It was cool inside the low-ceilinged building, even on a day as hot as this one.

'What can I get you?' a young girl about Grace's age said. She was wearing a cropped T-shirt and skinny jeans. A tea towel was slung over one shoulder.

'I'd like to see the landlord if he's around,' Lorraine said.

'He's upstairs,' the girl replied. 'Asleep.'

Lorraine held out her warrant card.

'Oh,' the girl said, staring at Lorraine as if she didn't believe her. She turned, went round the corner of the bar and opened a latched door. It was small and creaked as she pulled it open, revealing a narrow twisting staircase behind it. 'Da-*ad*!' she yelled up it. 'It's the police!'

Heads turned in Lorraine's direction, but she kept her eyes fixed on the rack of optics in front of her, not wanting to cause a stir. Jo would hate that.

'He'll be down in a tick,' the girl said. 'He gets tired.'

Her father emerged through the small doorway five minutes later wearing an untucked white shirt and black trousers. His grey hair, swept to one side, was clumped in misplaced strands across his crown.

'Sorry to bother you,' Lorraine said, and introduced herself.

The man came out from behind the bar and they sat at a small oak table beside the unlit fireplace.

'I noticed you have a CCTV camera in the car park,' she said. 'Is it operational?'

'That old thing?' he said, shaking his head. 'It's just meant to scare 'em off. Doesn't seem to work though. But if people will leave valuables in their cars.' He wiped his hands down his face.

'I'm here about the stolen motorbike last month.'

'Thought you were done with all that. I told them back then the camera wasn't real, that they ought to speak to Jim across the street.'

'Jim?' she asked.

'He's at number forty-two across the way. Place is like Fort Knox.'

'And did they ask Jim?' Lorraine said.

'No idea,' the landlord said. 'Ain't going to bring that poor lad back though, is it?'

'No,' Lorraine said, standing up to leave. 'It's not.'

✳

Jim was partially deaf. 'It's why I have all this stuff,' he said, silencing the screeching alarm as Lorraine stepped across the threshold of his bungalow. 'You can't be too careful these days, even in a place as sleepy as Radcote.' He was yelling until his wife told him to quieten down.

Lorraine asked if any of his cameras – she'd seen at least three on the front of his property – caught footage of the pub car park opposite.

'Not really,' he answered. 'But I get a bit of the road between my drive and the pub's.'

'Have you still got footage from a month or so ago?'

'Of course,' Jim said, riffling through a well-organised book of labelled CDs after Lorraine had told him the date of Dean's death. 'I keep it all, you know. They call me obsessive, but you never know when something will come in handy.'

'Exactly,' Lorraine said, glancing round the room. His wife had made her a cup of tea, balancing it on the edge of a dresser that was crowded with meticulously organised miniature china houses. The whole place seemed to be brimming with neat clutter.

'Right, let's see . . .' Jim plucked out a disc and inserted it into the drive of a desktop computer. A few moments later a grainy black and white image of his front drive was flickering on the screen. 'Late evening, you say? I can fast-forward it from here.'

Lorraine watched as the evening in question played out before them. The pub seemed busy and she could make out customers coming and going by the slowing of cars and the flaring of indicator lights as they turned into the car park, even though the camera had captured only the lower half of the vehicles, being mainly aimed at Jim's front garden. The legs of a few pedestrians, some with dogs, some in groups, were also visible as they walked past at top speed. The evening flashed past in minutes, turning from daylight to dusk to darkness. A couple of cats shot across the front garden.

'Stop,' Lorraine suddenly said. 'Go back a bit, will you?'

Jim rewound and played the footage again, this time at normal speed. A motorbike went into the pub car park. There was one person on it.

Jim sped the footage up again.

'Right, there, go back again.'

Jim did as he was instructed, his wife looming over his shoulder. They both seemed pleased to help.

Lorraine watched as the same motorbike slowly left the pub car park.

'Is the clock display set correctly?' she asked.

Jim nodded.

She told him to rewind and play it even slower. There it was again, the motorbike being stolen, at 11.12 p.m. She squinted at the screen, trying to improve the grainy resolution. There was no doubt about it, she could see two pairs of legs on the bike – a male wearing shorts sitting at the front, and a slim female, also with exposed legs, sitting to the rear.

'I'll need to take this with me,' Lorraine said.

Jim ejected the disc and slipped it into its protective sleeve.

As she was leaving, thanking them both, she said,

'Out of interest, have the police ever asked you for this footage before?'

Jim and his wife shook their heads decisively.

'Thanks again,' Lorraine said, thinking how much she despised Greg Burnley.

22

Freddie had exhaled with relief when they'd all left Gil's cottage earlier. He'd hidden himself beneath the pile of old clothes, bedding and curtains that had been dumped in the far corner of Gil's mezzanine sleeping area. It was a tip up there, but that had worked to his advantage: if anyone had peeked up, he'd have been well concealed within the mess. Every cell in his body had buzzed from lack of oxygen – he reckoned he'd pretty much not breathed properly the whole time they were there. His fingers had crept out first, reaching out from under the fusty fabric. Once he was fully out he'd stretched his back, cat-like, and pulled his pack out of the nest. He had no idea where Gil had gone, but was just glad that the place was finally empty after all the fuss.

Now, an hour later and still alone, Freddie was sitting on the edge of Gil's low bed. He took a bottle of water from his bag and drank half of it.

On the one hand, Gil had been a saviour, taking

him in earlier, giving him food, keeping quiet when everyone had burst into the tack room. But on the other, he'd been a liability, causing such a commotion with his ridiculous antics. Freddie had thankfully already been upstairs when it happened, snoozing, exhausted from the goings-on. He'd heard all the fuss and had been about to go downstairs to help Gil, but quickly retreated at the sound of someone running outside, and then Sonia had come bursting into the cottage, followed not long after that by the others. They'd immediately got Gil down, not realising Freddie was nearby. It would only have taken one wrong or careless word from Gil to reveal his whereabouts. He couldn't get caught yet.

After he'd left New Hope, he'd sat in an anonymous greasy spoon café at the other end of town, drinking tea and wondering whether running away was the answer. He'd spent the next two hours ambling back towards Radcote, but as he approached the village he'd ducked into a field and hid behind a hedge. That gang of lads was hanging out again, the same lot from the previous night. Were they waiting for him? He'd watched as they smoked weed, sitting on a gate.

Freddie had turned, unseen, and cut across the field that was bordered on one side by the railway line. It was then that Gil emerged from a small spinney.

'I am out searching for you,' he'd said matter-of-factly. 'But Tony would be cross if he knew I'd gone wandering off.'

Freddie had stared at him. 'Then perhaps you shouldn't tell anyone you've found me.'

Gil was nodding. 'Would you like me to help you hide?' His face lit up like a full moon. 'I am good at keeping secrets.'

Freddie had bitten his lip, glanced back across the field at those boys, then turned back to Gil. 'OK,' he'd said reluctantly. He didn't think he had any choice.

Now, alone in the tack room, Freddie took the stolen laptop from his pack. There was a power socket at the base of the eaves so he plugged it in with the cable Lana had given him.

He stared at the ceiling as the computer started up. *Lana.* For her sake, he prayed he wouldn't find anything.

He picked up where he'd left off. He'd already changed the computer's settings to reveal all folders, hidden or otherwise, as it had been previously set to conceal. The laptop clearly wasn't a hospital machine – Freddie was grateful for that – but it did contain records of files pertaining to patients that Tony had obviously viewed at home. He checked through them, and everything else that seemed to be related to work. There was nothing out of the ordinary.

He lingered over the family's Christmas snaps from the previous year. He stroked the cursor over Lana's face as she forced a smile for her father's camera – Simon had killed himself the Christmas before. The family had been setting off on a winter break. Freddie

240

imagined, as these pictures showed, that it would for evermore be a sombre time of year for them.

It was as Freddie was idly moving the cursor around the desktop, wondering where to check next, that it showed up, tucked away in the top right corner of the screen. A small ghost-like square of transparent white appeared then disappeared as the cursor touched it, giving itself away only to someone who knew what they were looking for.

'An *invisible* file,' Freddie whispered to himself, knowing they were quite different to hidden files.

Swallowing, he double-clicked it.

At first it appeared to contain nothing, but Freddie could see what Tony had done. Another invisible folder was concealed within the original, to put off anyone who'd stumbled across the first one accidentally.

He opened the second folder, which revealed three image files. Freddie double-clicked on the first, which automatically started up the picture viewing software. He stared blankly at the colour image. He went cold and numb. Then he opened the other two.

His eyes closed and tears pooled under his lids.

He needed to talk to Lana. He was about to call her, arrange a time to meet, when he heard a noise. It was coming from downstairs. He prayed it was just Gil coming back, but he shut the laptop lid and crawled under the pile of bedding and clothes to be safe. When he was well and truly hidden, he realised that his backpack was still on the bed.

'Hello, anyone here?' came the man's voice.

It was loud and authoritative, and Freddie recognised it instantly. It was Tony, and he was inside Gil's home.

He heard his footsteps clicking across the tiles, a grunt as he picked something up then put it down again.

Why had he come back? Had Gil revealed he was hiding here?

Freddie held his breath again, listening for sounds as Tony moved about. After what he'd just seen on the computer he couldn't face him ever again. He wasn't sure how Lana would be able to either. He knew how much she loved her dad, but this would change everything.

His nails dug into his palms as he fought to stay calm and still. Malc and his mum swept through his thoughts as he heard the first creak on the steps that led up to the mezzanine.

'Hello?' Tony said again.

Freddie could tell his voice was getting close. Another couple of creaks and he reckoned he was halfway up the narrow stairs, almost high enough to see into the sleeping area.

'Anyone up here?'

This time Freddie felt the floorboards shake and he knew that Tony was standing only a couple of feet away from him. Right beside his backpack on the bed.

23

I am bad for doing my exercises. They've taken me to the Manor kitchen and put me in a chair. Jo is making tea for everyone while Sonia wrings her hands. A short while ago Tony went outside but now he is back again looking puzzled.

'It's OK, love,' he says to Sonia. 'It's all going to be fine.'

But I can see that Sonia thinks it won't be. Since Simon, nothing's been OK for her.

Lana comes downstairs and my heart lights up as she enters the kitchen. She blusters in, red-faced and anxious. She can't seem to get out what she wants to say.

'You won't believe it, but I was followed by Frank this morning.' She's breathless. 'It was so scary and I didn't know what to do and . . .' She stops and looks at everyone, frowning, noticing how serious they all are. 'Is there news?' she asks.

'Nothing,' Jo says in a way that makes her sound

virtually dead. She is already going grey-skinned and empty like Sonia. But I promised Freddie I wouldn't tell and now I don't know what to do because I am already in lots of trouble and Tony will send me away to the place that's for people like me.

'The police are doing everything they can to find Freddie,' Sonia says, giving Lana a brief hug. She stays stiff in her mother's arms. 'He's not really been gone that long.'

'I know, but I wish he'd come back,' Lana says, placing her bag on a chair beside the back door and joining the group cautiously. She comes to stand near me.

'Gil gave us a bit of a fright,' Sonia says.

Then Lorraine comes back from wherever she went. She goes over to Stella, who is tapping away on her phone, looking bored. I wasn't really going to steal it.

'I was getting my muscles in shape for a girlfriend but now I'm not allowed to,' I tell Lana, but no one's listening. They're all looking at Lorraine. She stares at Adam, who's hardly said a word. It looks as if he's guarding the door. They are whispering. *We'll talk later* is all I hear.

Lorraine comes up to me. 'Gil, can you tell me how you came to have Stella's phone?' She isn't sunken or waxy-looking like Sonia.

'You need to think very carefully,' Adam says.

That's what Tony always says.

'Freddie gave it to me,' I say. It is the truth.

'When was this?' Lorraine asks.

'When I didn't want to help with the barbecue.' That is true, too.

'He went off for a walk, remember?' Tony says. 'Then Jo went to look for him, and Freddie.' He stares at Jo and she goes red.

'So you went for a walk and then what, Gil?' Lorraine asks. 'You saw Freddie? You know he is still missing, don't you?'

I nod although Freddie's not missing. 'I get muddled,' I tell them. 'I went walking through the village and then I saw Freddie.'

My legs start jumping up and down. I hate it when they do that.

'You just need to tell us the truth, Gil,' Adam says.

There are too many faces staring at me. It's frightening, like I don't even recognise them.

'Freddie gave the phone to me I didn't steal it like you all think I am not a thief.' My insides hurt like there's electricity in me. 'The smoke stings my eyes you see.'

'That's why he didn't want to help me cook,' Tony chips in.

'And I had all those little food things in my hand and I was getting sticky and greasy and I asked Freddie if he had a tissue and he told me to fuck off.'

'Then what happened?' Lorraine asked.

'I wiped my hands on my shorts and I licked them too because those things you made were yummy Sonia.' I smile at her but she doesn't see.

'Did Freddie say anything else to you?' Adam asked.

'He asked me if I was going back to the barbecue.' I press my hands on my knees to shut them up. 'I said yes I would be doing that because I'd only gone for a little stroll but I ended up in the village because I like walking you see and I walk everywhere,' I say to Lorraine and Adam. 'It makes my mind work more straightly. It helps me think and talk and I might meet a girlfriend to ask on a date.'

'What did Freddie say after that?' Jo said.

'He asked me to give the pink phone to Stella when I went back to the barbecue.'

Stella gives me a little smile.

In my mind I can see Freddie searching in his pack for the phone. He couldn't find it and things spilled out and I tried to help him and when I said *Hey, isn't that Tony's computer?* he suddenly went mad, telling me to get lost and piss off and then I went hot-red inside and started yelling back and waving my arms at him because when people are horrid to me I can't even help it.

'I am sorry I forgot to give you your phone Stella and I am sorry that I read some of your text messages and I am sorry that I was doing my exercises wrong and I am sorry that I ate too many of those things you made Sonia and then felt sick.' I cover my face with my hands. My legs start up again.

'Don't worry, Gil,' Stella says. 'I know you didn't mean to.'

She is nice.

'You've done really well,' Tony says. 'Did Freddie say where he was going?'

I shake my head.

'Which way did Freddie go after he'd given you the phone, Gil?' Adam says.

'I didn't see,' I tell him through my hands. I wish they'd leave me alone.

My arms start shaking so I clutch them round my body.

Then there is the slam of car doors and the crunch of gravel across the back courtyard.

'Thank God, it's the police,' Tony says, and goes to let them in.

❋

Sometimes I would like to go off, walk all the way to one of those other countries that are on the internet. One day I will go to Ecuador and China, see Victoria Falls and climb Ayers Rock. Then I won't have to do bad things any more.

Probably nothing to worry about . . . will send out alerts anyway . . . local search . . . depressed state of mind . . .

There are two more policemen in our kitchen. One is in a pale blue shirt and brown trousers and one is in a uniform.

'We'll need a recent photograph of your son,' the

policeman without the uniform says to Jo. 'If you're convinced he's missing.'

Jo nods her head and turns this way and that, searching in her bag. 'I've got one somewhere.' She pulls a passport-sized photograph from her purse. 'Here, keep it.'

'I am drawing a picture of Freddie,' I suddenly say without realising. 'It has snakes in it too.' My voice is loud and bumps around the kitchen.

Everyone stares at me.

They don't know what I notice, how I remember everything, how the inside of my head is ulcerated and sore from all the information it holds, every snippet of everything I see vying for space. The whole world lives in there, crawling inside me, tormenting me, twisting me up and making me into someone I'm not.

Their eyes drill into my skin.

'It has got your Stella in it too,' I tell Lorraine, while pointing at Stella. 'I am really good at drawing,' I say to the policeman.

'I see,' he says. 'I understand you saw Freddie last night?'

'Yes but I've never even killed anyone in the whole world, not even Simon.' My legs are off again.

'No one thinks anything of the sort, Gil,' Sonia says.

I see the sad look in her eye. I didn't mean to mention Simon and upset her, but sometimes I want to pull things apart.

Everyone is nodding in agreement and now I'm itching all over.

'Gil really is an amazing artist,' Sonia continues to the policeman. 'You see, he's autistic.'

'What we mustn't forget is that Freddie is an adult,' the policeman without a uniform says to Jo. 'It's not a crime to go off without telling anyone. I've got two boys in their twenties myself. I understand what you're going through.' He scratches his head.

Jo is staring at him and her eyes are blacker than ever.

'If his mother says he's missing, then he's bloody well missing,' Lorraine says. Her voice sounds like an angry wasp.

She doesn't look like a detective. Her Stella is my friend but not my girlfriend.

'Is there somewhere quiet I can sit with Mrs Curzon?' the man asks resignedly. 'I'll need to take a few details.'

'Of course,' Sonia says. 'You can use Tony's study, Jo.'

If I were to draw Sonia's face it would look tight and painful, like her skin was being stretched to almost tearing.

My eyes dart between them all, sizing them up, preparing a new picture in my mind. There's something building up inside me as I sew them all up, stitch it all together. They don't feel what I feel; don't see what I see.

'Dean didn't kill himself.'

The words explode from my mouth. A picture in words.

'You are all wrong and I am not wrong and I am going to do another drawing because it hurts too much just like last time.'

I stand up to leave but there are two hands on my shoulders, holding me. I feel the detective's warm breath on my face.

24

Lana had come downstairs to find the kitchen full of people. She still felt panic-stricken from being followed that morning, and now her parents, Gil, Lorraine, Adam, Stella and two policemen were crowded into the room. She was glad Lorraine was there for her mum's sake.

She wondered if she should tell these detectives about Frank, how he'd tailed her all the way home, looming large in her rear-view mirror. At one point she thought he was going to nudge her bumper he was so close behind her. Several times he dropped back, only to come close again. She had no idea why. In the end, she decided to say nothing.

The older, fatter detective pressed Gil back down into the chair. Lana saw the shock on Gil's face, saw how he implored her to help him as he stared at her, his cheeks drawing up into peach-coloured crests beneath his watery eyes. She had no idea what to do.

'You and I need to talk,' the detective said.

'Finally,' Lorraine muttered under her breath.

'I think there are some things about the Dean Watts case that need clarifying once and for all.'

Lana didn't like him. There was something greasy about him, something insensitive, too, as if he didn't care one bit about finding Freddie.

'It was a little over four weeks ago that the Dean Watts case hit my desk.' He was talking to everyone. Lana flinched as he caught her eye. 'Do you know why it was brought to the attention of CID?'

Lana glanced at Gil as a drop of spit flew from the detective's mouth and landed on his cheek. She prayed he would keep quiet about what he knew.

'Given what had happened around here, it's to be expected,' Adam said.

The detective drummed two fingers on Gil's shoulder. Lana knew that this would be driving him mad. 'Correct,' he said.

She felt strange, as if she was in someone else's body. She wasn't even conscious of holding herself upright.

'Any suicide cases within a five-mile radius of Wellesbury get special consideration. In the last year there have been thirty-seven suicides in the county. Three of them fell within the designated radius, and that's including Dean Watts and Lenny Jackman. This is well under the national rate but . . .' He paused, his eyes flicking everywhere. They settled on Lana. 'But of course we want to be certain there won't be another cluster.'

Lana braced herself, slowly, inwardly. She stared at her hands. They were shaking. She edged a step closer to the back door. The dogs were suddenly crowding around her legs as if she was going to take them for a walk. Instinctively, her hand reached for the two leads hanging on a hook. The small action sent them into a frenzy of circling bodies and wagging tales. Daisy let out a small bark.

'But it's OK because Dean didn't kill himself,' Gil said.

The detective was still looking at Lana intently. She broke his stare and turned to her mother, wondering if anyone else had spotted the tremors in her arms and legs or the twitch at her jaw. She wanted to grab her mum and run away.

Instead, she hooked the dogs' leads on to their collars.

'The investigation after Dean Watts' death followed strict guidelines,' the detective went on. 'In this case, I am completely satisfied that it was suicide. The post-mortem showed alcohol and drugs in his blood. The lack of tyre brake marks on the road and indentations in the verge were consistent with such an act. He wasn't wearing a helmet and no evasive action was taken. A full report was delivered by Traffic. Oh, and there was a suicide note,' he added smugly.

Lana wondered if he'd even heard what Gil had said. Her mum let out a choked sob.

'There is nothing we left out when investigating the Watts case,' he continued.

Lana watched as Lorraine whispered something in Adam's ear. Adam nodded. Poor Gil was still rocking and jiggling in his chair like a schoolkid with something urgent to say.

'DI Burnley, will you comment on Monday night's alleged suicide?' Lorraine said. 'You know as well as I do that there was evidence to suggest—'

'I'm not at liberty to discuss that,' Burnley replied.

The dogs tugged on their leads, dragging Lana closer to the door, to freedom.

Gil stuck his hand in the air. 'But Dean was riding on the motorbike with his girlfriend and they had a crash and his girlfriend ran away afterwards and I saw it and I have done a drawing of it.' He was almost in tears.

Burnley sighed and glanced at his watch. 'It's natural to seek a rational explanation. Especially those with a tendency towards . . .' He hesitated. 'Let's just say, I understand that your family will be more sensitive than most.'

'I'm interested to hear what Gil has to say,' Lorraine said, folding her arms.

'Let's not forget that the detective's here to find Freddie,' Jo said weakly from the corner.

'Shall I tell the policeman everything?' Gil said to Tony.

Lana watched her dad's mouth drop open, as if he didn't quite know what to say. The dogs tugged at the leads again, pulling her closer to the door.

'Yes, you should do that,' Lorraine said kindly, before Tony could reply.

'I was going for a walk in case I met a nice girlfriend and then I heard the motorbike and then I saw it crash into the tree. But Dean didn't kill himself because his girlfriend was driving it but she wasn't any good because she fell off and I saw it. I watched them. I watch everyone but that's OK because they don't know I'm there. I like to watch people, but if I had a girlfriend I wouldn't watch her in the shower because that would be—'

'Witness statements of people using the road put the time of death somewhere between twelve-thirty and one a.m. That's a very odd time for a walk.' The detective shifted his weight from one foot to the other. His partner remained silent.

'Yes it is,' Gil said earnestly.

Lana bowed her head. She clenched the tight weave of the dog's leads in her sweating palms.

'How do you know the other person was his girlfriend?'

'Because they kissed.' Gil made a throaty, embarrassed sound. 'And I saw her hand. It had Dean's ring on it.' Gil beamed at everyone. 'When you love someone you give them your ring.'

'Is that the skull ring in the picture you drew, Gil?' Lorraine asked.

Gil nodded. 'I will give my girlfriend a ring.' He held out the knuckles of his right hand and flashed a signet ring. 'I will give her this one.'

'Did you see Dean's girlfriend's face?' Lorraine asked.

Lana squirmed and glanced at her parents. *I'm sorry, Mum, I'm so sorry . . .*

Tony stepped in. 'What you have to understand about Gil, detective, is that his mind doesn't work quite like ours,' he said reasonably. 'He is severely autistic. He doesn't filter things the same way we would. Think of him as a collector of information, a hoarder of such minuscule detail that you or I wouldn't even notice, let alone file away to draw upon later. He can't help it. He also puts way more value on brief acquaintances than is appropriate.'

'Dean was my best friend,' Gil said, staring at Burnley earnestly.

'My point exactly,' Tony said. 'He'd only met Dean a couple of times but is still grieving as if he's lost a brother. Fabrications help him come to terms with that.'

Lana drew a deep breath in readiness.

'Do you remember what you did when the milkman passed away, Gil?' Tony went on.

'Don't tell them Tony. Please don't tell them about that.' Gil rocked fervently.

Tony shrugged at the detective.

'But Dean's girlfriend ran away from the crash,' Gil continued, suddenly reanimated. He looked at Lana, but she turned away. 'She didn't help Dean.'

'And that's when you found the visor, Gil?' Lorraine asked.

'Yes. I thought I could mend it. I'm good at mending things.'

'But you couldn't identify Dean's girlfriend?' Burnley asked. His impatience was palpable.

Gil didn't reply.

'Even though you were able to see her ring.'

'Yes.'

'Can you explain more?'

'Dean was my friend. He didn't kill himself—'

'Don't explain from the beginning again, for Christ's sake,' Burnley interrupted. 'How come you were close enough to see the ring yet not the girl's face?'

Gil's breath rasped in his chest. He was agitated. 'She was wearing the helmet but—'

'Stop!' Lana yelled.

Everyone stared at her as she stood by the door, dogs to heel, the leads yanked tight as she clamped her arms across her chest.

'It was me,' she stated calmly. 'I was the other person on the motorbike.'

25

Lana looked dejected and empty, her eyes huge in her white face.

'It's bad, isn't it?' she'd said to Lorraine as they followed Detective Inspector Burnley through the building. They ended up in a small interview room.

'Just tell us the truth, love,' was Lorraine's reply.

They'd gone to the Justice Centre in separate cars, Burnley agreeing that Lorraine could accompany Lana. It was an informal interview, but that could change without notice, he'd warned with a sour expression.

'So,' he said, squeezing into the small space between the table and the wall, half standing again to adjust his trousers and jolting the table. 'Tell me everything, then.'

Lorraine was sitting beside Lana. The interview wasn't being recorded but there was another officer present taking notes.

Lana glanced up at the mirrored glass set into the wall. 'Is there anyone behind there?' she asked.

Lorraine shook her head. 'Even if there was, it doesn't matter. We're on your side, love. We just want to know what happened. Start with the night you claim you were on the motorbike. Tell us about that.' She smiled, wanting to reach out and squeeze her hand, but knew it would set Burnley off.

'Claim?' Lana said softly. She tipped her head sideways and squinted at Lorraine. 'It's not a *claim*, it's the truth.'

'From the beginning,' Burnley said coldly. He leant forward on short, folded arms.

'Dean and I, you know, we liked each other. It was his idea, the bike. I think he wanted to show off. He wanted to . . .' Lana paused and drew in a big breath. 'He wanted to show me a good time.' It came out as a sigh.

'Can you remember what you were wearing?' Lorraine asked.

Burnley stared across at her as if she was mad, then stretched back his head and rubbed his neck.

Lana shrugged. 'Not really. It was a warm night. I usually live in my denim shorts, a T-shirt and my Converse in the holidays.' She looked down at her current attire. 'Maybe something like this?' It came out as a question.

'So Dean stole the motorbike,' Burnley said.

Lana nodded. 'It was so easy.' She tucked back her hair. 'I was scared, but he said we'd bring it back later so I thought that would be OK.'

'Where did you steal it from?' Burnley asked.

'A pub somewhere, I think. I can't remember much. I hit my head.'

Lorraine wanted to keep moving forward. 'So you got on the bike . . .'

'Yeah, and we, like, went off. He knew how to ride it. Said he'd been messing with bikes since he was a kid.'

'Did you have a helmet?' Lorraine asked.

Lana suddenly looked panic-stricken. 'Helmet?' she said, frowning. 'I was wearing one.' She paused. 'Yeah, Dean insisted I wear it. There was only one, you see.'

Burnley pushed back in his chair until his shoulders hit the wall. 'Tell me about the motorbike. Can you remember what make or colour it was?'

'It was dark,' Lana said slowly. 'I don't really know. It was just a bike. It was quite big, maybe blue. I don't know. And I don't know what colour the helmet was either. Dean put it on me before I saw it.'

'Who was driving the bike when you stole it?' Burnley asked.

'Dean.'

'Had you ever been on a motorbike before this?'

Lana shook her head. 'Not unless a quad bike counts. We have one at home. Dad uses it to get about the land. I've driven that before.'

Burnley nodded. 'Where did you go first?'

Lana frowned again. 'Just around. I was a bit scared.

He was going fast. He took us down the lanes, through some villages.'

'And what happened next?' Lorraine asked, watching her intently.

'I can't recall very well.' Lana touched the side of her head. 'We were at Devil's Mile, going really fast, and then . . .' Her hand went over her eyes. 'And then I just remember waking up. Everything hurt. Then I saw Dean and he was really badly injured. I panicked and didn't know what to do . . .'

She gave a loud sob. Lorraine noticed there were no tears.

'So you ran away,' Lorraine said.

'It was stupid and cowardly, I know, but I was so scared. I ran back home and pretended it had never happened.'

✻

'Do you believe her?' Lorraine asked Burnley later, with the familiar sounds of a busy department going on around them – a cacophony of ringing phones, layers of chatter, people sliding past each other in the narrow walkways between the rows of desks. Someone had brought in a tray of cakes – a birthday perhaps.

'No, I don't,' Burnley replied.

Lorraine reckoned it was the first time she'd ever heard him sound genuine.

She agreed with him, but kept it to herself.

'She was clueless,' Burnley continued, blowing ripples across the top of his coffee. 'Covering up for someone, or something.'

'And Freddie? You believe her about that?'

That had come right at the end of the interview and was the most important revelation as far as Lorraine was concerned. She hadn't phoned Jo yet, but it gave her hope they would find him soon. She hadn't known whether to hug or shake Lana when she'd confessed that she'd discovered Freddie sleeping at New Hope that morning.

Burnley was leaning across his desk. He looked like a bulldog, Lorraine thought. All neck and bad breath.

'You know what? I think I do believe her about that.' He grinned. 'I've already got some officers working on the town's CCTV but six of the cameras are down currently. Have been for months.'

'I reckon he's still local. This shouldn't be difficult.'

Lorraine was conscious that Lana was waiting for her downstairs. She'd been left in the care of a female officer, who'd taken her to get a drink.

'What's the stupid lad playing at, Fisher?' Burnley sounded almost compassionate. 'You know him better than me. Everything OK at home?'

Lorraine sighed. 'His mum's just split up with his stepdad. Freddie was very close to him.' She paused, reluctant to reveal personal information about Jo, but it had to be done. 'And when I spoke to Lana early this morning she told me Freddie's been having a hard time with some local kids. Online bullying, trouble at school.'

Burnley yawned, erasing any notion of compassion. 'Interesting,' he remarked.

'One more thing . . .' She was probably pushing her luck, but since she'd seen the CCTV footage of the bike leaving the pub and heard Lana's confession, she couldn't let it go. 'The Dean Watts file. I noticed there was no report about the suicide note that was found.'

'Correct,' Burnley said.

'You didn't think it was worth a handwriting analyst taking a look?'

'Nope.'

A young constable ducked into the office bearing a tray and Burnley grabbed a cube of yellow sponge cake. Lorraine shook her head at him politely.

'Then you won't mind if I do?' she said.

Burnley stared at her, his mouth full. He'd stopped chewing, as if thinking took up all his brain's capacity. 'I thought you were on holiday. Do you have a hard time relaxing?'

'I do when I see incomplete investigations prematurely closed. And I do when new evidence is made available and ignored. Believe me, I would love nothing more than to get out of here and be with my family but, if you remember, I spent seven months of my life chained to your cock-ups, so it would seem remiss of me now not to make certain you are keeping your new house in order.'

They stared at each other until Lorraine touched her lip pointedly and raised her eyes. Instinctively, Burnley drew the back of his hand across his mouth.

'And while we're at it, what did the pathology report reveal about Lenny Jackman? And the other scene forensics? There were plenty.'

She stood up to leave, trying to contain her thumping heart. She'd not wanted to become involved in these cases, and if it had been anyone, *anyone*, but Greg Burnley the other side of that desk, she'd have left well alone.

'Nothing's available yet,' he stated. 'I'll let you know when it is.'

He picked up his desk phone and jabbed a few numbers. 'Jane, bring the Dean Watts file to my office immediately, please.' He hung up. 'I'll get you copies of the suicide note and you can analyse it to your heart's content.' That laugh was back again. 'Comparing it to what, though, I have no idea. That's your problem.'

*

It was nearly midnight but Lorraine couldn't sleep. The guest room was hot and humid, the thick stone walls of Glebe House hanging on to every shred of the day's heat and transmitting it back at night like a giant storage heater.

'The stupid thing is, this place is freezing in winter,' she said to Adam, remembering nights from her child-hood bundled up in sweaters and woolly socks.

She slipped off her T-shirt and pulled the sheet up under her arms.

Adam smiled and raised his eyebrows.

'Stop it,' she said, shoving him in the shoulder. 'It was weird in the station,' she added after a short pause. 'Lana seemed relieved, as if a great weight had been lifted from her. Sonia was in a right state when I took her back though.'

When Lorraine dropped Lana home Sonia had been standing at the door, waiting for them. Lorraine wondered if she'd been there since the moment they'd left.

'For God's sake, what have you *done?*' were her first words to her daughter after they'd gone inside.

'It wasn't that bad, Mum,' Lana had said. 'Chill out.'

'*Chill out?* You have no idea what you're talking about.'

Sonia had seemed more fragile and thin than usual, her movements even more erratic, her mental state more frantic.

'The detective was really nice, actually.'

Lorraine had stifled a noise at this point.

'What, do you think he's going to put you on his Christmas card list? Wave if we bump into him in the supermarket? For God's sake, Lana, you've just confessed to *killing* someone. You've ruined your entire life.'

'You know,' Lorraine said to Adam, 'Sonia seemed

more concerned with Lana's medical school application being turned down because of a police record than anything else.'

'She's been through a lot,' was his drowsy reply.

'God, it's too hot in here.' Lorraine got out of bed and opened the window in the hope there might be a breeze.

The whole house seemed to creak and groan as she tried to settle again. She wondered if Jo had fallen asleep yet. The prospect of another night without Freddie filled them all with dread.

'At least we know now where Freddie was last night,' she went on. 'I just don't understand why Lana didn't tell us sooner.'

'Kids don't snitch on each other, remember? Anyway, it's clear that Freddie chose to leave home of his own accord. The question is *why*.'

Adam pulled up the floral bedspread. Lorraine kicked it off again.

'Jo's still out of her mind with worry,' she said, 'although she was comforted to know that Freddie had been at the shelter. I stopped off at the Job Centre in Wellesbury on the way home and managed to get copies of forms with Dean Watts' handwriting on. Something for our friends at the university to analyse tomorrow. I'll drive out and see Bill.'

Adam sighed and rolled over to face her. 'Has this all become a distraction for you, Ray, or do you really think there's some kind of a link?'

'Adam, the Watts case has new evidence. It needs re-examining. After what I went through last time I can't watch Burnley fuck up again. I'm hovering over the Lenny Jackman death like a hawk too. As for a link, unless Freddie does something stupid' – she sighed – 'then I don't see one. Even so, it's only a matter of time before some zealous reporter picks up the story. Two homeless lads kill themselves in a month, same area as the Wellesbury Six. It's too soon after that to ignore.'

'But if Dean's death was an accident, as Lana claims, then it's hardly the start of another spate, is it? Lenny whoever-he-was gets lumped in with the couple of hundred other railway jumpers each year, and on its own it isn't remarkable. Even in this area. You'd think Burnley would prefer to take the nicked-bike-and-accident option.' Adam curled an arm round her waist. 'Do you believe Lana was on the motorbike?'

'I don't know, to be honest,' Lorraine said. 'But one thing's for certain: either Lana's lying or Dean's suicide note is. I just don't know why she would confess to something she didn't do.'

'And if Lana is telling the truth, who wrote the note?'

They lay in silence for a few minutes, breathing in the night's thick heat. Adam batted away a mosquito.

'Earlier, at the Manor, Sonia implied Lana was protecting Gil by confessing, to save him from any inquiry.' Lorraine rubbed her eyes. She was tired but knew sleep was still a long way off.

'That sounds unlikely,' Adam said. 'Why not just defend him rather than implicate herself? Also, where are her injuries?'

'It's unlikely, yes, but not impossible,' Lorraine responded. 'As for her injuries, Gil said she fell off, didn't he? She could have been thrown clear before impact, landed on soft ground. We don't know that she hasn't recently suffered a bad back or a stiff neck or even cuts and bruises. The incident was a month ago now, kids are good at concealing things, and they heal quickly.'

She yawned.

'She wasn't wearing a ring like the one in Gil's picture, though I guess she could have got rid of it.'

Adam nodded. 'Confessions can take their time coming, especially if she reckoned she could get away with it to begin with. It was the dead of night, no witnesses – or so she thought – she panicked and ran.'

'It fits with what she said. Ever since her brother killed himself, Jo told me that Lana has been hot-housed for a medical career, almost like a replacement.'

'So doctor-in-the-making falls in love with the wrong boy. A *homeless* boy. There's no way her parents would approve.'

'Agreed,' Lorraine said. 'The pressure gets too much and she turns bad girl for a night – drinks, smokes weed, drives a stolen bike. Let's face it, our kids aren't always who we think they are.' She recalled what Grace had been through the previous year, and the problems she and Adam had had coming to terms with it.

'So Dean died instantly and there was nothing Lana could do. Her career was over before it had even begun. She panicked. She ran.'

'She could be covering up for someone else, but who, and why? Dean's *real* girlfriend?' Lorraine suggested, answering her own question. 'Let's face it, Lana with a homeless lad is pretty improbable, even as a rebellious strop.'

'Perhaps someone's blackmailing her.' Adam sounded sleepy. He eased himself down the bed. 'My gut says we should believe her for now.'

'Your gut?' Lorraine said sarcastically. 'That's ironic coming from the man who refuses to base anything on assumptions. *Ever.*'

'This is different,' Adam replied, glancing at his watch before unbuckling it and putting it on the bedside table.

'Why?'

'It's not my case.'

✴

Adam had fallen asleep within minutes, but Lorraine remained awake. At least she didn't think she'd dropped off: every so often she jerked upright and tried to focus on the small display of the bedside clock. She couldn't recall fretting over the time after 3.27, so when she opened her eyes after being woken by a noise downstairs she was dismayed to see light seeping in around the curtains already.

'What's going on, Jo?' The crying noises had drawn her to the kitchen. She'd forgotten to put on her slippers and the kitchen flagstones felt soothing and cool on her hot feet. 'Jo, what's the matter?'

She sat down beside her sister at the table.

'For God's sake, talk to me. Is there news?'

Dressed in yesterday's clothes, holding a piece of paper in one hand and a mug of coffee in the other, Jo turned slowly to Lorraine. 'It's Freddie,' she sobbed, staring at the paper again. 'He's left me a suicide note.'

26

'This is purgatory,' Sonia says. 'That's what it is.'

I don't know what that means but it's making Sonia unhappy. Her voice is stretched out thin and she is lying in bed. Tony is there too, looking after her.

They don't know about my secret hiding place behind the cupboard on the landing. They'd be cross if they knew I was listening but ever since the detectives took Lana to the police station yesterday my stomach has been churning. I don't know what to do.

'Take these,' Tony says.

I imagine him sitting on the edge of Sonia's bed. Tony sleeps in another bedroom. His duvet is brown and grey.

'Thanks,' Sonia says, and then it goes quiet as she sips water.

She's been different since Simon died, doing and saying things I don't understand. She said she wanted to find God. I offered to help, but not until I've found a girl-friend I told her. Neither of us have had any luck.

'I can't believe she did such a stupid thing,' Sonia says once her pills have gone down.

I hold my breath, listening to every word.

Tony makes a noise like he's blowing out all the air in his lungs. 'After everything,' he says, 'we don't need it.'

'It feels like it's happening all over again,' Sonia says.

My heart bangs heavily. I don't want that. I would get angry and not be nice any more.

'I know what you mean,' Tony replies. 'She's throwing her life away.'

They said that's what Simon did. Threw his life away. Wasted it. Chucked it out. They're wrong. He didn't. If he'd thrown it away we could have got it back for him. Sometimes I've thrown things away by mistake and it's easy to find them if you look. There's no bringing Simon back. His lips were blue. I saw them.

I butt my head against the wall to make the thoughts go away. Later I will do another drawing.

'Did you hear something?' Sonia says.

The floorboards creak as Tony comes out on to the landing. I press flat against the wall but he won't see me here. 'Probably just the dogs,' he says, going back into the bedroom. The bed springs squeak as he sits down again.

'What if they arrest her?' Sonia asks.

I imagine Lana in handcuffs, being put in a police

cell. I would draw a picture of her escaping if that happened.

'Then we get a bloody good lawyer.' Tony's sigh is deep and rasping, the kind that makes you feel guilty.

'She won't be able to go to uni—'

'Sonia, is that all you ever think about? Our daughter has just confessed to *killing* someone.'

I hear Tony walking about. His fingers tap on glass. If he's at the big window he'll see the horses in the fields.

'Since Simon . . .' Sonia trails off.

'For fuck's sake, woman.'

More walking. Tony's heels on the floorboards.

He is brave. He never cries. But he does shout and get angry. Sonia told me it's his way of coping. She said that my way is to draw things. I asked her what her way was but she said she didn't have one.

'You make it sound as if she's a murderer, Tony. Lana didn't kill anyone.' Sonia blows her nose.

After they took Lana away, Sonia went mad, as if she was fizzy inside and it was all coming out. She was doing a crazy dance around the kitchen, tripping on things. Tony grabbed her arms and she went quiet, falling to the floor, sobbing, saying she was sorry. Then, after Lana got back from the police station, Tony had finally put her to bed.

It's morning now.

'Drink your tea,' Tony says, and I hear the chink of china.

'I should have gone with her, but it's the police and—'

'I know. It's OK.'

'I wonder if there's news of Freddie,' Sonia says suddenly.

I clap my hand over my mouth to stop everything coming out. I am good at keeping secrets. If I tell, they'll be really cross with me.

'I should call Jo.'

'I already spoke to her,' Tony says. 'There's nothing to report.'

'You called her?'

I can hear a rustling of sheets. I think Sonia's sitting up.

'Briefly,' Tony says. 'I wanted to help. You know.'

Sonia is quiet for a bit. 'She's *my* friend,' she says after a while.

Tony doesn't answer.

'Did you ever think things would turn out like this?' Sonia has those little waves in her voice again.

'If I'd ever believed that my own son would do such a thing . . . *Jesus* . . . Nobody ever expects that.'

'We just didn't know him.'

'Fucking right we didn't.'

More silence. Downstairs, a dog whines in the kitchen. I hear claws scratching at the door.

'She's going off the rails like her brother.'

That's what Tony said Simon had done after he died. Gone off the rails. I think that means he went mad.

They once said that he'd been a mystery to them and who'd have ever known. They swore it would stay a secret that what he'd done was shameful. But I knew. I saw it. I see everything and I saw Simon hanging in the barn and it was horrid and it makes my insides hurt and it's only when I do drawings that I feel better although not properly better like before he was dead.

We were going on holiday. A winter break. Tony said it would do us good. Take Simon's mind off things, off all that nonsense he'd got in his head. Simon was going to be a vet although he didn't really want to be one and was unhappy.

Then we couldn't find him and everyone was panicking because we'd be late and miss the flight and we'd been searching for hours and then everything went horrid.

'And on top of everything, I'm worried about Gil,' Sonia says.

I shrink back against the wall even more.

'All this stuff about seeing that crash,' Sonia says.

She doesn't want to believe I was there, saw everything.

'It's nothing to do with us,' Tony says. 'And Jo's bloody sister could do with keeping her nose out.' I hear a rattle of pills again. 'I'll get you some more from the hospital.' Tony gets lots of pills.

'I don't know what I'd do without you,' Sonia says.

'I will *not* let this family fall apart,' he says, and that reminds me of what he said when they found him, when they were both wrapped up in each other's arms and were standing in the barn shaking and crying and unable to look at Simon. They didn't know I was watching through the small window at the end of the barn as if it was a horrid television show I couldn't turn off.

Simon had brown stuff on his legs. Simon had a rope round his neck. One eye was staring at me as if he knew I was there.

I drew a picture that night. Simon's ribs stuck out and his knees looked too big. I drew everything in that barn, even the other man hiding in the shadows. Underneath I wrote what Tony had said: 'Nothing will destroy my family. Not even this.'

When the police came they called Simon 'number five'.

27

Lorraine opened the door to Freddie's room. It still smelled of cheap body spray even though he hadn't been in it for two nights now. The curtains were closed – the end of one was hanging off the pole as if it had once been torn open too roughly – and his bed was unmade with the fitted sheet wrung off the mattress.

It was a typical teenager's room, she thought. She couldn't help feeling a sense of sadness, the tang of despair or hopelessness, as if he'd shrugged off a layer of gloom and dumped it with the damp towels on the floor. She swallowed and sighed. This was her *nephew*.

'Jo said he virtually lived up here,' she said. Every surface was cluttered with books and papers, cables and toiletries, as well as an assortment of dirty crockery and pie and pasty wrappers. 'This is the bedroom of a very fed-up young man. Not the Freddie I know.' She picked up some clothes and put them on the bed. 'Do you think it's even in here? Apparently, he's joined at the hip to it.'

Adam was already poking about in cupboards, having located a laptop charger cable amid the muddle on the desk. 'Then why didn't he take this?'

Lorraine shrugged. 'Surely his laptop would be on his desk if it was here.'

She lifted a few tatty folders and old textbooks and let them drop back into the muddle. Nothing, so she began searching the rest of the room. Jo had already found the letter addressed to her, so maybe there was a diary, or another letter, or something else that could undo the desperate thoughts and words the note had contained. It had been heartbreaking to read.

As she opened the wardrobe, the door half dropped off its hinges. The whole thing wobbled forward and Adam moved sharply to push it back. Inside was a jumble of clothes sliding off bent coat hangers, a collection of muddy and smelly old trainers that released a sour odour, and a shelf full of old papers and school books that clearly hadn't been touched in a long time given the dust on them.

Lorraine sighed. 'There's nothing here.'

Adam was now on his hands and knees, peering beneath the bed. Reaching under it, he pulled out a flattened sports bag with some stained football kit lying on top of it, crusted and dry, as well as several more plates and a few A level textbooks. He squinted into the dusty space.

'Nothing much under here either. Oh, hang on . . .'

He twisted his head round to look at the wooden

slats, then stood and grabbed the corner of the mattress, lifting it up out of the frame and pulling out a grey laptop.

'Not joined at the hip after all,' he remarked.

He sat on the bed and booted it up into safe mode. Lorraine had seen him do this several times before, not least on her laptop, when she'd forgotten her password. She turned away for a moment, not wanting to witness the forceful raid into Freddie's life, which felt inherently wrong, yet necessary at the same time.

'Right, password off,' Adam said, handing the machine over.

'Me? I have no idea where to begin,' Lorraine said, taking it. 'It's not as if we're going to be able to get into his Facebook account or email without some intervention.'

'OK then, let's just trawl through recent files, his browsing history, that kind of thing.'

Adam leant close as Lorraine methodically worked through the list of websites Freddie had visited.

'Social networking mostly,' she said as some familiar names reeled past onscreen. Lorraine reckoned any teenager's history would look similar. 'He's been buying stuff, look. He's been on music websites, there's his webmail, and what's this . . .'

Lorraine copied and pasted the address into a browser window and went to the website.

'Some kind of advice forum,' she said, not recognising the website name.

They both peered at the screen, speed-reading as Lorraine scrolled down.

'Oh God,' she whispered as it became clear what people were discussing. 'They're asking for advice about suicide.'

Adam reached out and took the laptop from her. He continued trawling through the site, sighing and making despairing noises as he worked.

'Can you see if he's posted anything?' Lorraine asked. 'Are there any usernames that could be Freddie?'

'That's what I'm looking for,' he replied, clicking the mouse several times. 'Do you think this could be him?'

Lorraine read where Adam was pointing. She closed her eyes briefly.

'Curzed95,' Adam said. 'A combination of Curzon and his birth year?'

Cursed, Lorraine thought. Is that how the poor boy feels about himself?

They were both silent again as they read through the short but pitiful message he'd posted. It reflected what was written in the letter he'd addressed to Jo, except the message revealed more about the bullying he'd been suffering, as well as asking questions about suicide. *I might as well be dead*, Freddie had typed. The answers he'd received had been quite detailed, describing the best methods depending on whether he really wanted to end it all or just wanted to make a cry for help. *Hanging is the real deal*, someone had written, *so only go there if you're sure. Pills or shallow cuts better for a gesture.*

Lorraine looked away, close to tears. She couldn't stand to read any more. 'Jo mustn't see this,' she said, thinking of her poor sister and how she had to stay strong.

'Look at the date and time he posted this,' Adam said. 'It's when we were at the Hawkeswells' barbecue, the night he disappeared.'

Adam opened up a few other websites that Freddie had visited, but they seemed unrelated. He moved on to some Word documents he'd opened in the last few days, the filename 'Chemistry Project' catching his eye. 'Why would he be looking at a chemistry project when he's finished his exams and left school?'

Lorraine agreed and was about to say something when Adam clicked on the file.

'Christ,' he said. 'Just look at this.'

The document was twenty-three pages long, each one containing images of what appeared to be a dedication to Freddie, as if he was already dead. First up was a picture of a gravestone with rotten flowers beside it. Lorraine noticed how someone had crudely drawn Freddie's name on the headstone with graffiti-style writing. Then there was a smaller mugshot of him beneath it. Again, it had been tampered with. Blood was dribbling from his eyes and mouth, and a noose had been put around his neck.

'Oh God, Adam, I'm not sure I can . . .'

'OK, I'll scan down,' Adam said as Lorraine turned away. 'This is one hell of a lot of shit for anyone to deal with, and it looks as though he's been targeted for months. It's nasty, Ray. Any one of these comments you'd be able to shrug off. But to have them coming at you for this long with images like this . . .' He blew out.

'He did well to save the screen shots,' Lorraine said.

She stole another glimpse at the laptop and was faced with slaughtered pig carcasses with Freddie's face superimposed over the animals' heads.

She turned away again.

'Ray, you should see this,' Adam said after a short while.

Lorraine turned back. The revolting images had gone and in their place were a couple of short emails.

'He's saved an email exchange with Lana,' Lorraine said after reading the messages quickly.

'Do you know what they're talking about?' Adam asked.

Lorraine thought for a moment. 'No. It sounds as if Lana's worried about something she's seen and Freddie has promised to help her. We could ask Jo or Sonia.'

She read the last line again: *If it's true, does this make us half brother and sister? Lana x*. Then, underneath, she reread Freddie's reply: *I really hope not . . .*

Adam logged into his own email account to send the files to himself.

'No wonder he left home,' Lorraine said. 'He must feel so alone, so desperate.' Her heart ached for him, and for Jo. It was such a tangled-up mess of emotion and . . . and there was something else, she thought, something else that was now bothering her.

She went over to the window and pulled back a curtain. Her sister was in the garden below talking to Malc. They were having a heated discussion by the looks of their hand gestures and body language. Jo looked tired and pale. Suddenly, Malc left.

'Put the laptop back where we found it,' Lorraine said quietly, closing the curtains again. 'Let me deal with Jo.'

*

'We'll find Freddie, you know. I promise.' Lorraine was standing in the living-room doorway. 'When did you speak to Malc?'

Jo looked up. Lorraine was shocked to see she had a tumbler of whisky rolling between her palms when the morning wasn't yet over. Her eyes were blistered from tears.

Lorraine sat down beside her on the old brown sofa.

Jo sniffed. 'He finally got my messages and called me back last night. He's gone out to talk to Freddie's mates. I told him he was wasting his time.'

'He wants to feel useful.'

'Well he should have bloody done that months ago then, shouldn't he?'

'Is he going to stay here tonight?' Lorraine asked after a pause.

Jo shrugged.

'Going back to London, then?'

Nothing.

'Jo . . . Adam and I went through Freddie's computer.' She paused. 'He's being bullied by some kids. It's been pretty bad.' She noticed the letter he'd written to his mum lying crumpled on the sofa beside her and wondered how much it mentioned of what had been going on. It looked as if she'd read it a thousand times.

Lorraine couldn't bring herself to tell her sister about the forum Freddie had posted on. Until now, she'd never believed he'd actually do anything desperate.

'There was something else we found, too, a few emails. It's probably nothing, but . . .' She took a deep breath. 'Freddie and Lana seemed to be troubled by something. Do you know what that might be?'

Jo slowly turned to her, tucked her feet beneath her, and hugged her arms around her body. As if she's trying to disappear, Lorraine thought.

'Sorry,' she finally whispered, tipping the rest of the whisky down her throat, pretty much confirming what Lorraine suspected.

'You always used to make things better for me,' Jo added after another pause. 'Get me out of messes.'

'Is that what you expect me to do now?'

Tears trickled slowly down Jo's face. 'Fucking police,' she said.

'Fucking sisters,' Lorraine said, trying to smile.

They sat in silence for a moment, listening to the creaks and groans of the old house heating up once again. The sun had already climbed high above the church, bathing its turreted tower in a golden glow. It reminded Lorraine of the summer holidays, of setting out on long bike rides and promising to be back for supper.

Jo suddenly stood up and swung round theatrically on her bare feet, her toes sinking into the pile of the carpet. 'You know what I fucking think? I think you're enjoying this. Sitting there, all pious and perfect in your squeaky clean life with your perfect fucking career, passing judgement over the sister who was supposed to have it all, but fucked up. *Again.*' She went over to the dresser to pour herself some more whisky. 'Well let me tell you something, Detective Inspector fucking Lorraine Fisher. I don't have it all and my life is not fucking perfect. It hasn't been for a long time.'

'Jo, stop it. Sit down.'

'Malc and I *grew apart.*' She overemphasised the words, as if they were a never-talked-about disease. 'We just fucking grew apart. Simple as that. Except he was too dumb to notice. Too dumb to be bothered to come home from work or have a decent conversation with me or remember a birthday or anniversary. How simple would all that have been to fix? What an easy problem to have!' She raised her glass, spilling some of her drink. 'And now look.'

'And you were too dumb not to go off with the first man who showed you some attention. Stop swearing.'

'We were at it like fucking rabbits,' Jo said in an increasingly slurred voice. 'Jealous?'

Her only defence, Lorraine thought sadly, was the drama.

'For God's sake, Jo. Freddie's out there somewhere, desperately unhappy, and you've been so wrapped up with your problems, you didn't notice.'

'That's what this is about all, isn't it?' Jo paused, frowned. She touched her forehead. 'All about, I mean. It's about what happened to *you* last year.'

Lorraine reached out towards Jo, wanting to calm her down.

'Go away!' Jo spat, ducking backwards. 'Well, I don't blame Adam, quite frankly.' She wobbled and staggered against the wall. 'You fucking deserved it, if you ask me.'

Lorraine's hand was swift and sharp, delivering a clean slap to Jo's left cheek. They stared at each other, breathing hard, no one daring to move. Finally, slowly, Jo brought her fingers up to the red welt on her face – then fell against Lorraine, sobbing hysterically.

'Please find Freddie, Lorraine. *Please*. I couldn't stand it if anything happened to him.'

'It's fine, it's OK,' Lorraine said softly. 'Calm down. You just need to calm down.'

Lorraine took her sister back to the sofa and they

sat there, Jo's face against Lorraine's blouse, Lorraine stroking her hair. Eventually the crying subsided.

'Is this a bad time?' Adam said from the doorway, shifting uncomfortably. 'Burnley just phoned. They've found Freddie's bicycle. It was in the woods where Lenny died.'

28

Once I'm back inside, I rattle the door to make certain it's locked. Freddie can't get out. And that means no one can get in either. He's banging about, being stupid because I left him alone.

'What are you doing, you fucking idiot?' he asks. He's just climbed down the steps and there's spit in the corner of his mouth.

I stand still, letting his horrid words bounce off me. That's what Sonia told me to do when people are mean to me. She says it will stop me getting angry and wanting to hurt them.

'I thought you were my mate.'

'I am your friend, Freddie,' I tell him. I have already said this many times, but perhaps he doesn't believe me. That makes my legs want to start up their jiggling again. I go itchy on my back. 'I am your friend. I am your friend. I am your friend.'

'Just shut up, right?' Freddie turns around and kicks the table leg.

'The door is locked and you can't get out. You are safe with me. I will make you food and keep you in here with me now.'

'You're fucking mental,' he says. 'You nearly killed yourself hanging up there yesterday.' He points to the beam. 'Nearly got me caught, too. I thought I could trust you.'

I don't answer him because if I did then I would get angry. I go to my fridge. I take out the cheese and eggs, hoping he likes omelettes. I like them. They make me feel good inside. Keeping him locked up makes me feel good inside too. I turn on the gas and carve out a chunk of butter. I drop it in the pan and watch it leak and froth in a runny circle.

'Tony came in here after they got you down, you know. Came right upstairs and nearly found me.'

He's still scared from what happened. He's clutching a laptop computer. I haven't got one of those. He puts it on my table and then goes to the window and drags my curtains closed.

'It's only lunchtime,' I say, looking at my watch. 'It won't be dark for ages.'

He looks at me and shakes his head and that makes me feel funny inside even more. I take an egg from the box, clutching it in my hand. I squeeze it really hard and it breaks and the slime oozes between my fingers. I am staring at Freddie and he has stopped really still and is watching me. He looks at my hand.

'I will make you an omelette now,' I tell him quietly.

Smudge threads between my ankles, licking up the spilt egg.

'Thank you,' Freddie says nicely.

Slowly, he turns back to the laptop. The screen is glowing. He slumps down in the chair, sliding my drawings across the table.

'Hey, that *is* Tony's computer,' I say, recognising it again. 'He will be cross with you.'

I am whisking lots of eggs together like Sonia showed me.

Freddie looks at me. 'Yeah, but I got it back for him, didn't I?' His grin is lopsided as if he's not sure. 'So he won't be cross and you'd better not fucking tell him, right?'

I shake my head from side to side until it hurts my brain. I tip the eggs into the pan and grate some cheese. I break a little wedge off for Smudge. He sniffs and pecks at it with his nose before walking away. He jumps up on Freddie's lap.

'He likes you,' I say.

'About the only one who fucking does,' Freddie says, rubbing Smudge's back. I can hear him purring.

Freddie has got lots of special words on the laptop screen and I don't understand it as I am not clever yet but I will be when I'm better.

'*I* like you,' I tell him. 'And so does Lana because I've seen it in the secret place at the back of her eyes.'

He swings round and curls up his nose at me.

I crumble the cheese into the pan and watch it melt into the egg. Then I fold the whole thing over on itself like Sonia showed me. It breaks up so I jab the spatula down into it and bite on my lip to stop myself getting cross.

'It's ready,' I say, sliding it on to the plate. I put a piece of bread next to it and take it over to the table.

Freddie has his head in his hands so I tap him on the shoulder.

'Are you sad?' I ask.

He looks up at me. 'No,' he says, and then thanks me when he sees the food. He whips the plate from my hands and shoves the bread into his mouth. I give him a fork and it's as if he's not eaten in days.

'I am a good cook, aren't I?' I say proudly. 'I could go on the telly on one of those cookery programmes that I watch with Sonia.'

I go over to the door and rattle it again to make sure it's still locked. Freddie stares at me, holding the plate under his chin, his mouth full of food.

'The key is in my pocket,' I tell him, patting it. 'You can't get out.'

'You've really locked me in?' He wipes his mouth on his hand. He looks at the door then back at me then at the door again.

'Yes,' I tell him. He is thinking about everything, about our adventure, about leaving, about going home, about our secrets. 'You are my friend now. You are going to stay with me.'

I sit down next to him and my leg jiggles under the table.

'Dean was my friend and he is dead and when I get a girlfriend and she marries me she will do the cooking and I will mow the grass and drive the car.'

Freddie chuckles and shakes his head, then wipes the crust around the plate.

'Tony says it's rude to do that with your bread.' I don't like it when people laugh at me. My good feeling inside is going away now.

He shrugs and stuffs the bread in his mouth. 'That's a bit bloody sexist, isn't it?' he says. Then he takes a cable from his backpack and plugs his phone into a socket. Half a minute later, the screen lights up.

'But it's what Tony says. He says that men should be men.' I pick up Freddie's empty plate. 'And that men should treat women nicely and then they will do what you want.'

'Is that what he says?'

Freddie leans really close to me and his face is only a few inches from mine. He grabs my arms.

I nod my head a lot. 'Let go,' I tell him, but he doesn't.

'Then he's an arrogant fucker, isn't he?'

I don't know what that means.

'Are you angry with Tony? Is that why you stole his computer?'

'I didn't steal it. I told you. I *found* it. So you can just keep your mouth shut.'

I nod lots more.

'And yes,' Freddie continues, 'I am angry with Tony.'

'Why? After Simon died he got really sad you know. It made him shout and punch and kick. Lots of things in the house got broken. He was cross at Simon for what he did.'

Freddie nods slowly. 'I don't know jack shit any more, pal.' He reaches into his pack again and pulls out a bottle of vodka. He swigs straight from it.

I know that's bad to do because Sonia cried when Tony did it once.

'Who's Jack Shit?' I ask.

Freddie is laughing again, but it's a laugh that doesn't sound happy. 'It just means I don't know anything.'

'Tony knows things. He's a doctor and doctors are clever. I'm not clever. I can only do drawings.'

Freddie is huffing out air all over the place now and I don't even know if it's laughing or nearly crying or if he's really angry. Maybe Jack Shit knows. I put my hand in my pocket and touch the lucky stone that Stella gave me.

'Lana will be just like Tony when she's a doctor.'

'I fucking very much doubt that.'

Freddie swigs again and does a burp. He holds out the bottle to me, but I turn my head away.

'You really don't know, do you, Gil?'

'What?' My palms are itching.

'Doesn't matter.'

Freddie stands up. He goes to the door, rattles the

handle. I am much bigger than him and step in the way.

'It's no use escaping,' I tell him. 'You have to stay with me now.'

Then his phone rings and we both stare at it, all lit up and buzzing next to the laptop. Jiggling across the table.

'Not again,' Freddie says. 'I don't want to speak to anyone.' He goes over to the table, yanks the power cable from the phone and presses the button to turn it off. 'Least of all my mum.'

His cheeks are red and his hands are curled up and tight, like hands go when people are about to cry. He is pacing about now, knocking into a chair.

I grab him by the shoulders. 'It's OK, Freddie. I will look after you.' I pluck a tissue from the box just like Sonia does for me.

He snatches it. 'Fucking adults, right?' He blows his nose and settles back down at the table, doing something on the computer that I don't understand.

I make a cup of tea. Sonia says it makes everything better.

When I put the mugs on the table, Freddie's face has gone really pale. He slowly shuts the laptop lid. 'Fucking *fucking* hell,' he says in a whisper. Then his cheeks burn red and he starts to rummage through all my drawings on the table. He's getting them all creased.

'Don't do that,' I tell him, but he doesn't listen.

'Where are they?' he says. 'The ones I saw earlier.

Show me.' His voice is louder now and he keeps saying *show me*, *show me* over and over until he's yelling it really loud.

'Show you what?' I ask, but it's as if he doesn't hear me and my drawings are going on the floor now and that's making me sad and cross. 'Stop it!' I say, and grab his arm. I can feel him shaking, right down to the bones deep inside his body.

He yanks out of my grip and shoves his phone and the computer into his backpack. 'Open the fucking door, you freak!' he screams. His whole body is shaking, even his voice.

'Oh no,' I say politely. I set my hands on his shoulders. 'You have to stay here with me now. You're my friend.'

29

'Jo's sleeping it off, so I'm going to see Bill. He said he was free this afternoon.'

Bill was an old family friend as well as an expert in document and digital forensics.

'I'll come with you, Ray. I want to see what he thinks. And I've cancelled meetings so I can stay on to help.'

'Thanks, Adam,' Lorraine replied.

Central Forensic Services was based in modern offices on the edge of Warwick University campus. Friday-afternoon traffic clogged the approach on the A45 and caused Lorraine to rummage in her handbag and fish out ten Silk Cut she wasn't even certain she had.

'I'll lean out,' she said, pre-empting Adam's disapproval, and lighting up.

They'd been stuck at a set of lights, waiting to turn left, for what seemed like an age. Finally, they were cruising down the long, leafy length of Kenilworth Road.

'Pull in there,' Lorraine said ten minutes later as they approached the two-storey building.

She and Adam got out of the car and went inside. The receptionist immediately showed them through to Bill's office.

'It has been too long,' Bill said in a loud, overstated voice, '*way* too long.' Beaming and red-faced, he grabbed Adam's hand, pulled him close and slapped him on the back with the other. Then he dragged Lorraine in for a kiss and a tight hug. For a moment, she couldn't breathe.

The last time they'd seen him was when he and his wife had invited them round for dinner at their home in Kenilworth.

'It's been about six months, I think,' Lorraine said, removing the clear plastic wallet from a brown envelope.

They sat down on two black leather sofas set at right angles to each other at one end of Bill's spacious office. A work experience lad brought in a tray of tea and a tin of biscuits. Lorraine noticed Bill had put on a bit of weight. His faded jeans strained around his girth and his green check shirt was slightly untucked. Bill never wore a suit.

'How's Sandy?' Adam asked.

'She's very well, thanks. Off on one of her charity dos soon. South America this time, I believe. A whole bunch of them cycling up some mountain.' Bill was shaking his head fondly. Sandy was always going on some adventure or another, raising money for good causes.

A network of tiny lines had deepened around his eyes at the mention of his wife, Lorraine noticed.

He clapped his hands together. 'So, what have you got for me?'

Bill's enthusiasm for his work was infectious; it was his drug. He'd dealt with thousands of cases for the police and other government agencies over the years, as well as working with solicitors both on a criminal and civil basis. What Bill didn't know about handwriting comparison or document analysis wasn't worth knowing. He'd appeared in court numerous times as an expert witness, including cases for Lorraine and Adam.

'It's a sad one, I'm afraid,' Lorraine began. She knew Bill had a couple of lads at university, one at Warwick studying Law, the other in Edinburgh reading English. 'It's a suicide note, homeless lad, nineteen, killed himself by crashing a stolen motorbike into a tree. Massive head injuries. The note was found in a locker where he kept his belongings at a homeless shelter. He was a regular there.'

Bill took the plastic wallet and looked at the photocopied note. He preferred to work from original documents, but Lorraine had made certain it was a clean copy. He shook his head slowly as he read. 'Sad indeed.' He placed it on the table. 'Easier to just take an overdose, surely?' His head retracted in disbelief. 'It's an elaborate way for a homeless lad to go.'

Lorraine made a similar gesture back and shrugged. 'Dean Watts was registered at the Job Centre in Wellesbury. He'd done a couple of courses – how to apply for jobs, that kind of thing. They were able to provide me with a few samples of his handwriting.'

Lorraine slipped another wallet from the envelope and handed it over. Bill curled in his lips as he read Dean's letter in which he tried to convince a builder to give him a job as a labourer.

'Who was the SIO on this?' Bill was almost smiling.

'Detective Inspector Greg Burnley,' Lorraine replied.

'Never heard of him,' Bill said, and picked up both samples, holding them side by side. 'But I can see why you wanted me to take a look.'

✻

'So the note is a fake,' Lorraine said half an hour later, back in the car. 'Which means Lana might be telling the truth.'

She hadn't been able to resist a second cigarette and was thankful Adam wasn't being high and mighty about it. It was just that the blend of work and home – something she'd never been comfortable with – had set her off. She was stressed, and she wanted her nephew back.

'Then who wrote it?' Adam said.

They were on their way to the Justice Centre to see Burnley, show him the handwriting comparison and give him Bill's off-the-record but adamant conclusion that Dean Watts had not written his own suicide note. *Not even close* were Bill's final words. Although, he'd added, someone had made a decent attempt to copy his style. 'I'd say they had access to something the deceased had previously written,' he said. 'But it's all in the tiny details, and they're dissimilar in every way.' Lorraine had suspected as much but wanted professional confirmation.

Burnley came out of his meeting especially when they arrived. Lorraine glanced up and thought he looked both inflamed and joyous as he approached them down the corridor, his short legs making hard work of the distance. She was leaning against a wall, finishing off a reply to a text from Grace.

'So, your nephew's bike,' Burnley began with a smug grin.

'Freddie's bicycle is significant in the "suicide", is it?' Lorraine put her phone in her jeans pocket and folded her arms. Between them, she and Adam were blocking the corridor.

'Happy to share opinions, as ever, although I'm still waiting for forensics on that one,' he said. 'You seem to be making yourselves right at home. *Mi casa* and all that.'

He stepped forward, clearly expecting them to move.

'Good, then you won't mind if I share a little titbit with you.' Lorraine wafted the envelope in his face.

'Dean Watts' suicide note was not written by him. An expert says it's a fake.'

Burnley's shoulders dropped an inch or two and his expression instantly changed – eyebrows raised, a pulled-back chin emphasising the stubbly flesh that hung beneath.

He ushered them through to his office, where Lorraine continued. 'We can take this through the proper channels, though that's such a drag and I'm more interested in finding my nephew rather than clearing up after your ineptitude. Again. Your full cooperation in all areas, therefore' – she lingered here – 'would really be appreciated.'

Burnley was back in his chair. He spread his hands out on his desk.

'And you might want to take a look at this,' Lorraine said, pulling a CD in a slipcase from her bag and dropping it on his desk. 'It's CCTV footage of the stolen motorbike leaving the pub in Radcote. I thought you might be interested to know that there were two people on the bike. Just like Gil said.'

✳

Twenty minutes later and Lorraine and Adam were alone, sifting through the case files from the six suicides that had occurred in the Wellesbury area. Burnley had swept them off into a private room. Even though many of the officers and staff were already leaving for the weekend, the department was always open.

'I still think it's distraction therapy for you,' Adam said, pulling Lorraine close. 'By the way, they're continuing to ping Freddie's phone periodically and there's been nothing so far.' He'd taken a call from their West Midlands office while Lorraine was waiting for the files to be gathered. 'And no movement on his bank account, either, cash machines or debit cards. It's eighteen pounds twenty-four in credit with no overdraft facility so he's not going very far on that.'

Lorraine nodded. 'I know you think I'm mad.' She looked up at the ceiling, a file open between her hands. 'If it wasn't Burnley . . . if it was anyone else . . .'

'I know,' Adam replied. 'You do what you need to do.'

Lorraine was grateful he understood. More often than not it was she who'd humour him when he veered off at tangents in an investigation, latched on to seemingly unrelated threads, trying to tie them up, to make sense of glimpses and morsels of information that others would have overlooked. It was what made them both good detectives.

'Dean's death was not a clear-cut suicide, I'm convinced of that. Even if Lana wasn't involved and she's covering up for someone, I'm certain there's some truth to Gil's claims.'

'Maybe she is telling the truth,' Adam said.

Lorraine rubbed her eyes and nodded. 'But you know

what else has really got to me? That message between Freddie and Lana, the one on his computer joking about being half brother and sister.' She sipped on a bottle of water, remembering how Jo had overreacted to her questions.

Between them they scanned through the paperwork which, Lorraine had to admit, was complete and thorough in most cases. Either Burnley had learnt a few lessons or he had an exemplary team behind him. She suspected the latter. It was only when they came to Simon Hawkeswell's file that her stomach tightened.

'Oh God, he looked just like his dad.'

She stared, almost mesmerised, at the dead boy's face – livid and bluey-purple, a snapshot of his last moments. The haemorrhaging was spotted about on his cheeks and eyelids like a disease. She plucked out a few of the scene photographs and looked at them, before sliding them across to Adam. Then she pulled one back again, studied it closely.

'Where's the pathologist's report?'

Adam drew it from the file and flipped through it. Lorraine lined up a few photographs of Simon. There were dozens of the scene.

'Do you see it too?' she said, running her finger along the ligature mark.

'Ray, leave it.' Adam clasped her wrist and Lorraine sensed that if they hadn't been where they were he'd have drawn her in for a tender kiss. It was what she needed. In fact, she ached for him. 'It's impossible to tell anything from photographs, love, and you know it.'

'You haven't even looked properly.'

She searched the document for the pathologist's name and nodded when she saw it, feeling slightly irrational at the way her thoughts were going.

'Didn't we hear something about him? Wasn't he hauled up for—'

'Ray . . .'

Lorraine noticed her hands were shaking. 'And look, here's the file of that boy Sonia mentioned at the barbecue. Jason Rees.'

More photographs were laid out on the table. Jason had also hanged himself.

'Adam, look at this, will you?'

'Why don't we call it a day?' he said. 'Get back to Jo, see how she's doing.'

Lorraine was already shaking her head. 'No,' she said, positioning her phone over the first file to photograph it. 'I've not even started.'

✲

Lorraine felt a sudden chill as they walked to the car. By the time they got back to Radcote, sheets of low swirling cloud had collected, forming a claustrophobic creamy-grey canopy over the village. Soon large drops of rain were pelting the car. A strange musty smell accompanied the early evening storm, along with an eerie glow reflecting off the ginger stone of the houses. They sat in the car on the front drive with lightning flashing above them. It reflected in the paned windows of Glebe House. A couple of seconds later, thunder rumbled above.

'Let's make a dash for it,' Lorraine said, opening the car door. A sudden gust of wind wrenched it from her grip. Adam got out too, hitching up the collar of his lightweight jacket, and they dashed towards the door. There was another flash of lightning and crack of thunder as they went inside.

Lorraine stood on the back doormat, dripping, her hair stuck to her face. 'It's crazy out there!' she said. 'I can't believe the weather changed so—'

Her breath caught in her lungs when she saw Jo's face.

'DI Burnley just phoned. They're sending round a family liaison officer. He said there'd been a development.'

'But we've only just come from the station.'

Lorraine grabbed a couple of towels from the utility room, tossing one at Adam. She rubbed her hair and shoulders then pulled Jo into her arms. The light was fading, in part due to the storm. It heralded the start of a third night without Freddie.

'Did he give details?'

Jo shook her head.

'Look, it's going to be OK. The FLO is just routine. Freddie will be fine.'

Lorraine felt a wave of nausea and glanced at Adam over Jo's back. He stared straight at her, sombre-faced.

'You read about things like this,' Jo said shakily. 'But you always think they're other people's nightmares.' She pulled away from Lorraine, looking lost in her own kitchen. 'People will be reading about my nightmare soon, wondering how I let my son get so depressed, how I never noticed, how he ran away to end—'

'Stop!' The voice filled the room.

Lorraine swung round, startled but then relieved when she saw Malc standing in the doorway.

'I won't have you talking like that, Jo,' he said, moving towards her. 'Freddie needs us to stay strong.' He took her in his arms and held her as if he'd never been away.

✴

'I'm Alison Black,' the young woman said to Lorraine. She shook out her umbrella and left it on the mat. It was still raining but not with the same tropical force. 'I'll be keeping you up to date on the investigation and can answer any questions you might have.'

Lorraine did the introductions, thinking that Alison seemed too young. Nice, well-mannered, sympathetic and clearly chosen so her middle-class background melded with that of Jo and Malc's, but she looked barely out of her twenties.

They all sat round the kitchen table, except Malc, who hovered uncertainly in the doorway.

'Are you working alone?' Adam asked.

'There's another officer assigned to this case and I'll be briefing him later.' She turned to look at Jo. 'Hopefully your son will be found soon enough and you won't be needing either of us.'

Her tone was light and jovial, and it caused an awkward silence.

A rushed risk assessment, Lorraine thought, probably drawn up that afternoon, informing Alison that she was safe to visit alone, that, as no body had been found, her presence would be welcomed rather than blamed. She noticed her large black shoulder bag, the contents of which she could predict: various liaison officer logs and information-gathering sheets to be delivered to the incident room if and when one was set up; packs from the Home Office explaining in bland yet still somehow confusing English the various stages of the legal system should the case progress to that level; information about appearing in court; witness protection leaflets; compensation claim details. She prayed they'd stay inside the bag and never become relevant for her sister.

Alison unbuckled the flap of her bag. She reached inside, took out a sheet of paper, and looked over at Malc. 'It's important you join us, Mr Curzon. Your input is valuable.'

'What are you implying?' His eyes had narrowed to incredulous slits. He was clearly upset.

'I just want to ask you about your son. Any little thing could be helpful to the investigating officers.'

'It's normal,' Lorraine assured him, beckoning him over. 'Alison's trained. She'll circulate anything useful on the Police National Computer and local information systems. It could really help. She's used to working with families who've had a loss and—'

'So Freddie's lost to us already, is he?' Malc's voice wavered.

Alison took over. 'It's really just a routine visit so we can keep you informed, give you all our phone numbers, plan some future meetings depending on where and how Freddie is found.'

'You mean if he's found *dead*,' Malc said, moving into the room to stand behind Jo's chair.

'We all want to find him safe and well, Mr Curzon,' Alison countered, shaking her head. Some of her mousy brown hair fell out of its clip. 'I'd like to start by asking you a bit about Freddie and his routine. What he likes to do. Who his friends are, that kind of thing. Then I'll take a look in his room, if I may.'

'I was told something had happened,' Jo said meekly. 'That there'd been a development.'

Alison smiled and pulled the cap off her pen. 'Let's just cover this first,' she said.

Lorraine listened as, between them, Jo and Malc did their best to convey their son's life to Alison. Jo's head hung forward, her shoulders rounded and her knees drawn up. Malc stood behind her, tentatively stroking her back as she spoke. Once or twice she flinched under his touch.

'So it's been very hard for him,' Jo said, finally, after explaining about the separation.

'For all of us,' Malc added.

'And given the time again, I wouldn't have . . . Well, I'd have been here more for Freddie.'

After Alison had taken down two pages of notes about what they knew about the bullying, Freddie's last year at school, who his friends were, his hobbies, his daily routines – everything from the names of his teachers to the address of his GP – she placed her pen on the table and took off her glasses.

'You're right about the development, Mrs Curzon. An item of significance has just been found in Blackdown Woods.'

'We already know about the bicycle,' Malc said.

'This is different,' Alison said. 'The bike's being sent for testing and will be preserved as evidence.'

Jo stood and paced the kitchen. 'Evidence of what? Who found it? What is it?'

'We've had a team conducting a thorough search of the woods. I don't have details of the officer who found the item, I'm afraid. And until the lab sends through results, we won't know what it may be evidence of.'

Alison had been careful to keep to a comforting tone, but now she flushed a little – red peaks on her pale, young, freckled cheeks.

Jo's face crumpled. 'Just *tell* us,' she implored.

'They found a hooded top near where they believe a scuffle took place,' Alison said. 'There was a considerable amount of blood on it.'

'Blood?' Jo said. Her eyes grew wide as the implications sunk in.

'There was a student railcard in the pocket,' Alison continued, glancing at her notes. 'I'm afraid it had Freddie's name on it.'

30

Freddie stared up at Gil, his shoulder smarting from where he'd been shoved down into the sofa as he'd tried yet again to escape. 'You're crazy,' he said. 'You can't keep me locked up in here any longer. I'll call the police.'

Gil paced about, his right hand shoved in his back pocket, fingering the key. Freddie forced himself not to stare at it.

Another night had passed – he'd barely slept, while Gil had guarded the door – and it was now early on Saturday morning. He tried to keep his voice level, not knowing how far Gil would go. All he could think of were those disgusting drawings he'd seen yesterday, and what he'd found on the laptop. It didn't make sense – or did it? Was that why they kept Gil out here? He would have to play this very carefully.

'Don't call me crazy,' Gil responded. 'I am your friend I want to be your friend.'

He suddenly bent forward, wrapping his arms around his body. Freddie thought he was going to cry.

'Gil, look, I'm sorry, right? I didn't mean to upset you, mate.' He eased the pack on to his shoulder and slowly stood up. He didn't want to make any sudden moves. 'I *am* your friend, Gil. But friends don't lock each other up, do they? Why don't you give me the key and I can let us out?'

He moved closer to Gil.

'No, because then you would leave and I won't have a friend any more. Apart from Smudge the cat. He is my friend.'

Freddie stared into Gil's eyes. They were an un-remarkable shade of pale blue. They looked just like anyone else's – but there was something else about them. Something dangerous.

'Lana is your friend, too. Don't forget that.'

Freddie wondered where she was, if she was OK. He desperately needed to get a message to her. He wasn't sure if his phone had held on to enough charge from yesterday to send her a text. It had only been plugged in a few minutes.

'She is going away to university soon then I will be all alone.'

Gil picked up a tea towel and wound it around the knuckles of each hand. His fingers swelled and bulged purple from the pressure, reminding Freddie of what was on the computer.

'She'll visit you in the holidays, Gil.'

Freddie slowly eased himself back towards the sofa, trying not to seem threatening. Gil was rocking from one foot to the other, a slow sideways motion, the tea towel still a taut band between his hands.

Freddie reached for his backpack and slowly opened the flap.

'No!' Gil cried out.

Freddie retracted and folded his arms.

'No, she will make new friends and forget about me.'

Freddie breathed out and tried again, this time managing to get his hand into the pack, feeling around for his phone. He wondered if he could text from inside the bag. He pressed the power button, coughing several times to mask the beep.

'Simon was my friend and he is dead. Dean was my friend and he is dead. Lenny was your friend and he is dead.' Gil's voice was monotonous.

Freddie's heart kicked up. He could see the glow of his phone's screen inside the bag. His thumb was hovering over the keys and, with another cough, he managed to turn off the keypad sounds without Gil noticing.

'You will be dead too if I don't keep you safe and locked up. You don't understand. No one does.'

Gil's shoulders jerked up and down, and he began to move away from the door. The key was still in his pocket.

'But those pictures . . .' Freddie said, hoping to distract him.

Gil turned slowly to face Freddie. His nose and cheeks were an angry red.

'Those ones in the barn . . . why did you draw them?'

Gil dragged a chair over to the door and sat down, blocking the only exit. Freddie took the opportunity to glance into the pack and toggle through his texts until he came to the last one from Lana. He hit reply.

Gil pummelled the side of his head. 'No one knows how much it hurts,' he said. The tea towel was still wrapped around his knuckles, snapping tightly between his fists. 'If I don't draw my pictures it will get really, really bad.'

Freddie knew he had to get help – Lana, maybe Aunty Lorraine, *anyone*. But it was all such a mess with the computer, with Lenny. He'd be arrested for sure and end up in prison. But maybe that was the best place for him anyway. Locked up again, but away from all this shit.

He fumbled with the touchscreen on his phone inside his pack while Gil went on repeating himself.

saw them togthr. u wre rite. nd got me hear llocked up send smne helpgil

He hit send, stealing a glimpse at the screen. Damn, did it make enough sense? He prayed Lana would figure it out.

'It wasn't my fault that Simon died it was that other man's fault but then he died too.' A couple of tears dribbled down Gil's cheeks, curling around the soft flesh of his stubbly jowls. For a moment, Freddie felt sorry for him.

Christ, he hadn't put where he was in the text. How would she know where to send help?

'No one's saying it's your fault, Gil,' Freddie managed to reply.

His throat was tight, as if a fist were gripping his windpipe. He would send another text, tell Lana to get his Uncle Adam to come to the cottage. But when he reached in for the phone again the screen was blank. He jabbed a couple of buttons. The battery had died.

'You think I am bad and that's why I am locking you up but I didn't lock Dean in or lock Simon in did I and they still died.'

Freddie was forcing himself to think. He'd already spotted the window bars, so making an escape by that route was impossible. There was no way out of the loft apart from a skylight, and Gil would grab him before he even got up there. He'd have to either con Gil into letting him go free, or overpower him and get the key. He didn't fancy his chances at either.

'I'm sorry, Gil, I'm just confused,' Freddie said, withdrawing his hand from the pack and fastening it in readiness. Whatever happened, he mustn't leave it behind. It contained the laptop.

'It wasn't my fault he died we were going on holiday and I was excited. But then no one was excited because Simon was hanging.' Gil rubbed his face.

The holiday made sense. Freddie had seen the suitcase twice. Once in the pictures on the computer . . .

Oh God, that poor naked man, his dick on show and that brown stuff that was probably shit . . . the photographer's shadow cast from the low winter sun streaming into the barn . . . the other person cowering in the dark corner, watching on . . .

And he'd seen it again in Gil's drawing. It was old-fashioned-looking, battered, had a sticker of the Eiffel Tower on it. Gil had copied it meticulously. He'd noticed it when Gil first allowed him to hide in the cottage. His pictures were everywhere and Freddie had flicked through them, not seeing the really nasty ones until later. Apart from being grotesque, they wouldn't have meant much until he'd seen the actual photographs, secreted in layers of invisible files on the computer. And even then, the implications weren't certain.

Oh God, why had he ever left his bedroom?

Fleetingly, he thought of his mum, how she must be feeling. He'd been gone three nights now and he knew she'd be in a state.

'Did you hear that?' Freddie said. The rumble of a rough-sounding vehicle passing the tack-room doorway.

Gil shook his head. 'I will not let them take you.'

It was definitely a car. Freddie prayed it was his Aunty Lorraine. She'd understand about the bullying and he could make up some excuse about why he'd been in the woods. Lenny could hardly say differently, not now.

He stood up, but Gil was up in a flash and shoving him back down on the sofa.

'I just wanted to see whose car it was,' Freddie said.

'You are a secret I am good at keeping secrets,' Gil replied. It came out as a chant, as if it was pre-programmed and he couldn't say anything else.

Freddie strained his ears, thought he heard a car door slam nearby.

'Tony said I mustn't tell anyone and that if I do bad things will happen and I will go to the place for people like me. I can't let you go.'

The worried expression on Gil's face temporarily slowed Freddie's heart. He realised that, like him, Gil was a prisoner too. Freddie had never bothered to ask Lana what was wrong with him, but now they had something in common. Except Gil was trapped inside his own mind with no chance of ever escaping.

'Tony won't send you away,' Freddie tried to re-assure him. 'You can trust me.' This time when he stood up, pack slung on his shoulder again, Gil didn't shove him, and when he opened his arms for a broth-erly embrace, Gil walked right into them.

Slowly, carefully, Freddie slipped his hand into Gil's back pocket and retrieved the key.

'Shall we have another cuppa?' Freddie said, closing his fingers around the metal. 'Now that we're best mates.' He pulled away.

'That is a good idea,' Gil said, moving into the galley kitchen area.

'I'll just make sure the door's secure so no one can get in.'

Gil nodded as he grabbed the kettle.

It all happened so quickly – the sound of the water running, the kettle filling, Gil's happy whistling, the key sliding into the lock, turning easily, the cool evening air on his face as the door opened, Gil's angry yell as he realised what was happening.

Freddie almost felt bad, running out, leaving him bewildered, but there was no time for that as images of Lenny, of the woods, of the rock pounding, pounding, pounding Lenny to a pulp flashed through his mind.

A crow flapped out of a tall tree as he charged across the gravel, his heart burning from adrenalin.

When he saw the battered truck, it didn't register at first. Not until the hands grabbed him, almost caught him from falling as he went dizzy with fear.

Strong, sinewy tattooed arms wound around his body, his neck.

'And where do you think you're going?' Frank said, black teeth grinning down.

31

Lana was standing in the Manor kitchen, holding her phone, not knowing what to do. She jumped as the door opened and her father came in from the yard. The dogs wrapped around his legs, getting in the way.

'Hi,' she said tentatively, trying to gauge his mood, watching him as he washed his hands, scrubbing them several times.

She looked surreptitiously again at Freddie's text.

saw them togthr

Did Freddie mean their parents?

'Hello,' her dad said. He seemed preoccupied, distracted. 'Where's your mother?'

'Maybe with the horses,' Lana whispered.

Her dad dried his hands, tossed the towel over the back of a wooden chair.

u wre rite

She didn't want to be right, didn't want her dad and Jo to have been doing those things together. She'd seen the photos by accident, walked in on her dad one evening when he was in his study. He'd been working late, so he'd said, and she'd brought him a cup of tea before she went up to bed. It was only a glimpse, just a flash, but the images were burnt on her mind. Had Freddie found them on her dad's laptop? Had he got the proof?

Thing is, they hadn't really thought out what to do next.

'I'm sorry, Dad,' Lana said.

He swung round, looking as if he'd just told a patient or their family bad news. She always knew when he'd done that – he came home pretty much reeking of death. She thought she smelled it on him now.

'I'm sorry for getting into trouble,' she explained.

He grunted, poured himself a Scotch despite the time of day. 'It's Saturday,' he said, sensing her disapproval. 'I'm winding down.'

Her father paced up and down the kitchen, one hand shoved in his pocket, one hand holding the tumbler. The dogs continued to follow him until he shoved Daisy's rump with his foot. Then they skulked off to their beds.

'I don't understand why you were so fucking stupid, Lana.' He slugged more whisky.

'The motorbike?' she said, just in case he meant something else. She wasn't sure how much he knew.

Her dad nodded, finished his drink and poured another one straight away. Lana noticed the soft redness of his cheeks bleed upwards, towards his eyes.

'It was stupid,' she said. She felt sick even talking about it.

'I don't understand why you'd do something like that.'

He sounded sad, which made Lana feel even worse. For a moment she wondered if he was about to hug her, tell her she'd always be safe, like he used to do when she was little.

But the hug didn't come. He just drank more whisky, then stalked off.

got me hear llocked up send smne helpgil

What did Freddie mean? Was she supposed to send help, and if so, where? Had he meant to put Gil's name at the end? She could hardly ask her dad for help. Maybe her mum would know what to do; or perhaps she should speak to Lorraine? The text was worrying her, though – the broken words, the brevity, the urgency.

She clasped the phone tightly then slid it in her back pocket. Daisy came out of her bed and skirted around her. Lana pulled her close, gripping on to the barrel of her body in the hope the dog might tell her what to do.

'Where the hell are you, Freddie?' she whispered into the dog's fur. 'I need to know where you are.'

❈

'Where the hell is your father?' Freddie had said. They were in the middle of their exams, and he was jittery and nervous, unable to sit still. He hadn't even commented on the paper they'd just taken. 'I'm going to the hospital to find him. I'm going to . . . to . . .' But they'd got only one hour before their next A level and Lana was trying to calm him down. She wished she'd never mentioned what she'd seen the night before.

The school café table was wedged between them, two Diet Cokes, two sausage, chips and peas sitting on it untouched. Lana had felt an urgent need to reach out and hold Freddie's hand. 'You have to forget about it,' she'd said. 'Let's concentrate on our exams and sort out this mess when they're over. We'll do some revision together tonight, OK?'

But Freddie had just stared at her, turning the can of Coke round and round between his hands. He was shocked, Lana could see that. Shocked and very upset.

'Oi, fuckhead, you're in my place.' A boy in their year loomed over them, and was quickly joined by several others.

Resignedly, Freddie had stood up, head bowed, and lifted his tray of food to move; but the boy had swung up his arm and knocked it from his grip. Chips and peas shot everywhere. Instinctively, Lana had made a grab for his sausage before it hit the floor.

'Just leave it,' Freddie had said and walked off, his books clutched to his chest.

Lana had followed, and they'd gone to sit at another table, listening to the jeers and cruel comments from the group of boys as they went.

'Ignore them,' Lana had said. 'They're idiots. And look, I probably made a mistake about what I thought I saw.' This time she had taken Freddie's hand. He hadn't responded.

If she was perfectly honest, Lana didn't think she'd made a mistake at all. She hadn't slept at all last night. Her mind kept going over and over what it meant, trying to find a rational explanation. There wasn't one.

His mum. Her dad. They'd been together. And someone had taken pictures.

✱

The exam had been a long one. Chemistry. Lana knew she had to do better than average. She had to get an A grade minimum – for her mother, for herself, for the rest of her life. Several times she'd glanced furtively at Freddie on the next row. Every time he'd been writing frantically, head bowed, arm curled round his paper.

At the end of the session she'd put down her pen, her papers sitting squarely in front of her. She reckoned she'd done what she had to do.

✱

'I don't believe it,' Freddie had said later that day, head in hands. They were back in Radcote, revising in Lana's garden near the lake so that Freddie could smoke. The grass made her legs itch. At that moment she'd wished she smoked, wished she was a rebellious teenager who got pissed, went to clubs, took Ecstasy, and didn't come home until five in the morning.

'I'm going to sort it out, make it all OK,' he'd added, stubbing out his cigarette and lighting another. 'I'm not going to let this happen.'

'But it already has,' Lana had said, wishing she could erase the pictures from her mind.

'Look, my mum, she doesn't know what she's doing. Sometimes she . . .'

Freddie had bowed his head.

'And my dad's been messed up since Simon.' Lana hadn't wanted to make excuses for him, but it was the only explanation. 'What will you do?'

Later, she wished she hadn't asked.

Freddie had flicked through the pages of his English notes and stuck a finger in a certain place.

'We're best off leaving them to it,' Lana had continued. Her family didn't need any more trouble, especially not from her.

'No,' Freddie had said, snapping his English book closed. He'd stood up, looming over her in his crumpled school clothes, his stubby tie. 'First I want to see what you saw, make certain that you're right. Then we work out what to do.'

✳

'Dad, please don't drink any more,' Lana said as her father returned to the kitchen to pour a third glass of whisky.

Sonia opened the back door. 'What's wrong with Gil?' she said, coming inside and pulling off her boots.

Lana thought she looked ill, pale, washed-out. She didn't know how she'd had the strength to muck out the stables.

'How the hell do I know?' Tony snapped.

'I just found him wandering around the courtyard mumbling stuff to himself. He was in a state. I asked him to come over here, but he wouldn't. I settled him inside his house with some tea.'

'What was he saying?' Lana asked.

'It was hard to tell. He was so upset. Stuff about—'

'Shut up, woman, for Christ's sake!'

Lana stared at her father, horrified, as he slammed down his glass. His face was red.

'Dad—'

'And you be quiet too. I need to think.'

He paced about the kitchen, his fists balled up at his sides.

'Tony, Lana was only trying to help. Don't be so rude.'

It was the first time Lana had ever seen her mother stand up to her dad. Lana held her breath.

'We need to help Gil, not argue. He's very upset about something. You should have seen him. He was going on about it being his fault that Freddie was missing, that he didn't keep him safe—'

Lana screamed as her dad lunged forward and his hand lashed out at her mum. For a second, everything fell silent. Sonia held her face, her mouth fell open.

'Dad, *stop* it!' Lana yelled.

He looked at her as if he hadn't realised she was still there, before striding out of the back door, slamming it shut. She heard his footsteps on the gravel, then silence. She went up to her mum and hugged her.

'Mum, I don't know what to do,' she said, pulling her phone from her pocket with shaking hands. 'I think someone's got Freddie.'

32

'Where were you the night Dean died, Abby?' Lorraine asked.

After breakfast, she and Adam had gone straight to New Hope. Lorraine had been tempted to sit on the bunk beside Abby, but had pulled the one opposite closer instead. She was leaning forward, elbows on knees, trying to cajole some sense from the girl.

Adam had refused to sit and towered above Abby, who was huddled under the folds of her unzipped sleeping bag. By the look of her, she was hoping the camp bed would collapse and swallow her up.

'We can discuss it at the police station if you prefer. Perhaps you'll remember more there.'

There was only silence from Abby.

'It's important, love,' Lorraine said, frowning up at Adam.

'I can't remember,' she replied. 'Probably here. Or my mate's place. My mum kicked me out a few months ago.'

'There's a logbook for the shelter we can check,' Adam said. 'What's your friend's name?'

'I really miss him,' Abby said, ignoring the question. She touched the ring that hung on a cheap chain around her neck. 'I loved him.'

Lorraine reached out to Abby's arm, and gave it a little stroke. 'It must still be terribly hard for you. I'm so sorry. But we need the name of the person you were with that night.' She wanted Abby to realise that they were on her side.

Abby shrugged. 'Gem Mason. She lives on the Westlands estate. Forty-three Coundon Drive. OK?' She scowled at Lorraine.

'Yes, thanks, love,' Lorraine said. 'It's just that sometimes, when people die, it can turn out they didn't always want to.'

'But they said he left a note. He killed himself, didn't he?' A tear trickled down her cheek. 'I thought he loved me back.'

'That's what we're trying to find out, and we're hoping you can help us. If Dean's death wasn't suicide, we need to work out exactly what happened.'

Abby was shaking her head. The gothic skull ring trembled at her neck. 'I didn't have nothing to do with it.'

'What if someone had already told us that they were on the motorbike with Dean when he died?' Adam said. 'That it was an accident, not a suicide.'

Abby gave a little jump of shock. 'Like who?'

'A girl about your age, actually.'

'Then it's a lie!' She sounded distressed. 'Dean wouldn't have taken no other girl apart from me on the bike.' She pulled up her sleeping bag and drew it around her shoulders, leaving only her head and skinny legs exposed. The black gladiator sandals she wore were too big around her bony ankles.

'Let's just suppose for a moment he did. Do you have any idea who it could have been?' Lorraine asked.

Abby shrugged.

'And you really can't remember where you got Dean's ring from?'

Abby twisted away from them. She clearly wanted them to leave so she could burrow back into her pit of misery, even though she wasn't supposed to be in the shelter at this time. The volunteer on duty, Derek, hadn't insisted Abby leave with the others. It was hard not to feel sorry for her.

Suddenly, Abby sat up straight. 'That girl who works here, there's this boy she hangs out with, yeah?'

'Go on,' Lorraine said, interested suddenly.

'He gave me the ring. He told me Dean would have wanted me to have it.'

'What does the boy look like?' Adam asked.

'You know, just a boy. Skinny, shaggy blond hair. He's the one gave Lenny money to nick the laptop. Everyone here knows that.'

Lorraine took her purse from her bag and pulled out a photograph. 'Is this him?' she said, showing her a picture of Freddie.

'Yeah, that's him,' Abby said confidently.

Lorraine and Adam looked at each other.

'And the girl he hangs out with, what's her name?'

'Lana,' Abby said. 'Lana Hawkeswell.'

There was a flash of pleasure on her skinny face before she burrowed back down under the bag. It was clear the chat was over.

＊

'Now what?' Lorraine said, buckling up her seatbelt and starting the car.

Adam opened a bottle of water and drank half of it in one gulp. He shook his head. Neither of them wanted to believe the implications. 'Freddie gets Lenny to steal a computer. Let's assume it's not because he just wanted a computer, rather he wanted *that* computer.'

'But we know Sonia was borrowing Tony's laptop that day because hers was being repaired. So which one was he after?'

'If Lana was involved in the theft, she would have known which computer was which and told Freddie.'

'And Freddie's bike was found where Lenny died, and his top too,' Lorraine said with a sigh as they headed up the hill towards Radcote and home. 'Greg should get the lab results on the blood back any time now.'

＊

Ten minutes later they were back in Jo's kitchen. Jo was sobbing. Alison, the FLO, was there, trying to comfort her. Another young male officer in uniform was standing awkwardly beside them.

'What's happened?' Lorraine said, crouching next to Jo.

It was only then that she noticed Greg Burnley in the corner by the cluttered pine dresser. She caught his eye and nodded perfunctorily.

'It's about the blood on the jacket, ma'am,' Alison said.

The other officer cleared his throat.

'What about it?' Lorraine steadied herself on a chair, caught suddenly by a rush of adrenalin.

'The lab has confirmed it as Lenny Jackman's blood,' Burnley said, stepping out of the corner. 'I'm afraid Freddie is now a suspect in relation to Lenny's death.'

'Not the suicide you were so certain of then?' Lorraine said, having detected a note of satisfaction in his voice as he condemned her nephew.

'Plus the pathologist's report conclusively shows that Lenny died of head injuries before the train hit him.' Burnley's hands were clasped in front of his stomach, where his belly strained over his belt. 'So not a suicide, no.'

Jo gasped. Alison offered her a sip of water, tissues, a hand to clasp, but she refused them all.

Lorraine frowned, thinking everything through. 'It's hard to believe that Freddie was involved, but . . .'

She took a deep breath, feeling faint suddenly. Work and home had finally merged – something she'd always tried to avoid. She and Jo looked at each other, although they weren't really seeing themselves. Between them, they were seeing Freddie.

Adam handed her a glass of water, and Lorraine took a couple of sips. She was hot, dehydrated, and felt very tired.

'I believe Freddie's laptop is in his bedroom,' Burnley went on with a nod to Alison, who had been up there on her previous visit.

Jo looked up. Clumps of mascara had made U shapes beneath her eyes. 'Yes,' she said weakly.

'We'll be seizing it and any other property we see fit,' Burnley informed them. 'It's in yours and Freddie's interests, so we can rule him out.'

Alison and the other officer took this as their cue and left the room with a large bag, no doubt containing an evidence kit.

Lorraine put her head in her hands. She didn't know whether to stay with Jo or go after them. In the end, she decided Jo needed her more.

33

'I can't believe he hasn't come home,' Jo said. She'd barely eaten the last few days, although between her and Adam, they'd made sure she'd sipped water, taken showers, changed her clothes. Apart from that, her existence was on lock-down.

'Jo . . .' Lorraine said. A piece of limp pizza sat on her plate. Adam had been out to fetch it, but only Stella was eating. She'd taken several slices and gone into the living room to watch television. 'We need to talk, Jo.'

Lorraine glanced at Adam and he got up and left, taking his wine with him. They'd opened a lunchtime bottle in the hope it would help them relax, perhaps allow Jo a few hours' sleep. Lorraine was also hoping it might get her to confide a few things. They were finally alone, Malc having gone to door-knock around the village again. Clearly, he couldn't bear to be idle.

'We went to the shelter earlier, wanting to find out about Dean's mystery girlfriend.'

Jo looked at her sister, heavy-eyed, picking at the crust of her pizza with her nail. She obviously had no intention of eating it. 'What's that got to do with finding Freddie?'

'Hear me out. There were a few lads hanging around the shelter and they told us Dean had been seeing someone called Abby. She was there so we chatted to her.'

'I still don't understand.'

'Do you know anyone called Abby Grey?'

Jo shrugged. 'Sonia will, I expect. She knows everyone at New Hope.'

'The thing is, Jo, she was wearing a ring on a chain.'

'So?'

'It was exactly the same skull ring that Gil put in his drawing. Abby described the person who gave it to her and it sounded just like Freddie. I showed her a photograph of him and she confirmed it was him.' Lorraine waited for it to sink in. 'Apparently Freddie told Abby that Dean had wanted her to have the ring, meaning he must have had contact with Dean before he died.'

Jo was crying again. 'Why is everyone out to blame Freddie for everything? Are you saying he killed Dean too?'

Lorraine shook her head. 'No, no, of course I'm not, but this is too significant to ignore. Abby was also certain that the boy who gave her the ring was the one who paid Lenny to steal the computer from New Hope.'

Jo was silent. Lorraine could see it in her eyes, batting about the news, just as she was in her own mind.

'Jo, can you think of any reason why Freddie would want to get hold of Tony's laptop?'

'No,' Jo replied immediately. 'Freddie's not a thief.'

'No, but he's your son and he loves you. He might want to protect you or help you if he thought—'

'How would he know Sonia just happened to have Tony's computer that day?' she said indignantly. 'If he'd wanted to delete pictures or whatever, surely there are easier ways to do it – by visiting Lana for instance or . . . or—'

'What pictures, love?'

Jo frowned. 'I don't know. For Christ's sake!'

'Jo—'

'Lana probably told him to nick it. I don't know. Maybe she wanted her dad's computer for something. Stop fucking blaming Freddie for everything!'

'No one is, Jo. And I agree, I think Lana *is* involved in some way. With her admitting to being on the motorbike with Dean, and now this, it's puzzling. But if you know there's something on that computer that Freddie wanted to get hold of, then it's vital you tell me. *Now*, Jo.' Lorraine leant in close to her sister. 'For Freddie's sake.'

SAMANTHA HAYES

'At least she admitted she'd done something stupid,' Lorraine said later. She and Adam were in their bedroom because Jo was downstairs having a much-needed sleep, the wine having done its job. 'It's worrying, Adam. Very worrying indeed. You don't think Freddie really did harm Lenny, do you?'

'Shh,' he said, pulling her close.

'But what if Lenny turned nasty, demanded loads of money for stealing the laptop, and Freddie hurt him accidentally?'

'Then it was probably self-defence.'

'And that damned visor helmet.' Lorraine shook her head. 'Burnley actually did his homework. It was confirmed as exactly the same make and type as the helmet that was stolen with the bike. Along with his drawing, I don't doubt Gil was at the scene.'

Lorraine sat down at the dressing table. She'd brought Jo's laptop up to the bedroom, wanting to take another look at the CCTV footage of the front of the pub. Since they'd spoken to Abby, there was something about it that was troubling her.

'I can slow it right down,' she said, adjusting the settings in the movie player. The scene resolved on the screen and Lorraine sped through it until she got to the point where the motorbike was leaving the pub.

Adam was checking his phone, keeping half an eye on the footage.

'Here they come,' Lorraine said. 'Two people on the bike – a male and a female.' She slowed the speed

336

right down, played it back several times. 'There. Did you see?' she said finally.

Adam leant in and watched as she played it again.

'Look at the girl's shoes,' she said. 'Recognise them?'

She waited while Adam thought.

'No, I don't,' he said.

Lorraine half laughed, shaking her head in disbelief. 'Well, I recognise them,' she said. 'They're the sandals Abby was wearing earlier. No doubt.'

34

'Abby's alibi checked out,' Lorraine said, hanging up from the phone call. The French doors were open and she and Adam were sitting out on the terrace. She stared down at the mossy flagstones her father had laid decades ago. 'Gem Mason and her mother both confirmed that Abby was with them the night Dean died. Apparently Gem is on probation at the moment so was being overly helpful. She showed the attending officer Facebook pictures of the two of them together that night. He was satisfied she was telling the truth.'

Adam nodded thoughtfully. They could hear Jo banging about in the kitchen. She hadn't slept for much more than an hour and was now keeping busy by hacking up and throwing every vegetable in the fridge into a huge pot along with some chicken and red wine. The smell of frying onions and garlic drifted outside.

Lorraine glanced through the doors at her and then leant in towards Adam. 'The photos Jo told me about of her and Tony,' she whispered. 'She said they were pretty, you know, hardcore.'

'Oh, for heaven's sake,' Adam said, rolling his eyes.

'They'd had a fair bit to drink, apparently. It happened here, when Malc was working in London.'

Lorraine felt sorry for Jo, but was also furious with her. She understood that she must have been very unhappy to do something so reckless, but allowing Tony to take those pictures was inexcusable.

'Put them on Facebook, did he?' Adam asked.

'He might as well have done. Jo says he began to pressure her soon afterwards. You know, wanting to see her more often, take more risks. He told her he was lonely, that Sonia had become cold and empty.'

Lorraine gazed around the garden. It seemed an age since she'd sat there with Jo on their first morning the previous weekend. They'd had so much planned and she'd been looking forward to it – a week in the country soaking up some sun and relaxing. How wrong she'd been.

'I take it he'd threatened to tell Malc if she didn't comply.'

Lorraine nodded sadly.

They quietened as Malc came out through the glass-paned doors. His usually neat dark hair was messy and standing up, and his skin had lost its natural tan, seeming sallow and washed-out. Even his six-foot height seemed diminished as he stood there, hands shoved in the front pockets of his jeans. His expression showed just how concerned he was about his stepson.

'Isn't there anything else the local police can do?' he said, dropping down into one of the wrought-iron chairs. He leant back and closed his eyes.

'Greg Burnley might be a git, but he's not going to mess up procedure on this one,' Lorraine told him. 'He's got a good team supporting him. They're doing all the right things.'

Malc opened his eyes. 'If you don't mind me saying,' he said slowly, 'you both seem quite preoccupied with those two deaths that happened around here recently. Should I be worried too?'

'It's all been rather surprising, Malc, to tell you the truth,' Lorraine said. 'Not long after I arrived with Stella last weekend, Gil told me something that made the Dean Watts suicide theory seem pretty unstable.'

'I read about him dying in the paper,' Malc said, sighing. 'You do know about the six kids from around here who all did the same thing eighteen months ago, don't you?'

Lorraine was already nodding. 'Yes, and I was there when Lenny stole Tony's laptop from the homeless shelter. Again, at first glance, his death appeared to be a suicide. But not now. As you know, Freddie seems to have been involved, plus we have other forensics results. It certainly wasn't suicide.'

'I just can't believe Freddie would hurt anyone,' Malc said, helping himself to some of the tea from the pot on the table.

'Me neither,' Lorraine replied.

'What if the other deaths weren't suicide either?'

'Malc, mate, you should have joined the force.' Adam laughed. They'd always got on well.

'I'd be a useless cop,' Malc said. 'Too trusting, me. But don't tell me you haven't considered it.'

'You're right,' Lorraine said, holding up her hands, 'we have considered it. I've even spent hours at the Justice Centre going over the old files, looking for possible links, but the only thing that stood out was that the final two boys, Simon and a lad called Jason Rees, were about three or four years older than the others. They didn't really fit the age demographic.'

Malc was thoughtful for a moment. 'You do know about those two, I take it?'

'Know what?' Lorraine leant forward in her chair.

'Well, I mean, don't hold me to it. Kids talking, hearsay and all that.' Malc seemed slightly embarrassed.

'*What*, Malc?'

'Brian – I play darts with him,' Malc explained. 'His son started the rumour.' He drank some of his tea. 'Jason Rees was a regular at New Hope. He was a right drop-out by all accounts, although hadn't always been. Apparently he came from a well-heeled background at one time. Anyway, he lost the plot, got into drugs, and ended up at the shelter. This was before Sonia got involved with the place, by the way. That only happened after she lost Simon.'

'You know an awful lot about village goings-on for a City man,' Adam remarked.

'One night a week in the Old Dog was all it took. What else do you talk about over a pint and a few games of darts?' He grinned fondly, as if he wished he could take time back. 'Turns out that Jason and Simon had a thing together. God knows how or where they met as their lives were worlds apart.'

'That's even more tragic,' Lorraine said.

'Simon wasn't happy at university, everyone knew that. He was planning on quitting and going travelling with Jason as soon as they'd got some money together. The word was, after Simon died, Jason couldn't bear to live without him so killed himself too.'

There was silence, just the occasional sounds of Jo clattering in the kitchen, as Lorraine thought through the implications.

'That makes me even more certain that those two deaths were unrelated to the previous four,' she said after a short while.

'Maybe you're right,' Malc said. 'Brian told me Tony was bereft losing his son. But he never talked about him being gay.' Malc shook his head. 'You've met Tony. You know what I mean.'

'I do,' Lorraine replied thoughtfully, sipping on her tea.

*

Greg Burnley almost seemed pleased to see them, Lorraine thought as they walked through the open door of his office. He looked up from his desk and smiled, his eyes narrowing to wrinkly slits in his tired, puffy face. She knew he'd been working extra-long hours recently.

'News?' she said. Burnley had summoned them to the office.

'Not of Freddie, I'm afraid. But Sonia's alibi for Gil doesn't check out.'

'Didn't she say she was with him on the night of the crash?' Lorraine said, thinking back several days.

Burnley nodded. 'One of my constables investigated. She claimed she'd rented two movies from the shop in Wellesbury that afternoon and then gone to the grocery store next door to get ingredients for a curry. She was having a night at home with Gil, apparently.'

'Sounds plausible enough,' Lorraine commented. She understood why Sonia would want to protect Gil.

'Yes, except that the rental shop had no record of anyone from Sonia's address taking out movies that night, or even that week. She claimed she paid for the groceries in cash.'

'Gil's prone to wandering off,' Lorraine said. 'He

could easily have gone walkabout when Sonia and Tony were asleep.'

'True again,' Burnley said. 'Although she says she locked all the doors and Gil doesn't have access to the keys.'

'Gil's story stacks up, though. Whether he was there or not, we know that two people left the pub on the motorbike and—'

'Doesn't mean two people were on it when it crashed,' Burnley said, scratching his chin.

'Fair play,' Lorraine said. She couldn't believe she and Adam were actually brainstorming with the man she once hoped she'd never see again. 'My theory about the girl on the bike being Abby didn't stand up to much scrutiny. It's just those sandals . . . And Lana said she was wearing Converse trainers when I asked her what she had on that night.'

'Surely the sandals aren't unique,' Burnley suggested.

Lorraine had to agree. 'True. But the ones Abby was wearing looked expensive,' she said. 'They were real leather, designer I think. Where would a homeless girl get the money to buy them?'

'Charity shop?' Adam said.

'Or the donations bags that came into the shelter?' Lorraine felt a little stab of excitement. 'The Hawkeswells have been having a big clear-out recently.'

'Which would fit with Lana's story of her being on the bike if they were once her sandals,' Burnley said, folding his arms.

Lorraine sighed. 'There were a dozen or so dustbin sacks of clothes and boxes of bric-a-brac at New Hope when I visited a few days back. Some were for the charity event Sonia's organising, and I think some were to give to the homeless.'

'Then we need to speak to Frank,' Adam said.

He glanced at his watch. Another day was fast slipping away.

'One step ahead,' Burnley said with a satisfied grin. 'A couple of my officers went out to see him yesterday. Not about the charity donations, of course.'

'And?' Lorraine and Adam both said it at the same time.

'Turns out he had a son once.'

'Once?'

'He disappeared aged fourteen. Frank Butler was arrested on suspicion of his murder.'

✤

Jo and Malc were deep in conversation when Lorraine and Adam arrived back at Glebe House. Lorraine dumped her bag on the kitchen table and Stella rushed up to her, clearly unsettled by Freddie's continuing absence.

'We'll stay here tonight now,' Lorraine said, stroking her daughter's hair as she leant against her, arms wrapped around her waist.

She filled Jo and Malc in on the news, especially

about Frank's arrest. 'It happened twenty years ago and a body was never found.'

'He's always given me the creeps, if I'm honest,' Jo said flatly.

'Why don't you go and find the chessboard, Stella?' Lorraine thought it best to change the subject. 'I bet your Uncle Malc will give you a game.'

A moment later, Stella yelled out from the living room that she couldn't find it.

'I'll go,' Lorraine said, walking across the hall flagstones and into the big room at the other end of the house. It seemed cold and desolate, reflective of the family's situation. 'I know what your searching's like,' she said, giving Stella a mini-tickle.

Stella pouted. 'The games always used to be kept in this cupboard,' she said, 'but it's all changed.'

'You're right,' Lorraine said, poking about in a mess of papers and photograph albums. A shoe box fell off a shelf and spilled its contents. 'Oh great,' she muttered, gathering up the bits of paper. They were mostly cards and letters, plus a few newspaper cuttings and saved recipes. 'Look in the bottom drawer of the bureau,' she told Stella, pointing across the room.

'Found it,' Stella said a moment later. She held up the chessboard and a wooden box of playing pieces Lorraine remembered using as a kid.

'Take it through while I clear up this mess.'

Lorraine was on her knees, gathering up the cards, resisting the temptation to peek at the messages. One,

346

however, caught her attention. It was a poem, unsigned, written on a floral postcard, dated only weeks earlier. A few phrases stood out – *simply adore you . . . can't live without you . . . please don't end it . . . you make my heart beat . . .*

'How very sad,' she said to herself, thinking. She guessed they were Malc's desperate words of love to Jo, and that he'd sent the poem soon after leaving the house.

She was about to put it back in the box with the others when something made her look at the card again. She stood up and took it over to the window to study it in the light, trying to recall what Bill from Central Forensics had pointed out to her about spotting specific similarities and differences between scripts, especially the unique traits and quirks of an individual.

'What is it, love?' Adam was suddenly beside her.

Lorraine glanced at him. 'Just a poem.' She sighed. 'But look at the flourishes on the Ys and the Fs. And there, too.'

She gave the card to Adam to read.

'OK. What about them?'

'As far as I remember, they're identical to the letters on Lenny Jackman's suicide note.'

35

Freddie had no idea how long he'd been gagged and tied up. He ached all over, his right shoulder still agony from where he'd been dragged along by the arm from Gil's cottage. He reckoned it was dislocated.

'You fucking pig!' he'd screamed when he'd first been shoved in the barn.

The bastard had clamped his hand over his mouth, taken his backpack from him, and tipped out the contents.

'Is this the computer nicked from New Hope?' he'd growled.

'Fuck you,' Freddie had said.

Another blinding pain had ripped through him as his shoulders were wrenched back, and his wrists bound up tightly with twine.

'Keep quiet, or you'll feel this around your head,' the man had said, brandishing a shovel a few feet from Freddie's face. 'I asked you if this was the computer nicked from New Hope.'

Freddie cowered back into the pile of straw he'd been shoved into, and nodded. 'But it wasn't me who took it,' he cried. He squirmed, feeling he was going to pass out. 'Oh God . . . look, this is agony . . . please untie my hands. I think my shoulder is broken or dislocated . . . *please* untie me. I won't escape.' He was choking on the sobs now.

'Nice try, son. Now shut the fuck up, or I'll make you.'

Freddie smelled his sour breath, felt the cold metal of the Swiss Army knife blade against the skin of his neck. Then a pain in his thigh as he was kicked hard.

'Shouldn't go around snooping into business that's not yours, should you?'

Freddie ducked to avoid being hit round the head.

'I'm sorry, I'm sorry,' he sobbed. 'Please don't hurt me any more.'

Freddie thought of his mother at home in their kitchen. He'd do anything to be back with her.

'You've no idea what you're messing with, you fucking idiot.'

It was true, although Freddie was beginning to work it out. Getting Lenny to nick the computer had felt like the right thing to do at the time, but seemed plain reckless now, after what he'd found. Surely only the police had those kinds of photographs? He felt sick thinking about what had happened, what it all meant – and it had taken place in this very barn, too. By the time he'd pieced it all together, seen Gil's drawings and figured it out, it was too late. He'd been caught.

Freddie had then been tightly gagged and hauled by his legs into a dark corner. The barn doors had slammed shut and he'd been alone ever since, dozing fitfully. It was still daylight, but he'd been grabbed early in the morning so he could have been lying there for five hours or seven hours, or longer.

He woke to a noise – doors opening and shutting. Someone was coming.

Him.

Freddie watched on in horror as the man walked in and began dragging bales of straw from their storage place into the middle of the barn. He made a choked sound but his throat was so dry, the gag so tight, he could hardly be heard. He heard grunts and curses as the precarious stack of bales grew. As each one was shifted, clouds of dust filled the dank air. Freddie's lungs burned as he watched the tower get taller.

Just minutes later the man was cutting his gag away and he was gasping for breath. He opened and shut his stiff jaw, rubbing at his cracked lips.

'What are you doing?' he begged, feeling terrified.

'Stand up.'

Freddie's heart hammered in his chest as he stared up at the tall structure. He pushed himself further back towards the wall, his feet scuffing frantically on the floor, trying to get away even though it was futile. He was shaking, had no idea what to do.

'I said fucking get up.'

He was yanked up by his bad arm, and even though

the pain was excruciating, it didn't compare to the fear he now felt inside, for he had seen the rope – thick, coiled, trailing along the floor, one end knotted and looped. He couldn't take his eyes off it.

'What are you doing with that?' Freddie said, praying his text had got through to Lana and she'd understood his garbled words and would somehow find him. 'Please, just tell me what's going on.'

His heart thumped in his chest and his limbs felt icy cold from adrenalin. He scanned around, searching for a way to escape, but was dragged towards the stack of straw, the grip on his arm vice-like.

'Everyone knows you're a miserable little fucker. And lovesick, too, I would bet.' The rope was right in front of him now. 'I've seen the way you look at her.'

Freddie tried to shake his head, pull back, but he was frozen.

'So no one will be very surprised to find' – he picked up the rope by the noose, looked up at the thick cross beam above – 'that you decided to end it all.'

'What? What are you on about?' Freddie's eyes were saucers as the loop, wide and gaping, was slipped over his head. 'Stop it! I don't want to die!' he shrieked, but the knife came up to his face, threatening, and the rope pulled tight around his neck.

'Get up on the bales. *Now!*'

Freddie wanted to run for it, make a dash for the door, but he'd have to get the rope off somehow first and his hands were still tied.

'You're crazy. You can't do this.' He wriggled, but it was no good. '*Help!*' he yelled, fighting as much as he could. 'I don't want to die, I don't want to die . . .' His voice was buckling now, cracking like a fourteen-year-old's. 'Please, God, someone, help me . . .'

A vicious kick to his knee dropped him to the floor. His face was suddenly in the dirt, and almost in the same instant he was hauled back up by the neck like a puppet, his screams of pain mercilessly ignored. He watched in horror as the long end of the rope was slung over the beam above the stack of bales and pulled tight. Then he was being shoved towards the tower and made to get on to the first tier with a sharp kick up his backside.

The scent of straw filled his nostrils as his face hit the bales – perhaps the last thing he'd ever smell, Freddie thought. It was almost impossible to climb with the taut rope throttling him, but he was forced to scramble up using his legs alone. If he didn't, he'd be strangled instantly. One of the lower bales gave way when he was ten feet up and he felt himself drop. He'd never felt so terrified or alone in his entire life. He tried to scream, but couldn't.

'Keep climbing!'

Freddie's only option was to do as he was told.

Finally, he reached the top. The rope was still tight and the beam directly above him now. Another bale fell out of the now leaning tower, making him hardly dare breathe, let alone move. If the whole lot fell, he'd be hanging, dead within minutes.

Briefly, the photographs he'd found of Simon flashed through his mind. He could see quite clearly now what had happened. Simon hadn't killed himself, just as he knew Lenny hadn't killed himself either. Freddie didn't want to go the same way as them.

His ears pounded with the blood being forced into his head – a *woosh-woosh* in time with his panicked heartbeat – and his lips bulged and his eyeballs throbbed as the rope bit deeper. The tower swayed beneath him as he teetered on tiptoes, trying to release some of the pressure in his head. He stared down in disbelief and saw that the rope was lashed on to a metal hook in the wall.

Oh God, please don't let me die.

Then he was left alone, and the warmth came, spreading through his trousers as he pissed himself, knowing that if one more bale slipped, it would all be over.

36

I slap my head until it hurts. Freddie is gone and if he dies like Simon and Dean and Lenny it will be my fault. It hurts when I breathe, a stabbing pain in my lungs. Sometimes Sonia takes me to the hospital because of my chest but I don't care about that now. I just want Freddie to come back.

Slowly, I open the door of my house and look out. It was hours ago when he ran away from me and charged straight into Frank's arms. I've been hiding ever since, scared of what would happen. I know they went off towards the big barn. I know every sound around here. I haven't dared go outside since.

Eventually, I step out of my house, knowing I should have stopped them. But I wasn't sure how. That's why I hid. Tony would tell me that I was a coward, that I should be ashamed of myself. He's right and that is why I am going to get Freddie. I have got some courage now.

Smudge pads across the gravel with me. I wish Sonia was here to help me.

I go around the edge of the courtyard towards the barn, keeping my back close to the wall, weaving between the shrubs, creeping along the rotting wood of the garage doors until I have to go out into the open to get across the grass to the barn. I am shaking, praying no one will see me, because then they would ask questions and my voice wouldn't work.

I peer through the barn window and my fingers sink into the spongy wood of the rotten windowsill. Thick cobwebs across the glass block most of my view. It's dark inside but I can still see there's a mess in there. I go round to the big doors at the end and pull them open.

'Hello?' I say nervously, going inside.

Something touches my ankles and I jump. When I look down, it's only Smudge. He makes a croaky meow.

'Is anyone in here?' I call out, going further in.

The heavy doors swing shut behind me and everything goes darker again.

It's as though someone's been fighting. Sonia will be cross when she sees all the straw stacked up in the wrong place. All her tools for taking care of the horses' hooves have been tipped out of their box too. I gather up the picks and the files and put them away neatly and then I see the knife sitting on the crate. It's the one Sonia uses for cutting the twine on the bales. It used to live in the kitchen drawer but now it lives out here. I pick it up slowly, turning it over and over, staring at the razor-sharp blade. This could kill someone, I think, putting it back down again.

'Freddie?' I call out, a bit louder now, venturing round the other side of the big stack. 'Are you in here will you come back with me because I want to keep you safe and we can have another omelette?'

'Help . . .'

The voice is small and weak and coming from up high. I stare up, going right round the tower of bales, accidentally kicking one.

'Get back . . .'

Around the other side of the bales I see Freddie balanced on top of them. He has a rope tied around his neck and his face is purple. He can hardly speak.

'What are you doing up there, Freddie?' I ask, frowning. 'Don't you know that's dangerous?' Sonia always tells me to learn from my mistakes. I learnt that I shouldn't do my exercises up high any more. 'You are silly and need to get down right now.'

'Please . . . get me . . . down . . . help me . . .'

'It serves you right if you are stuck,' I say. 'Though I will help you because you are my friend and I would like you to come back to my house and we can cook more food together.'

I go back and get the knife from the crate and stare up, frowning at the stack of bales. They don't look very safe, but I will have to climb up there if I'm to save Freddie. I give the bottom one a kick, to see how sturdy it is, but then some straw breaks away and it half caves in. Freddie drops down a few inches, his legs writhing and kicking, searching for something to stand on. Finally, he gets his feet back on a bale again. He's making a funny noise in his throat.

'Wait Freddie, I am coming up,' I say, hoisting myself up on to the first bale.

He's trying to speak but I can't understand him. It's hard to climb with the big knife in my hand, and I'm worried that someone will hear me, or Frank will come back and then when I think of that my chest hurts again and I get frightened.

A bale gives way.

'*Watch . . . out . . .*' Freddie gasps.

His bulging eyes stare down at me as I get closer. It feels as if we could topple over at any moment.

'Don't worry Freddie,' I say, nearing the top. There's not much room for us both up there but I need to get all the way up to cut the rope. 'You mustn't do your exercises like this any more.'

I am panting and my arms are tired. I stretch my leg up to the final bale, but a chunk of the one I'm standing on falls away, making me grab the twine of another. That slips too, and I drop down a few feet.

Freddie is sobbing as I haul myself up again. I'm finally at the top, and it's just as I'm standing up, wobbling, trying to get my balance, the knife only inches away from Freddie's neck, that I notice the face staring in at the window.

37

Lana had rattled the door handle hard, close to tears. Everything was her fault, and she didn't know how to make it better.

'It's locked,' she'd said to her mum, wishing they'd come to look for Gil sooner.

They pushed through the weeds to get round to the window. Lana rubbed at the glass with her sweatshirt sleeve. 'I can't see him,' she said. A sinking feeling gripped her from the inside out. 'Freddie's text message this morning . . . you don't think he meant that Gil had got him, do you?'

Lana was relieved when her mother laughed, despite the red welt blooming on her cheek. 'Of course not. Gil wouldn't hurt a fly.'

'That's what I thought,' Lana said quietly, staring at the ground a few feet away from the tack room. 'What's that?'

Sonia tracked her gaze and bent down to pick up the bright red rubber band.

'Looks like one of those charity wristbands,' she said. 'Someone must have dropped it.'

Lana took it from her. 'It's Freddie's, I'm certain of it.' She read the words around the edge. 'I was there when he bought it. I have one too, look, in a different colour.' She flashed her wrist. 'Do you think he dropped it on purpose?'

Sonia shrugged. 'If he's run away, he's not going to hang around here. He must know everyone's out looking for him.'

'But he didn't *want* to run away,' Lana said. 'I'm certain of that. Freddie loves his mum and . . . and . . .' And I love him too, she thought, not knowing how to begin telling her mum everything. She'd been through enough this last year.

'Look,' Sonia said, staring twenty feet further on. 'There's another one.' The sun had come out from behind a cloud and caught the bright yellow colour.

'That belongs to Freddie, too,' Lana exclaimed, running over to it. 'He *has* been here, hasn't he?'

'It is strange, I admit.' Sonia paused. 'I wouldn't bank on him being here now, though. And that fits with what Gil was saying, that it was his fault he'd been taken away.'

'Did he say who by?'

'No. I thought it was just Gil piling the guilt on to himself, as usual. Things have been so unsettled these last few days.' She sighed. 'Let's keep looking, shall we?'

Slowly they walked away from Gil's house across the courtyard and towards the barn.

Lana sprinted ahead suddenly, stopped and picked something else off the gravel. 'Mum, this is Freddie's too.' She held up a small metal key ring in the shape of a peace symbol. There was one key attached to it. 'I bet if you try this in Jo's back door, it'll fit.'

Sonia stared at it thoughtfully and nodded. 'OK, this changes things,' she said, looking around.

Lana felt her trepidation; it was almost as if they were being watched. She stared up at the big house behind her. She'd lived there half her life, but suddenly it seemed cold and foreboding.

'Mum, are you and Dad going to split—'

'Not now, Lana,' Sonia interrupted. 'If you're right about these things and Freddie left some kind of trail then it leads from Gil's house right across to the barn. Frank was due to come round earlier and swap some charity bags. He took the wrong ones the other day. I wonder if he's been or if he saw anything.'

Sonia told Lana to wait there and strode back across the yard before disappearing behind the tack room. A few moments later she was back, slightly breathless. 'That's odd. His truck's parked there but I haven't seen him about.' She put her hands on her hips and stared down into the paddocks in case he'd gone to see the horses. He'd recently shown an interest in buying their foal.

'You could try phoning him,' Lana suggested, not

really caring about Frank. She just wanted to find Freddie, and know what was going to happen to her mum and dad. She'd never seen him lash out that hard before.

She didn't know whether to tell her mum about the photographs she and Freddie had found.

Lana sighed. 'I'm going to check the barn,' she said, making her way towards the red-brick building. She couldn't ignore the things Freddie had dropped.

The sun slipped behind another cloud, and a crow flew from the old cedar tree to sit on the gable end of the barn roof. The screeching noise it made sounded sinister in the still afternoon air.

'Can you see anything?' Sonia said, coming up beside her.

'It's hard to tell,' Lana whispered, looking in through the window. She thought she'd spotted some kind of movement but it could have been a reflection. The big door was on the opposite end and seemed to be closed, making it hard to see. 'Did you move all the bales, Mum?'

'No, why?' Sonia came closer.

'They're dumped all over the place . . .'

Lana looked again and gasped. She pushed her mother back against the rough brick. 'Get back.'

'What's wrong?'

'Oh Mum . . . Oh my God . . .' Lana broke down into tears.

'What's going *on*?' Sonia said, trying to look through

the window again, but her daughter wouldn't let her. This time she pulled her down to the ground.

'You're shaking, sweetheart. What on earth is it?'

'It's Gil, Mum, and he's got a knife at Freddie's throat.'

38

Lana was breathless, crouching beneath the window.

'*What?*' Sonia said.

Lana tried to keep her mum hidden down low but she forced her way up, staring in and gasping. She clapped both hands over her mouth. 'Oh my *God*,' she said as she dropped back down next to Lana again. 'We have to do something.'

'I'll call the police,' Lana said shakily.

'No, wait. *We* have to handle this.' Her mum took hold of her shoulders. 'I want you to go to your dad's gun cabinet. Bring the short-barrelled shotgun. You know the one?'

Lana nodded, terrified about what she had to do.

'And, love,' Sonia said, catching Lana's wrist as she scrambled up, 'be careful.'

Lana ran off towards the house. She knew her dad kept the keys to the cabinet under some old clay pots in the boot room, remembering how he'd always warned her off touching them. Her fingers fumbled as she swept them up. She went straight to her dad's study where the gun cabinet was built into the wall, hidden behind carved wooden doors, and unlocked both sets, swinging open the heavy metal inner doors to reveal the rack of guns.

Lana's heart clenched. She'd never held one before. *This little beauty is always loaded and ready to go.*

She took a deep breath before grabbing the short-barrelled gun, pulling it from its rack. Briefly, she spotted the phone on her dad's desk, wondered whether to dial 999, but she had to do as her mother had told her so she ran back to the barn, keeping the gun pointing upwards.

She'd only been gone a few minutes yet it felt like a lifetime. Lana's arms trembled as she held the gun, crossing the courtyard.

'Mum?' she called out when she couldn't see her.

She looked around, panicking, praying it wasn't too late.

'Mum, where are you?' she said as loudly as she dared. 'I've got it.'

There was no reply, so she ventured round to the big doors at the other end of the barn. She hovered outside, swallowing down her fear, before pushing against the wood and going in.

She kept the gun pointing up, moving forward slowly, and crept around the stack of bales she'd seen Freddie standing on. She hardly dared look up, but when she did she saw that his face was purple, his feet unstable on the straw, and his hands were tied behind his back. He was gasping for breath. Then she heard voices and her parents came into view.

'Mum?' she said, not believing her eyes.

Her dad had his hands outstretched, cajoling Sonia into giving up the knife she was threatening him with.

'What are you doing?' Lana screamed. 'Stop it!'

'Your mum's not well, love,' her dad said, glancing quickly at her. He took another step towards Sonia. 'I was trying to rescue Freddie but your mother turned on me.' He was shaking, sweating, as scared as she was. 'She's gone mad. Keep away from her.'

Lana nodded, wide-eyed, and glanced up at Freddie again, the gun swinging round in her hands.

'Mum?' she said. 'Why are you doing this? Just give Dad the knife. Please, Mum.'

Sonia turned to face her. Her eyes were crazy and spit foamed on her lips. Her father was right.

'He's lying, Lana,' she said, jabbing the knife in her dad's direction. '*He's* the crazy one. For Christ's sake, Lana, you have to believe me!'

Then Lana heard snivelling and crying coming from the corner. Her head whipped round and she saw Gil curled up beside some old crates, his hands over his face, his head bowed.

'Lana, listen to me,' her dad said. 'I need you to give me the gun. I don't want anyone to get hurt.'

He reached out his hands to her, shuffling forward a couple of steps, glancing at her mum then looking back at her earnestly. For a second, the images on the laptop flashed into Lana's mind; but this was different now, this was her dad trying to help.

'OK, OK Dad,' she said quietly, her voice barely working.

She stole one last glance up at Freddie before stepping towards her dad. His eyes were huge and staring and his face had swollen to the colour of ripe plums.

Sonia rushed to get between them, brandishing the knife at Tony. 'Lana, no! Don't be stupid. You've *got* to listen to me. Do *not* give him the gun. Pass it to me, then take Gil and get out of here. Lock yourselves in the house.'

Lana was in tears again, switching her gaze between her parents. 'Mum, I can't. You're not well.'

The gun was almost in Tony's hands when Sonia suddenly lashed out at him with the knife, slicing his forearm. The wound seeped blood as he recoiled, shrieking.

'You stupid woman!' he yelled, doubling up, before reaching out for the gun again. He got his fingers around the barrel.

'Lana, no! Your father killed Simon and he's going to kill Freddie too! You *have* to listen to me!'

Lana froze, then with a scream yanked the gun away.

For a moment everything was quiet. Then Tony went mad, kicking and swiping at the bales and destroying the stack beneath Freddie. Sonia leapt on his back, trying to stop him, plunging the knife into his shoulder, but the tower swayed and collapsed.

Lana screamed, watching helplessly as Freddie suddenly dropped and hung above them all by his neck.

39

Lorraine was sitting with Jo in the garden while Adam took Malc to the Old Dog and Fox for an hour. 'It'll take his mind off things,' he'd said. Lorraine had urged him to find out about the card, as well as where Malc had been on the night of Lenny's death, even though she felt treacherous doing so.

'I've been thinking about you and Malc,' she said.

'That's nice,' Jo responded sourly, taking a slug from her wine glass. 'What did you conclude?'

'That he loves you,' Lorraine said honestly, hoping against hope that it was pure coincidence Malc's writing seemed identical to Lenny's suicide note.

'And how did you work that out, *detective*?'

Lorraine sighed. 'I wasn't snooping, I promise, but . . .' She saw the look on Jo's face and decided not to mention the poem. 'Don't you think there's any chance you could work things out with him? When Freddie comes home, it'll be good for him, too.'

Jo closed her eyes. '*If* he comes home,' she said quietly.

'He will.'

Lorraine moved closer to her sister.

'To be honest, I want to work things out with Malc. I miss him, you know.' She laughed. 'Ironic, isn't it?'

'No, it's natural,' Lorraine said kindly, hoping to God she'd got this all wrong.

'I tried to end it recently,' Jo said. 'With Tony, I mean. But . . .' Her face crumpled with worry. 'He got really possessive. He told me no one ever left him. That he owned me.'

'That's scary,' Lorraine said.

'When I said our affair had to stop, he kept phoning me, hanging around outside the house, following me whenever I went out.'

'Why didn't you tell me? I could have done something.'

Jo shook her head. 'Why do you think?' She sipped more wine. 'He kept sending me texts, emails; he wrote me notes and poems. He said things like "you flow in my veins" and "you make my heart beat".'

Lorraine sat up. 'He said *what*?'

❋

Lorraine glanced at Gil's cottage as they approached, having run all the way with Jo. The door was locked so she peered through the window. She couldn't see anyone in the single room downstairs, and they'd already tried banging on the Manor's front and back doors with no reply. She glanced at her phone. Adam hadn't replied to her text.

'How did the affair kick off?' she asked her sister as they walked briskly towards the courtyard.

'Malc and I were in the pub having a quiet dinner a few months ago. Sonia and Tony were at another table. I knew Sonia, but we didn't socialise as couples. That came about after Tony and I started seeing each other. He thought it would be good cover if Sonia and I became good frien—'

Lorraine had held her hand up to silence Jo. 'Did you hear something?' They were in the middle of the courtyard.

'No,' Jo said.

They both stopped to listen. Lorraine strained her ears, turned to face the house, then towards the old barn ahead. The gardens and paddocks lay beyond.

'I swear I just heard someone cry out. Sorry, you were saying . . .'

They walked on.

'Well, Tony kept looking over at me and smiling. Not a smile like just "hi", but a smile that had real meaning. Malc's smiles never—'

They both heard the scream this time.

'Hurry,' Lorraine said, running off in the direction of the barn.

There was another scream, shrill and piercing, as she flung open the wooden doors. It took a moment for her eyes to adjust, but when they did she stuck out an arm preventing Jo from getting any closer.

Jo became hysterical when she saw her son hanging from the beam. 'Freddie, oh God no, Freddie!' Lana was screaming too, pressed against the back wall of the barn.

'Stay back!' Lorraine cried, but Jo ignored her and charged over to where Sonia was standing on some fallen bales, holding on to Freddie's legs, desperately trying to lift him up, prevent him from choking. Her face was scarlet with the effort.

Lorraine searched around for something to stand on, not immediately noticing that Tony Hawkeswell was holding a shotgun, and pointing it straight at her.

'Get out,' Tony yelled, 'or I'll shoot.'

'No,' Lorraine said, angry but trying to stay calm, refusing to be stopped. Her eyes flicked down to the knife lying on the floor. Her heart thumped in her chest as she grabbed it and shouted, 'Drop the gun!'

The weapon was only a few feet from her face. She stared into Tony's eyes – a dark and bitter place – and then saw where the rope was secured to the wall behind him. She had to get to that hook.

'The police will be here any moment, Tony, so just put the gun down,' she ordered, praying that Adam had called for backup.

'No . . . no . . .' he muttered, his voice faltering, the barrel unsteady. 'I . . . I . . .'

There was simply no time for delay. Lorraine charged past Tony, intent on hacking through the rope. The shot momentarily stopped her in her tracks, the deafening sound ricocheting through her head, but she forged on and sawed frantically at the rope with the knife until it was cut in two. She swung round in time to see Freddie falling into the straw and Tony drop to the ground. She leapt over him to get to Freddie, kneeling down beside her nephew. Jo was already there, stroking her son's hair, burying her face into his shoulder.

'Is he breathing?' Lorraine said, grappling the noose away from his neck. He was bruised and in shock, but she heard the rasping in his throat as his lungs gulped in air.

'Mum?' he murmured, already beginning to return to his normal colour. He rubbed at his neck.

'Get him into the recovery position,' Lorraine said, dialling for an ambulance.

She turned and stared back at where Tony lay. Most of his face and the top of his head were blown open from where he'd shot himself, fragments of blood and flesh spread in a circle around him.

40

Lorraine had to work hard to encourage Gil to come out of the corner. His arms were clamped round his body as he stood up, terrified, trying not to look at Tony lying on the ground. Slowly, he walked towards Lorraine, keeping his eyes fixed low. Sonia had already taken Lana off to the house.

'Everything's OK,' Lorraine said to Gil, putting her arm around him and leading him towards the doors. 'You're safe now.'

She turned back to Freddie, who was sitting up, his mother refusing to leave his side. 'Can you walk?' she asked him.

'I think so,' he said, nodding and wincing as Jo helped him to stand, and hooking his arm over her shoulder.

'Tony can't be angry with me now, can he?' Gil asked Lorraine as he pushed the big doors open. 'After I saw him kill Simon he forced me to keep quiet. I tried to stop Tony going into the barn and finding

Simon with his boyfriend because it was a secret but I didn't so it was my fault he killed Simon and Jason and now I just draw pictures to make everything better otherwise it hurts too much.' He took a big breath.

'No, he can't get angry with you now,' Lorraine said.

'Tony said I had to keep quiet for ever or else Lana and Sonia would get hurt, but Sonia knew that Tony killed Simon too, that's why she is always sad.' Gil was panting, pulling at his clothes. 'And then I saw the motorbike crash and Lana told me I had to keep quiet about that as well but it was really hard because things kept bursting out. And I'm sorry Freddie, I didn't mean to scare you with the knife. I was trying to cut you down but then Tony and Sonia came and were fighting so I just went and hid because I was scared too.' Gil stretched his mouth wide and covered his face. 'I would like to go to bed soon if that's OK.'

'You'll be able to shortly, Gil. Come back into the house with us now.'

Lorraine glanced at Jo and reached over to give her hand a squeeze before she ushered them all inside the back door. She sent them on in and waited outside because she'd spotted Adam running down the drive. His eyes were wide as he skidded to a stop beside her. Malc was following on behind.

'You OK?' he said, grabbing Lorraine with both arms.

'I'm fine. We found Freddie. He's safe.'

Lorraine explained quickly what had happened, including what Gil had just told her.

Inside the crowded kitchen, Lana was sitting beside Freddie, staring down at her fingers. Gil was on the other side of her, his big arms ensnaring her. Lana had tears in her eyes and Freddie was comforting her. She looked up when Lorraine went over to them.

'It's all our fault,' Lana said. 'We should never have got Lenny to steal the laptop. Now him and my dad are . . . are dead.' She fell into another sobbing fit. 'I should never have told you to give that ring to Abby either, Freddie. When I found it, I should have just chucked it in the lake.'

Lorraine did her best to reassure her, knowing now wasn't the time to press her for more details. That would come later, when she made a statement.

Freddie stood up, clutching his shoulder, hugged his mother and Malc, then took his aunt aside.

'I'm sorry for all the trouble I caused, but it wasn't without good reason,' he told her.

He looked utterly exhausted, and his voice was not much more than a croak, but Lorraine thought how grown up he suddenly seemed.

'I was hiding at Gil's place and found some awful pictures on Tony's laptop.'

Lorraine held up her hands to spare him. 'Yes, I know, love. Your mum and Tony.'

'No, there was more than that,' he said quietly. 'I discovered an invisible folder.' His cheeks reddened.

'There were some really vile pictures in it. As Gil said, Simon was murdered, and that's why Tony was after me.' He bowed his head. 'The laptop is still in the barn.'

'Oh, come here,' Lorraine said, embracing him tightly. 'We were worried sick about you.'

The sound of sirens outside broke them up. A moment later there were two paramedics in the kitchen. Lorraine explained to them what had happened and left them to check Freddie out, even though he was protesting that he was absolutely fine. She went over to Sonia who was leaning against the sink, looking terrified.

'I've let everyone down,' she said. Her face was slick with tears and her eyes flared. 'It nearly happened again.' She took a moment to blow her nose. 'I'll never forget that day. We were all packed and about to go on holiday, but couldn't find Simon anywhere. Then I discovered him hanging. He didn't look like my boy.' She wiped her face on her shirt sleeve. 'Lana was waiting in the car, and Gil was out helping to look.'

Lorraine allowed her to speak, aware of the police arriving outside.

'I didn't register what had happened at first.' She paused, swallowing a couple of times. 'He was staring above my head, across the barn. Then Tony appeared, drenched in sweat, glaring at Simon with crazy eyes. I didn't believe him when he told me he'd just found him like that.'

Sonia fixed her eyes on Lorraine, ignoring everyone else in the kitchen.

'Then Tony grabbed me, told me not to call the police. When I saw the scratches on his cheeks, the grazes on his knuckles, I knew he'd killed our son. There was something in his eyes, too. He'd found Simon and Jason together, strangled Simon with a belt.'

Lorraine recalled the pathologist's report, how it had mentioned a second, fainter ligature mark, possibly consistent with a badly tied knot slipping, in effect hanging him twice. Burnley had missed the obvious, concealed within the spate.

'Tony told me that he'd found them at it, said it had been going on right under our noses, that it was disgusting, and that he'd had no choice but to put a stop to it. He went after Jason a few days later.'

'I'm so sorry,' Lorraine said.

'But then something strange happened.' Sonia's eyes narrowed. 'He said there was a suicide note, that Simon had been depressed and wanted to end his life. I didn't understand at first.'

'Go on,' Lorraine said, glancing out of the window.

'He kept saying it over and over, making it into something believable, a better alternative to the truth. When I told him to show me the note, he said we had to write one, that we would do it for Simon. I told him no, said he had to give himself up, but then I began to wonder if he was right. How would I manage if he went to prison?'

She covered her face again.

'When I went to fetch a pen and paper from my bag in the car, Lana was still in there, listening to music, scowling because we were late. Gil was sitting beside her by then, stiff and white, staring straight ahead. I knew immediately that he knew. From that moment, he became part of our secret. I hated myself for it. But knowing that Simon had been in love was some comfort.'

Sonia's face seemed calmer now, as if that thought combined with telling the truth was a relief.

'He'd planned on dropping out of university, going travelling with Jason.' She gripped Lorraine's hands. 'Tony wrote the words. It's hard knowing what to put in your son's suicide note.'

Lorraine shuddered, realising just how much danger Freddie had been in the night Lenny was killed. It could so easily have been him on the railway tracks – his faked suicide note instead.

*

When Lorraine went outside, the courtyard was filled with the tick-tick of blue flashing lights, and Adam was briefing the officers present. Several others were stepping into white forensics suits ready to enter the barn once the SIO arrived – Greg Burnley, Lorraine assumed. Another was unravelling tape, cordoning off the courtyard in a wide circumference, logbook already in hand to record all comings and goings.

A car came down the drive and a woman, about Lorraine's age and wearing a dark suit, got out. Lorraine went over to introduce herself.

'And Greg Burnley?' she said after learning that DI Walton had been assigned as the SIO.

'I understand he's been suspended from duty, pending an investigation,' she replied, glancing around.

Lorraine nodded slowly and briefed her on what had happened.

She was about to head back into the house to see if the paramedics had finished with Freddie when she saw a figure lumbering up the drive. He slowed momentarily when he saw all the police.

'Frank,' Lorraine said. 'There's been an incident, I'm afraid.' She stared at the dustbin sacks he was holding.

'I was in the pub when I heard,' he said. 'I came as fast as I could, but couldn't keep up.' He was out of breath and dumped the sacks on the ground. 'I came round earlier to bring these back, but I couldn't find Sonia. I collected the wrong ones the other day. I feel awful because the lads at New Hope already took some of the stuff.'

'Under the circumstances, I'm sure Sonia won't mind,' Lorraine said.

Frank bowed his head. 'I was guilty myself,' he said quietly. 'I feel like a vulture.' He hesitated. 'I don't blame you if you press charges, but I took a mobile phone. I couldn't believe it was in the charity bag, but Sonia's so kind-hearted and I couldn't afford a new one.'

'Frank, you've done the right thing.'

'The phone's back here in the bag,' he said, looking relieved. 'And I reckon I gave Freddie a right old fright when I called round this morning. He nearly knocked me over, charging out of Gil's place. Tony was nearby and marched him straight off, giving him a good telling off, I shouldn't wonder.'

Lorraine nodded thoughtfully, said goodbye to Frank and went back into the house.

Alison Black had arrived and was talking to Lana and Gil.

'And how are you feeling?' she said, turning to Freddie. Jo was still sitting beside him, holding his hand.

'They said I'm fine, that I can go home,' he answered. He was certainly looking much better.

'The detective has agreed to take your statements tomorrow,' Lorraine said to Freddie, Lana and Gil. Then she held out her hands to Freddie and Jo. 'We should go home now. And you must both come with us,' she added, looking at Lana and Gil. Alison agreed.

Sonia was still standing rigid against the sink, with a uniformed officer beside her. DI Walton came in and said a few words to the constable before leading Sonia away by the arm.

'Mum?' Lana said.

'It's routine, love,' Lorraine told her. 'They'll need

to question her at the station, perhaps keep her overnight, but I'm certain the courts will be lenient in this
case. Try not to worry.'

As they passed through the courtyard, her instincts
were telling her to help, to organise, to interview and
take statements, but Lorraine had a quick word with
Adam and he agreed to stay behind for a while. She
told DI Walton she'd be in touch. It was more
important for her to provide support to Jo, Freddie,
Lana and Gil now, as well as making sure Stella wasn't
too distressed. Malc had already gone back to Glebe
House to be with her.

The sun was beginning to set as they walked off
down the long drive, leaving the blue and white crime-
scene tape spiralling behind them and the car lights
flashing. Lorraine couldn't help noticing how Lana's
hand slipped into Freddie's, how her head briefly rested
on his shoulder.

✳

'Hungry?' Jo asked Freddie as they went into the
kitchen. He was staring around as if he'd been away
for ever.

'Er, yeah,' he said with a sheepish laugh.

'Lucky I made that chicken casserole then, isn't it?'
Jo said, as if she didn't quite believe her son was home.

Malc crushed him in another embrace. 'Good to
have you back, mate.'

The kitchen was filled with the scent of wine and herbs and Jo busied about, trying to make Gil and Lana feel at home, even though there was nothing anyone could do to ease their pain, take away what had happened.

Lorraine left them to it and went to see Stella. She found her asleep in the living room, a book spread open on her lap. She sat down beside her and gently stroked her head.

'Love, it's me.'

'Mum?' Stella sat bolt upright, bleary-eyed.

'Come here,' she said, pulling her close for a hug. It was what she needed.

'Are we going home soon?' Stella asked in a sleepy voice. 'It's really boring here.'

'Soon, love,' she replied. 'Soon.'

41

The next morning Adam returned to Birmingham, promising not only to contact the appropriate authorities to ensure the offensive content about Freddie was removed from the internet, but also that they would bring a case against the perpetrators, as well as alert the school and their parents.

'I should have asked for help sooner,' Freddie admitted as they all sat in the garden to have lunch.

'That's how the bullies get away with it, love,' Lorraine said, serving the salad and quiche Jo had brought out. 'They bank on the threats keeping you quiet, that the shame will silence you.'

Freddie was nodding, having already agreed to chat to a counsellor about it. 'I thought I'd have a look at universities online later,' he said. Lorraine noticed the smile on Jo's face. Freddie was thinking of the future already, planning what he wanted to do. 'I like the idea of studying Economics.'

'Get you,' Lana said, squeezing his hand. A phone

call from her mum earlier had cheered her up: Sonia was going to be allowed home that afternoon.

'And what about you, Lana?' Lorraine said. 'You'll be off to medical school before too long, won't you?'

Lana blushed and looked at Freddie. 'Mum's not going to be very pleased,' she said, sipping her water.

'Just tell them,' Freddie said. 'The truth's always better.'

Lana nodded and took a breath. 'I never wanted to be a doctor,' she confessed. 'It was . . . it was Dad's idea initially. Then Mum latched on to it, hoping I'd be as clever as Simon. The truth is, I didn't actually write a single word on my exam papers. I'm not going to be a doctor.'

There was a moment's silence.

'You're very brave to do that Lana but now I won't get better,' Gil said, munching his food.

'You don't *need* to get better, Gil,' she replied, taking his hand. 'There's nothing wrong with you.'

They ate the meal, enjoying being together despite the shadow cast by the week's events. Malc promised he'd stay in Radcote for another week, adding to Jo's growing relief, and Lorraine also promised not to leave for a couple more days.

✳

Later, Lorraine offered to take Lana to fetch her mum from the Justice Centre. Lana was nervous but agreed it was the right thing to do.

'She's been released on bail,' Lorraine explained on the journey there. 'There'll be a court case, but not for a while yet. Taking everything into account, how she helped save Freddie, I think things will be OK for her.'

Lana nodded, taking it all in. 'Thanks for everything,' she said earnestly as they walked up the steps of the police station.

When they all got back to the Manor, Gil was waiting at the door, excited to tell Sonia that he'd moved back into the main house.

*

Early on Wednesday morning, Stella sat bleary-eyed in the passenger seat next to Lorraine. She had to get back for work meetings. In the last couple of days they'd been on two outings, including coaxing Freddie out on a narrow boat day trip. He'd come willingly, knowing Lana would be joining them.

'Go, go!' Jo said with a laugh, pretending to shoo them away. 'Get yourselves out of here while you can!'

The last few days had done her the world of good. Lorraine hadn't said anything on Monday morning when Jo and Malc had come down for breakfast together in their dressing gowns.

'I'm coming back to see you for the day on Sunday, OK?' Lorraine said through the open car window. 'And I'll phone later tonight.'

Jo grabbed her arm through the window. 'I'm sorry it's been so awful.'

'Oh, Jo . . .' Lorraine got out of the car again. 'It's been pretty awful, yes – pretty much the most awful you've managed yet.' They fell into a hug. 'Let's keep in touch. We're all we've got.'

Jo agreed, nodding furiously against Lorraine's shoulder, fighting the tears.

'Are you sure you'll be OK?' Lorraine asked.

'Malc's staying for a bit.'

Lorraine held her at arm's length. 'Do you think you two will . . . ?'

'I really hope so. It's made Freddie so much happier already. I just hope Malc will be able to forgive me.'

'Keep talking to each other,' Lorraine said. 'And look after that nephew of mine.'

She got back into the car, and Jo stepped back towards the house. Malc and Freddie had also come outside to see them off. The three of them stood in a huddle, Freddie in the middle, taller than both his mum and stepdad. He'd already said his goodbyes, thanking Lorraine profusely for sorting things out with DI Walton. As long as he was helpful and gave detailed and accurate statements, no charges would be brought against him.

Lorraine tooted the horn, crunching over the gravel as she turned out on to the lane. Soon they were leaving Radcote, heading back the way they'd come the best part of two weeks earlier.

'Is this Devil's Mile again?' Stella asked, pulling open a bag of crisps she'd found on the back seat.

'It is,' Lorraine replied.

She glanced in her rear-view mirror before speeding up. She wanted to get out, get home. Leave events behind, though not leave her sister. Things would be different now. Closer, better. They'd see each other more.

'Is it where that boy killed himself?' Stella asked.

Lorraine slowed as they passed the wilted flowers tied to the tree. She turned sideways, catching a glimpse of a fresh bunch that had been put there – the colours were vibrant reds and yellows, the wrapping paper equally bright and new.

'Yes, it is,' she said.

'Do you know what happened to him?' Stella went on, crunching. Crumbs showered down her front.

Lorraine glanced at Stella, and stuck her hand in the crisp packet, pulling one out. 'In all honesty, love, I don't think I do.'

EPILOGUE

I'd never felt so alive, but that's what Dean did to me. It had been a long time since I'd smiled like that. He convinced me, laughing, encouraging, kissing, that I could do things. He had such white teeth. His smile was one of the things that had drawn me to him. We'd met at New Hope, of course, where desperate souls collide.

I'd wanted to prove something on that stolen bike that night. I thought it was to Dean, but I was wrong. It was to myself.

You're a natural!

He never saw my grin. I wanted to go faster. Much faster. That's why I twisted the accelerator towards me as far as it would go. My entire life – and his – gripped in one hand.

Then came that seemingly interminable tumble, every part of me jarring and twisting and tearing. A battering noise inside my skull. A taste of blood inside my mouth. An engine rumbling, resonating through the ground.

Dean? Dean, where are you?

No reply.

I was about to scream but stopped. Was someone there?

The engine cut out and everything was quiet.

Hello?

When I found him, I barely recognised him.

Keep calm.

And then something kicked in, I grabbed the broken helmet, paused again, listened. The crack of a twig, the thud of footsteps, the rasp of breath even more terrified than mine.

Without stopping, I managed to get myself home, limping across the fields the back way, ducking into hedges or shadows whenever cars came along the village lane. I crept towards the house and clicked open the back door. Everything was silent, and I slipped the broken helmet through the loft hatch where no one would look. The visor was missing but I daren't go back for it.

Reluctantly, I removed the ring Dean had given me and stashed it in an old handbag at the back of my wardrobe. I didn't have the heart to throw it away, although I should have done.

I got in the shower and scrubbed Dean off my body. The water swirled with mud and red and flecks of grass.

It was late – or early – but there was no way I could have slept. Soon, a band of orange-pink light filtered through, making it seem as if nothing bad had actually happened, as if the birds weren't singing out what I'd done, the dogs weren't whining to the tune of my crime in the kitchen below, the bin men weren't trundling through the village collecting up the trash of my life.

'Morning,' I said cheerily at breakfast. I was so stiff I could hardly walk.

'Morning,' they all said back.

The day had begun and I drove to New Hope, early for my shift.

Dean, of course, wasn't there.

'What's got into you?' Frank asked cheerily, but I ignored him, claiming a headache. That much was true. Every time the door opened to the church hall, every time a phone rang, my heart skittered and stalled.

Then I remembered the stuff Dean said he'd got in a locker. There was a master key hidden in the kitchen. The boys were always losing their keys.

Dean's life consisted of the contents of a holdall. His scent wafted out when I opened the locker – sweat mixed with the powdery smell of value-brand deodorant. A balled-up sock tumbled to the floor so I picked it up, put it back in his bag along with the note I'd just written. Someone would eventually find it.

'You look awful,' Frank said. 'Sit down and have a cuppa.'

It was true. I felt sick. Dead inside. I could have

shown him the bruises blooming on my back, let him see my purple swollen ankle beneath my trousers, have a feel of what I'm certain was a cracked rib. But I didn't. It all remained concealed. Besides, I wanted the pain. It was punishment.

Something about the way Dean had looked at me, the way he smelled, the way he walked, those long limbs never knowing quite where to put themselves – it reminded me so much of Simon. The youthful and carefree way Dean breezed through life. I'd half expected him to pick me up, spin me around. For a few months that summer it had been like having Simon back.

But then the horror of what I'd done wound back, and I'd feel more alone, more scared than ever before.

Steal a bike, he'd said. *Steal some fun*, I'd agreed. Steal some precious hours together.

But now it was over and Dean was dead. Just like Simon.

Then the police came.

And they found Dean's note.

They said they were sorry, told us that he'd killed himself, took his stuff away.

I was sorry, too.

'Mum,' Lana said when she arrived at New Hope later, 'you look terrible. Didn't you sleep?'

'I'm fine,' I said, sitting down so she couldn't see how I was shaking.

I told her what had happened, that Dean had killed

himself. She was shocked. We sat in silence for a while, thinking about him. When she glanced at my arms, I pulled down my sleeves to cover the bruises. I told her about the nightmare that had kept me awake, how I'd dreamt about Simon. How he'd died all over again and there'd been nothing I could do to save him.

But how I was glad I'd had him back, just for one night.